D0777271

THE SUNFLOWER PLOT

By the Same Author

A Bouquet of Thorns
Menacing Groves
Flowers of Evil
The Mantrap Garden
A Botanist at Bay
Green Trigger Fingers

Charles Scribner's Sons
Macmillan Publishing Company
866 Third Avenue. New York. NY 10022

Printed in the United States of America

THE SUNFLOWER PLOT

John Sherwood

Charles Scribner's Sons
New York

Maxwell Macmillan International
New York   Oxford   Singapore   Sydney

THE SUNFLOWER PLOT

ONE

Theodore Stratton looked back furtively. He had not been followed. The lane was empty, right down to the bend at the edge of the wood, where open fields sloped down to the valley. No one would be 'following' him in the sinister meaning of the word. Not unless they knew why he was there, and that was very unlikely. The danger was from a casual passer-by. The lane was narrow, almost a farm track really, and little used by cars. But it was popular with ramblers, because it gave access above the wood to the public footpath along the ridge of the Sussex Downs, with marvellous views to the English Channel on one side and across rolling farmland on the other. On a fine weekend the place would be swarming with walkers on their way up to the ridge. But it was a Tuesday, with overcast skies and a sharp wind to discourage health-giving exercise. On the climb up the valley he had had a noisy party of hikers in front of him. But at the point where the lane entered the wood he had paused, leaning on his stick as if exhausted, till they were out of sight.

With a last short-sighted glance behind him, Theo advanced into the ditch and hoisted himself awkwardly over the wire into the wood. After taking a few steps, he turned to scatter fallen leaves over the footprints he had made, to hide them. An unnecessary precaution, perhaps, but an observant countryman who saw them might wonder who had gone into the wood at that point, and why. On thinking it over he decided to cache his walking-stick there. He had needed it on the climb up from the valley, but it would be a nuisance scrambling through the undergrowth on the steep slope between the trees.

He hid the stick in some ivy behind the trunk of a tree, and set off clumsily up the slope. He was in his sixties and surprisingly vigorous for a man of his scrawny build, though perhaps eager stealth had released extra reserves of energy. He was panting now with the climb. His raincoat kept catching on brambles and a low branch removed his tweed hat, revealing sparse grey hair in disorder. He replaced it crossly, unsettling his gold-rimmed spectacles in the process, and hurried on up the slope.

He was looking now for the landmarks he had memorised from his previous visit; the beech tree with a broken branch, the patch of dog mercury; just to the right of it, the empty fertiliser sack abandoned on the chalky downland pasture above the wood, and blown down into it by some storm.

Last time he had hesitated about the sack, whether or not to remove it in case its bright blue plastic attracted attention to the spot. In the end he had left it, afraid that without it as a guide, he would fail to find his way there again. But he would certainly remove it now, to keep his secret discovery safe.

When he first stumbled on it, the buds were just beginning to show colour. Now it was in full flower, standing up straight as a soldier with its spike of pale purple flowers shaped like helmeted men, with the four lobes on the lip to represent arms and legs; *Orchis militaris*, the Soldier Orchid.

It was listed as 'in woods on chalk, very rare'. As far as he knew it was almost extinct in its main habitat, East Anglia. It had never been recorded as far west as this.

In the first flush of discovery he had thought of notifying the local botanical society, then decided not to risk it. If too many people knew the secret, some hooligan botanist would steal it and try to grow it on in his garden. To prevent that, the society would have to mount a twenty-four-hour guard over it till it had finished setting seed, and he did not trust them to do that. Far better to keep the secret to himself.

Apart from being rare, the orchid was a beautiful thing. He knelt down beside it and let the pleasure of it sink in. It was moments like this that made life worthwhile and lately there had been too few of them.

A scholar by temperament, he had always lived dangerously in the material sense, taking teaching jobs at starvation wages that left him free to pursue the pleasures of the mind. His last job,

8

teaching botany for five hours a week at a boys' prep school, had ended five years ago when the school collapsed into bankruptcy. Since then he had been living as a dependant in the household of his rich nephew, Victor. But the life of a courtier bored him. To overcome boredom, one had to live dangerously; even to the point of frightening oneself from time to time.

His camera, with the special lens for close-ups, hung on a strap round his neck, under his raincoat. It was the most expensive that money could buy, but not his. Victor had passed it on to him after his own craze for botany and plant photography had been dropped in favour of his next enthusiasm. When handing it over, he had made it crystal clear that it was only on loan and not a present.

He lavished a whole reel of film on the orchid, photographing it from various distances and every possible angle. Then he scattered fallen leaves over the ground he had disturbed, removed the blue sack to a safe distance, and started back down the slope. At the fence he paused to retrieve his walking-stick and obliterate the traces he left at the point where he climbed back into the lane. This took some time, and as he finished a pair of walkers on their way up to the Downs appeared round the bend below. Had they seen him come out of the wood? If so, perhaps they would come to the obvious but incorrect conclusion: a call of nature.

Up to now, living dangerously had meant, specifically, saying things to Victor which would have been better left unsaid, and getting a kick out of his reaction. A greater danger threatened now. If things went wrong, Victor would throw him out of the house and leave him to fend for himself with no money and no roof over his head. He was getting old. He had not intended to live as dangerously as that.

He had set off down the lane towards his car, which he had left near the main road where it would not attract attention. The two walkers on the way up were a teenager and his girlfriend, who gave him a cheery good afternoon as they passed him. He tried to reply. But his mind was elsewhere and what came out was a loud barking sound.

Struggling on up the lane beside her boyfriend Kevin, Samantha Mason decided that she was in two minds about him. He was not very dishy, but one couldn't expect everything and as an

9

apprentice with an electrical engineering firm he could look forward to a solid future ahead. What worried her was that he had ideas, such as wanting to go for a walk on the Downs on a miserably cold day. He read books, too. Not useful books like the ones her dad read, about do-it-yourself and car maintenance, but the life-stories of famous people who had been dead for years, what was the point of that? She had once caught him reading poetry, of all things. The worst of it was that she was now labelled as his girlfriend, which meant that village boys she felt more at home with kept off the grass. But she had no excuse for giving him the push, and was not sure she wanted to.

Kevin, shortening his stride so that she could keep up, had decided some days ago that Samantha was a bit of a bore. She made a disgusted face when he mentioned anything out of the ordinary, and when she said 'book' she meant a woman's magazine. He had every intention of dumping her, but it would have to be done gracefully. She had wanted to spend the afternoon snogging on her parents' sofa, but he was deliberately going easy on the sex and had insisted on this walk instead. It was the first step in his campaign to put her off him. In a few days he would follow it up with a carefully engineered quarrel, then another till she broke it off.

They strode on up the hill in glum silence, each deep in thought. Suddenly Kevin stopped. 'What's that?'

'A bird making a noise,' Samantha suggested.

The sound was repeated. This time there was no doubt about it. A woman was screaming in mortal terror.

They looked back. The noise seemed to come from somewhere near a car they had noticed on the way up, parked on the verge a hundred yards back down the lane. The old gentleman with the walking-stick was just passing it, and he too had taken alarm. After peering into the car and finding nothing amiss, he had traced the source of the cries to the wood on the downward slope from the lane and was scrambling over the wire to go to the rescue.

Kevin and Samantha ran back down the lane to help. The driver's door of the car was open and a pair of glasses, a handbag and a half-eaten sandwich had tumbled out of it on to the ground. They hurried over to the fence and found themselves looking down a steep bank into the wood. At the bottom of it a woman with her dress torn open from top to bottom was sobbing wildly as she tried to pull it together round her. Near her a heavily built man with red hair lay sprawled on the ground face down, with a pair of naked buttocks facing the sky. His slacks were nowhere to be seen.

'You down there, what's up then?' Kevin called, then realised that this was a silly question with an obvious answer.

The woman with the torn dress was staring at a spot a few feet away, where an ugly-looking kitchen knife lay on the ground, 'Oh, filthy, horrible!' she shouted hoarsely between sobs. She was in her fifties, Samantha decided, but even quite old women got raped. She had a long, distinguished-looking face and her dark hair had been subjected to what Samantha, who worked as a junior at a hairdresser's, recognised at once as an expensive London cut. Kevin, meanwhile, was concentrating on a different tableau. The old gentleman was bent double, peering down short-sightedly at the red-haired man. 'Oh my God, he's not moving, what have I done?' he moaned. Kneeling, he shook the man's shoulders as he lay face down. This made the head fall to one side at an unnatural angle.

'Oh Kevin, his neck's funny,' cried Samantha. 'It's creepy, come away.'

Ignoring her, Kevin scrambled over the fence and slid down the bank to join the group at the bottom, where he narrowly avoided treading on the knife. 'Kiss of life,' he said, preparing to turn the casualty over. 'They taught me how at First Aid.'

'No!' the old gentleman cried anxiously. 'Never move a person who may have a spinal injury.'

'D'you think that's what's wrong with him?' Kevin asked.

'I'm very much afraid I've broken his neck.'

'You did?' Kevin sounded admiring but incredulous. Had this shambling old wrinkly really grappled with a rapist armed with a knife? 'How come?' he asked.

Theo Stratton picked up his walking-stick which lay on the ground at his feet. 'I did it with this.'

In halting, broken tones he described how he had found the rapist brandishing the knife to terrify his victim as he pressed her against the bank and half lay on top of her. The only weapon to hand was the walking-stick. Gripping it by the wrong end, Theo

11

had hooked the crook of its handle round the red-haired man's throat. Then he had tugged sharply, intending only to drag the brute away and put a stop to his obscene performance. 'I should have used less force,' he lamented, 'but how was I to know it would break his neck?'

'He's dead, isn't he?' said the woman, still shaken by sobs. 'Serve him right.'

'He is and all,' said Kevin, rising from beside the corpse and speaking with the assurance born of six first-aid lessons.

'I shall never forgive myself,' Theo moaned. 'He was committing a horrible crime, but capital punishment disgusts me. What I have just done is worse.'

'Look at that knife,' the woman blurted out amid her tears. 'If it wasn't him, it would have been me. Thank you, whoever you are.'

'My name is Theodore Stratton. Theo for short.'

'Oh dear, I suppose introductions are in order even when one's clothes are in shreds. I'm Alison Montgomery. Mrs.'

Kevin gave his name, and added, 'That's Samantha up there.'

In Samantha's mind, the clientele at the hairdresser's was divided into three categories: proper ladies, posh women and normal. Mrs Montgomery's speech, and her whole attitude, labelled her at once as a proper lady.

'I'm sorry, it's the shock, I'm going to vomit,' said Theo, and moved away. But only a dry retching came. He had eaten nothing since breakfast.

Kevin took him kindly by the arm. 'Come over here and sit down, Theo, you'll feel better. It's not your fault, you weren't to know.'

Mrs Montgomery was still clutching the remains of her dress round her. She was shivering, and Kevin turned his attention to her. 'You got a mac or anything in the car, Alison, that you could put on?'

'Oh, what a good idea. Thank you, it's on the back seat.'

'You hear that, Samantha? Get it.'

Samantha obeyed, noting incidentally that Mrs Montgomery's raincoat was an expensive Burberry, and that the interior of her car smelt luxuriously of leather.

Mrs Montgomery was still shivering as she put it on. 'I was

eating my sandwiches in the car, and this awful creature came rushing out of the wood and dragged me down here . . . '

The corpse's only garment was a shirt in a loud red and black check. Its feet were bare, and rather dirty from the earth in the wood. 'I wonder who he is,' Theo murmured sadly.

'The police will find out quick enough,' said Kevin.

'Oh, no, damn it,' lamented Mrs Montgomery. 'Do we really have to go through all that, the publicity and morbid excitement? He was interrupted in time; he didn't even get my tights down, I shan't complain.'

'You have to have the police when someone's dead,' said Kevin. 'Now. Let's get organised. We'd better get Alison into the warm, she's still shivering. There's a farm down the bottom of the lane, she can be looked after there. And they'll have a phone to call the police on. Theo, you know how to drive a car?'

'Of course.'

'Then give him your car keys, Alison, so he can drive you down to the farm.'

'I'll drive. I'm feeling much better now,' she told him.

'Okay then, you take Theo and Samantha down to the farm, and you, Theo, use their phone to call the police. I'll stay here till they come.'

'Oh, why?' Samantha complained.

'You're not supposed to leave a body unattended till the police arrive to take over,' he explained. 'They never do in books.'

Books, he's always on about books, Samantha told herself crossly as she climbed into the car. But she was still in two minds about him. It would be silly to dump a boyfriend who could take control so competently in a crisis.

Kevin watched Mrs Montgomery make a neat three-point turn and drive away towards the valley. Then he settled down beside the corpse to think out ways of dumping Samantha.

At the bottom of the hill, Mrs Montgomery drove up to the picturesque half-timbered farmhouse and everyone got out. It had obviously escaped gentrification and survived as a working farm where everything happened in the kitchen, so she ignored the disused-looking front door and knocked round at the back. The comfortably stout woman who answered was horrified when she heard what had happened. 'Come in, dear, come in. I'll make

13

you a cuppa. Hot strong sweet tea, that's what you need after a
nasty experience like that.'

Mrs Montgomery rejected this form of therapy, but asked if she
might get her suitcase from the car and go upstairs to change out
of her torn dress. Theo asked for permission to use the phone to
call the police, and after some thought Samantha offered to fetch
the suitcase. But she was too late: Mrs Montgomery was half out
of the door already.

Theo dialled 999 and gave an outline of what had happened. The
policeman at the other end promised to send the proper people
at once, including a counsellor who specialised in consoling rape
victims, and someone to take a specimen of semen.

'There isn't any semen,' he explained. 'I interrupted him before
that happened.'

'You're sure?'

'She says he hadn't even got as far as pulling her tights down.'

He wanted to explain how distressed he was at the fatal result
of his intervention, but the policeman cut him off to get the wheels
of justice moving. He settled down to wait, parrying a volley
of questions from the farmer's wife, whose appetite for sordid
detail he found distasteful. Presently Mrs Montgomery reappeared
from upstairs, wearing an admirably cut summer suit which made
Samantha green with envy, and said firmly that she would prefer
not to dwell on her experience, so could they please talk about
something else. Frustrated, the farmer's wife, brooking no refusal,
dosed everyone with her alarmingly strong sweet tea.

The police arrived in force. After getting directions from
the farm, a scene-of-crime team drove on up the hill to relieve
Kevin at his post by the corpse. A policewoman and social worker
whisked Mrs Montgomery away into a musty front parlour where
she refused firmly to be counselled, assured them that no semen
was available, and said she was ready to make a formal statement.

Her given names, she told them, were Alison Margaret. She
gave two addresses in London: a business one at an antique shop
she owned in King Street, off St James's Square, and a flat in
Battersea.

The policewoman made notes in longhand. 'And you thought
you'd enjoy a day in the country and a walk on the Downs?'

14

'Not exactly. I deal in antiques and a friend of mine in Steyning had a break-front bookcase she wanted to sell, so I came down to give her a valuation. She gave me a bed for the night, and this morning I thought I might as well have a breath of fresh air before I headed back to London. In view of what's happened that was obviously a rotten idea. I suppose there will be court proceedings?'

'Yes, dear,' said the policewoman gently. 'An inquest.'

'Hell. I hate the idea of the publicity, with the media pandering to their readers' morbid excitement and feminists forming support groups and beating their propaganda drums. Rape victims are allowed to be anonymous, aren't they?'

'In the normal way, perhaps. I'm not sure if a coroner would allow the name of a witness at an inquest to be withheld. Now if you could bear to tell us exactly what happened, though I know this will distress you.'

'I'm not distressed, I'm bloody angry,' she replied, and launched into her narrative.

Up the hill in the wood, Kevin had found that he was not as hard-boiled about death as he had expected to be, and was sitting some way away from the corpse with his back to it when the police arrived. When the detective in charge said, 'Right, lad. You can get along down to the farm now where the others are,' he was relieved, and made off down the lane at once.

The scene-of-crime team got to work. Time of death, between one and one and a half hours ago. Photographs of the body lying on its face and of the knife. Long shot of the body and the knife, to show their relative positions. 'Where's the rest of his clothes then?' someone asked. 'He won't have walked up the hill starkers from the waist down.'

They were found deeper in the wood, lying on the ground: a bomber jacket, underpants, jeans, socks with a hole in one toe, a pair of not very clean trainers. The hip pocket of the jeans yielded a set of dog-eared, postcard sized, pornographic photographs, mostly close-ups of male and female genitals in perverse attitudes. The two detectives, both clean-living married men, were shocked. The photographer pretended to be, though he was neither married nor clean-living.

15

The time came for the corpse to be removed to the mortuary. 'Turn him over, then, will we?' said the senior detective.

As they laid him on his back on the stretcher the photographer shouted, 'Cor, look at that!'

They all stared. What surprised them was not the neck, lolling obscenely to one side, but what was revealed when the shirt, which was unbuttoned from top to bottom, fell open. The whole of the corpse's chest and belly was covered with an elaborate tattoo of dragons, butterflies, snakes and contorted foliage, with two enormous flowers centred on his nipples.

'Never seen anything like that before, have you, Sarge?' said the photographer.

'Army or navy blokes go in for it, get it done somewhere abroad. Come on, lads, let's get him back to the morgue.'

'He should be in a museum with all that artwork on him,' said the photographer.

Back at the farm, Mrs Montgomery had driven away, after saying with a shudder that no doubt she would see them all at the inquest. Samantha was giving the police a statement which consisted largely of her own ultra-sensitive reaction to the events under inquiry. Theo Stratton waited his turn in the kitchen. He was still sorting out his emotions, which were complex and anxious. He was also suffering from some sort of physical distress, which he diagnosed in the end as hunger. The farmer's wife had offered him more of the disgusting tea but no solid refreshment, evidently thinking it improper for people to eat in the presence of death. His packed lunch was in his raincoat pocket, but it was socially impossible to get it out and eat it.

Soon Kevin arrived from his post up the hill. Theo took his mind off his hunger by exerting his charm on the young man, who proved happy to talk about his career plans and surprisingly well read for a boy of his age. But he had just got this going nicely when Samantha came out of the musty front parlour and he was summoned in.

'My name is Theodore Alfred Stratton,' he said, 'and I live at Clintbury Park, Clintbury, near Mayhurst.' By courtesy of my nephew Victor, he added mentally.

'Been walking up on the Downs, had you, sir?'

'Yes,' said Theo, lying unhappily.

'Quite a long way from home, aren't you? It must be all of thirty miles from here to Mayhurst.'

'Oh dear, that last answer of mine wasn't quite accurate, I'm still very shaken up after what happened. I came here for a particular reason, to see a very rare orchid that's growing in the wood up the lane. But could you please not put that in any statement that will be made public. It's a protected plant, and if too many people know about it someone will steal it.'

'Very well, sir, we'll see that you aren't asked about that at the inquest. Now if you could just tell me exactly what happened. The lady said something about you attacking the deceased with a walking-stick.'

'Yes, it's in the kitchen somewhere. Oh dear, I blame myself dreadfully for what happened.'

'I wouldn't distress myself if I was you, sir. By all accounts he deserved it. Now if you could just give me the details.'

Theo launched into his narrative. He was uneasy about this whole episode and his part in it. But despite vague forebodings he had no clear picture of the mayhem and turmoil it would bring in its train. As he described his exploit with the walking-stick, he wished he could have played the shy hero, who hurries away from the scene without giving his name.

17

TWO

'You don't remember him at all?' asked Sir Hugo.

At the other end of the telephone, Celia Grant tried to conjure up a mental picture of Victor Stratton. 'At the Arundels, you say?'

'Yes. He sat next to you at dinner and you fascinated him.'

'Oh dear. Did I, Uncle Hugo? Was he an elderly lawyer from Los Angeles with a passion for the royal family? Short and enormously fat?'

'Stratton is fortyish and a normal size and shape,' her uncle protested. 'He's not American, either. South African, by origin at least.'

'Oh dear.'

'Not necessarily. He's very civilised. His father got out before things there went sour and made his home in England, and when the old man died Victor inherited a financial empire consisting largely of diamonds and beer. He's settled down in a lovely house near Mayhurst and he wants to meet you again.'

'No, Uncle Hugo, no, and no, and no. I'm not in the business of fascinating rich South Africans who live in lovely houses near Mayhurst. I'm quite happy as I am, and this sort of thing only leads to complications.'

'I don't see why it should.'

'I do.'

Over the years since her husband's death, Celia had suffered some alarming experiences at the hands of men who decided that a fragile-looking little widow with white hair and a pink-and-white complexion and a youthful figure must be in need of male protection. As the creator and owner of a well-known nursery garden she needed to be, and was, as tough as old boots. But to her regret she did not look it.

'I see no reason why you should fear the worst,' argued Sir Hugo. 'The fascination was horticultural rather than sexual. Apparently you revealed an exhaustive knowledge of Elizabethan garden flowers.'

'Oh, I begin to remember him now. He has a thing about Shakespeare, is that it? And he quizzed me about what the Elizabethans meant by a gillyflower.' *

'Quite right, he's a sort of amateur Shakespearean expert, and he's been doing quite a lot of work on flower symbolism in the plays. I think you can expect scholarly interest rather than unbridled passions. In fact he hinted at some business proposition that he wants to put to you. Do come.'

'Come to what?' Celia asked crossly.

'I'm sorry, didn't I explain? He and I are on a charity committee that meets in Brighton, and as it's a long slog back to Mayhurst from there I invited him to dine with me afterwards and spend the night. It was his suggestion that you should join us for dinner. Why don't you?'

Celia hesitated.

'I'll ask some other people,' Sir Hugo urged, 'and you can hide behind them if he gets embarrassing.'

What could the 'business proposition' possibly be? Curiosity, her besetting sin, proved stronger than her native caution. She accepted, then decided it was probably unnecessary to remind her uncle that her embarrassing tendency to find herself involved in crime was a secret to be kept from casual acquaintances. She entered the date in her diary, then carried on with the despairing conference with her head gardener which Sir Hugo's phone call had interrupted.

'Sorry, Bill. Where were we?'

'In the glooms,' said Bill Wilkins.

---

* Henry Lyte, writing in 1578 in his *Niewe Herball or Historie of Plantes*, says that 'gillyflower' covers not only the carnation proper and the rest of the dianthus family, but also wallflowers and various other *cruciferae*. But in everyday usage the term seems to have been limited to the carnation and its immediate relatives.

Bill had come to work for Celia when Archerscroft was in its infancy, a pretty boy with golden curls and a passionate interest in plants. He had developed into a handsome man, and her principal adviser as well as her head gardener. They had been through many crises together, but this one was a stinker. Archerscroft Nurseries was losing trade to a big new garden centre which had opened up in a commanding main road position just outside the village, selling bedding plants, shrubs, hideous concrete garden ornaments and the like, and even some of the rather unusual things which Archerscroft specialised in. The downturn in business at Archerscroft had reached alarming proportions and something had to be done.

'We got too big for our boots, Celia, that's what, sellin' all them bedding plants and stuff that people can get anywhere. We was better off before, when we was little.'

True, Celia decided. As a small specialist nursery selling rarities unobtainable elsewhere, the business had been a roaring success. The absence of competition had encouraged her to expand. She had borrowed heavily from the bank to enlarge the car park and add more glasshouses. In the new competitive situation the interest payments were a nightmare, and crisis point had been reached. They would have to cut down and lay off staff, but she hated the idea.

'Me too, Celia, but we got to,' said Bill. 'There's no other way.'

'Unless we branch out into some sideline that the competition hasn't thought of.'

'Such as what?'

'Goodness knows. Tropical fish.'

'Oh no, Celia, they're tricky. My auntie had one. It made a disgusting mess in its bowl and died; we'd never make a profit. It's them alpines, that's the trouble, they're the millstone round our neck.'

The venture into alpines, a notoriously unprofitable field, had been one of their worst mistakes. They were beautiful and Celia loved them, but they had to go. If she sold the stock she had built up, and the special alpine house she had bought to contain it, the proceeds would pay off the arrears of interest and part of the loan. But getting a decent price was not proving easy. A partner from one of the big growers had come

20

to look at the stock, and offered her less than half what it was worth.

'We'll get the same story tomorrow when the man from Hilbury's comes,' said Bill gloomily. 'He'll cotton on that we're skint and can't afford to refuse.'

They went on wrestling with the problem for almost an hour, but reached only one conclusion: next day Celia would exercise her feminine wiles at the bank and try to gain a respite.

That evening, her uncle phoned again. 'I rang Stratton back to tell him you were coming, and made an alarming discovery. He wants you to lay out his garden for him.'

'Oh!'

'So I thought I'd better warn you. I know you don't want to get involved in that sort of thing, but you can always say Mayhurst's too far.'

'It isn't as far as all that,' said Celia, suddenly seeing the dawn of salvation. A big contract to landscape a garden would get the bank off her back for a time.

'You don't mean you'd consider it?' Sir Hugo asked.

'I might.'

'But I thought you said landscape gardening was more trouble than it was worth.'

'The point is I need the money. How rich is he?'

'Very.'

Suddenly she had cold feet. 'Soaking the rich isn't easy. They think value for money consists of changing their minds halfway through at no extra cost, and you end up making a loss instead of a fat profit. Would he be that sort, do you think?'

'I hardly know him. Why don't you wait till you've met him, and decide then?'

'On the basis of what? Chaps with perfect table manners can behave like hogs at the trough when it comes to a business deal.'

The silence at the other end was followed by a mouse-like scrabbling sound. Sir Hugo was searching for something on his desk.

'Listen, Celia, I've had an idea, if only I can find . . . ah yes, here we are, it's on Wednesday evening. Victor Stratton's giving a lecture to the Mayhurst Literary and Historical Society. He sent me a card. I can't make it, but if you're doubtful about him you could go, and try to size him up.'

'What's he lecturing about?'

'Let me see. It says here "The Floral Bard: A Study of Flower Symbolism in the Plays of William Shakespeare".'

'I think I'll go, Uncle Hugo. Mayhurst's a long way but it might be quite a good idea.'

'On second thoughts, no. He might spot you in the audience and wonder why you were there.'

'No problem. I shall go in fancy dress and a false nose.'

'So we've no idea who he is?' asked Inspector Grainger.

'No, sir.'

'How about his clothes?'

'Bomber jacket. Jeans. Marks and Spencer shirt. Trainers. Not much help to us.'

'Pockets?'

'Handkerchief. Key ring with two Yale keys fitting different locks. Three pounds sixty in small change. Obscene photos in the hip pocket of the jeans. Wallet in the bomber jacket containing three ten-pound notes and the return half of a ticket from London to Worthing. Day return.'

'No credit cards? Nothing?'

'Two receipts from the checkouts of supermarkets in Lewisham. One dated the day before he died, the other a week earlier.'

'Okay then, let's take a look at him.'

'Very well, sir. He's quite a picture.'

A whole gallery of pictures, Inspector Grainger thought as he gazed down at the heavily tattooed torso lying on the mortuary slab and studied the naked women, dragons and fantastic butterflies and flowers on his chest and belly.

'There's more of the same on his back, sir.'

'Good. Get him photographed front and back and have two dozen prints made. With luck we'll find the tattooist who did it to him.'

'Won't it have been done abroad?'

'Maybe, but there are tattooists in seaports like Liverpool and some in London. And run a check with Records for tattooed men with red hair and a sex offence history. We might get a line on him that way.'

About to go, Inspector Grainger took another look at the uncircumcised corpse. 'Funny. Considering what he was up to, you'd think . . . '

'No, sir. Not necessarily, the pathologist says. Not after death.'

It was a spying mission and Celia dressed accordingly, in an inconspicuous mouse-coloured blouse and skirt. An unbecoming beret hid her mop of prematurely white hair, and the bottom drawer of her desk had yielded up a pair of half-moon reading glasses which she never wore because they made her look idiotic. Thus arrayed, she joined the members of the Mayhurst Literary and Historical Society in a depressing church hall and waited for the lecturer to appear. Most of the society's members were elderly, but they had been joined in the audience by a mob of teenage schoolchildren, probably at the behest of teachers shepherding their charges through one of the Shakespeare plays on the examination syllabus. Evidently the lecture was to be illustrated with slides. A projector and screen had been set up.

Victor Stratton appeared, and was greeted by officials of the society. He was running to fat, and slightly below average height. Sir Hugo had probably been right to put him down as fortyish. His fresh, clean-shaven face still gave a reminder of the good-looking fair-haired youngster he had once been, but it was overlaid with the faintly discontented expression which went with inherited wealth. Accompanied by the officials and followed by a uniformed chauffeur carrying a cartridge of slides, he approached the projector. When the little procession reached it, Stratton took the slides from the chauffeur, like a priest taking something from an acolyte. Why, Celia wondered, had he not carried them in from the car himself? Did the arms of the very rich atrophy and become useless for carrying anything heavier than a golf club?

A tall, scrawny man in his sixties brought up the tail end of the procession. Stratton turned and introduced him curtly to the others. 'My Uncle Theo.'

Theo was anxious. Victor had a brain which could mop up information rapidly and make him an expert on any subject which interested him. But he had no long-term memory, and nothing

23

interested him for long. Theo had acted as his tutor through a series of enthusiasms ranging from bird life and wild flowers to medieval church brasses and the eighteenth-century novel. The lecture on the botanical references in Shakespeare had formed part of the last craze but one. After being delivered to a number of audiences during the previous winter, it had languished forgotten in a drawer, and Victor had switched his interest elsewhere. While he stuck to the typewritten text he could hardly go wrong. But there would be questions afterwards. Would he remember enough to handle the tricky ones? Hopefully, there would be no real expert on the subject in the audience.

In due course Stratton took his place on the platform beside the chairman, who introduced him as 'a distinguished amateur botanist and admirer of Shakespeare, who has made a special study of flower symbolism in the plays'. Stratton listened with a mock-modest smile which did not disguise the fact that he was very pleased with himself.

When the introduction was over he rose and warmed up his audience with practised ease, thanking the chairman 'for putting so elegantly the truth of the matter, which is that I'm a half-baked enthusiast with no real qualifications for lecturing anyone about anything'. Plunging into his subject, he explained that the Elizabethans were enormously superstitious about the curative properties of plants, many of which also had symbolic or sentimental associations which had since been forgotten. The botanical allusions in the plays formed a sort of secret language which he would now try to decipher.

He asked for the lights to be put down and the first slide appeared on the screen. It was a photograph of a rosemary bush.

'You remember what Ophelia says about this bush in her mad scene. "Here's rosemary, that's for remembrance." It also appears in *Romeo and Juliet* in connection with remembrance of the dead and in many other contexts as symbolising remembrance between lovers. But why is rosemary associated with remembrance? Perhaps because of a belief recorded in 1607 by a certain Doctor Roger Halketh, who maintained, surprisingly enough in a sermon, that rosemary "helpeth the braine, strengtheneth the memory and is very medicinable for the head".'

24

After quoting other authorities to the same effect, he went on: 'The text of Ophelia's mad scene makes it clear that she is to hand the rosemary, and also some pansies, or *pensées* for thoughts, to her brother Laertes. But Shakespeare has provided her with more flowers and herbs to be handed to other members of the cast who happen to be on the stage at the time. Unfortunately the text doesn't say which of the bystanders is to have what, and Shakespeare didn't provide posterity with a stage direction to tell the poor, wretched actress how to distribute all these bits and pieces. So how can she decide what to do? Only by considering the medicinal properties or sentimental associations attached to each plant in Shakespeare's day. Take rue, for instance.'

A bush of it appeared on the screen. Rue, Stratton explained, stood for repentance and was also recommended in a medical work of 1584 as a specific 'for the abating of carnal lust'. The rue could have been intended for King Claudius, who was in need of it on both counts. But so too was the Queen: which of them was to have it? Who was to have columbines, whose long nectaries resembled cuckold's horns? Or fennel, associated with flattery but said to have 'a wonderful property to take away the film or web that overcasteth and dimmeth our eyes'. There were various theories about the daisy. But in Stratton's view it symbolised forsaken love, and Shakespeare meant Ophelia to keep it for herself. Who, though, was to have the withered violets? There were more botanical specimens than people to receive them, and the number of possible solutions was almost endless.

The audience was enjoying itself. Theo, who had written the lecture for Victor to deliver, had heard him deliver it four times. It always went well, even the schoolchildren were lapping it up.

Celia too was favourably impressed, but found her attention being distracted from the speaker's remarks by the behaviour of a couple sitting in the row in front. The woman, heavily built with a rich mahogany hair-do, seemed to be bullying the much smaller man who sat beside her. Presently she began talking to him quite loudly, and it was clear that she was urging him to some course of action.

'Not yet,' he murmured. 'Later, I'm not ready.'

'Why not? Hurry, or he will finish.'

What was he to hurry up and do, Celia wondered in alarm.

Create a disturbance? He was fiddling with something in his lap. What? It was too dark to see.

Stratton was dealing with the funereal associations of the flowers that Ophelia had gathered before she drowned in the brook.

> . . . fantastic garlands did she make
> Of crow-flowers, nettles, daisies, and long purples
> That liberal shepherds gave a grosser name,
> But our cold maids do dead men's fingers call them.

The 'long purples', he said, came from the Early Purple Orchid, *Orchis mascula*. A botanical diagram of the plant, with its fleshy flower shoot rising from the ground between two testicle-shaped tubers, explained vividly why the shepherds had 'a grosser name' for it. This delighted the schoolchildren.

As Stratton dealt with the problem of the Dead Men's Fingers, the fierce nudging still went on in front of Celia as the mahogany-haired woman tried unsuccessfully to spur her neighbour into action. What action? Some sort of outrage, clearly. A stink-bomb? Celia half stood up to see what he was fiddling with in his lap. He was furiously taking notes.

Stratton dealt with the other flowers in the funeral wreath, and pointed out that the willow, from a branch of which Ophelia had fallen into the brook, was associated with mourning for lost love. As the willow tree appeared on the screen, an even fiercer nudge launched the man in front of Celia into action. He groaned loudly and said, 'Oh dear, what nonsense.'

'Certainly, it is nonsense,' agreed the woman beside him in a strong foreign accent.

Ignoring the interruption, Victor Stratton switched from *Hamlet* to *The Winter's Tale* and quoted Perdita's condemnation of 'carnations and streaked gillyvors, which some call nature's bastards'. She disliked them, he explained, because they were man-made hybrids. This was an allusion to the great controversy of the time about the value of art as opposed to nature. It had been touched off by the recent discovery across the Atlantic of beings in an uncorrupted state of nature, surrounded by wild fruits which, to quote Montaigne's famous essay 'Of the Cannibales', possessed 'the most true and profitable vertues'. Montaigne contrasted these with European produce which had been 'altered by our artificial devises' and 'bastardised, to the pleasure of our corrupted taste'.

The man in the row in front had been groaning loudly throughout all this. Egged on by his companion, he suddenly stood up. 'May we have the lights on, please? This really must stop.'

Someone switched on the lights in the hall.

'I'm sorry,' he added. 'But I really can't allow this farrago of misinformation to continue.'

The chairman looked startled. 'If you disagree with what the speaker is saying, you can make your points at the end of the lecture, when he has agreed to answer questions.'

'The only question that arises, Mr Chairman, is whether the speaker knows anything at all about the subject.'

The chairman glared down at the interrupter. 'You're not a member of the society, I believe?'

'No. But the lecture was open to the public.'

'Quite. But may we have your name?'

'I am the horticultural correspondent of a national newspaper. But as I am here in my private capacity, I would prefer not to give my name.'

Stratton's face was scarlet with anger, and not at all pretty. He tried to say something, but the heckler swept on. 'The lecturer tells us that the "long purples" in *Hamlet* were *Orchis mascula*. The name "Dead Men's Fingers" points to one of the long-rooted *Dactylorhizas*. The lecturer says Shakespeare confused the two.'

Theo was aghast. Victor had no long-term memory. Would he remember enough to deal with a knowledgeable heckler?

'How could he have "confused the two"?' cried the heckler indignantly. 'Shakespeare loved the country and its flowers. He would never have made such a crude botanical error.'

'You're wrong,' Stratton snapped back venomously. 'There are some botanical errors in the plays.'

'Name one.'

Stratton stammered something, then fell silent. His face was now an ugly purple.

In a flurry of agitation, Theo came to the rescue. 'In *Cymbeline* Shakespeare says the spots in the throat of a cowslip are crimson. That's a crude botanical error if anything is.'

'How do we know that they weren't crimson in his day?

27

Another thing, the speaker illustrated his remarks about the sad associations of the willow with a slide of the common *Salix alba*, whereas it is clear that the weeping willow, *Salix babylonica*, was intended. It has been associated with sorrow as early as biblical times and is mentioned in the Psalms.'

'So you say,' Stratton snapped. 'But you've no evidence, it's a matter of opinion which tree he meant.'

This feeble answer astonished Celia. Anyone who knew the subject thoroughly enough to lecture about it would have been able to point out that *Salix babylonica* (which came from China anyway, the specific name was a mistake) was introduced into Europe long after Shakespeare's day. As for the Psalms, the translators of the Bible were probably guessing wildly when they wrote down 'willow' against the Hebrew word which they decided from the context must stand for some sort of Old Testament tree.

The heckler pressed his attack relentlessly. 'What evidence have you that Shakespeare ever read Montaigne's essay "Of the Cannibales", and do you know when it was first published in English?'

'The question's irrelevant,' Victor managed after some thought. 'The ideas in it were being discussed everywhere in the sixteen hundreds.'

'You've only answered half the question. When was it published?'

Stratton was stumped. His mouth opened and shut, but no sound came out.

The heckler addressed the audience directly. 'He doesn't know! He doesn't know the date. Typical. His truest remark came right at the beginning, when he confessed that he had no qualifications for lecturing on this or any other subject.'

Theo, sitting in the front row of the audience, wondered desperately what to do. Victor had looked daggers at him when he came to the rescue with the crimson-throated cowslip; it was obviously the wrong thing to do. An unobtrusive prompt would be better. He moved up, half-crouching, to the foot of the platform and supplied the missing date in a hoarse whisper.

'Montaigne's essay "Of the Cannibales" was first published in English in 1603,' Stratton announced, 'seven years before *The Winter's Tale* was written.'

'Ah, my point is proved!' cried the heckler. 'Mr Stratton didn't write this lecture himself, it was ghost-written for him. And there, unless I am much mistaken, is the true author, who has to prompt him when questions are asked.'

'I did *not* write the lecture,' Theo lied in a voice hoarse with distress. 'I only gave some advice and criticism.'

'Bad advice and not enough criticism,' snapped the heckler. 'There is a great deal more I could say, but never mind. Ladies and gentlemen, you are wasting your time here, I suggest that you follow our example and leave.'

'Yes, we are going,' proclaimed his massive companion. 'One cannot breathe, the air is infected here.'

The hall buzzed with excitement. The schoolchildren, for whom the fracas was an unexpected bonus, were delighted. Everyone watched the pair leave the hall. At the door they turned, and Celia saw the woman full-face for the first time. She was about sixty, the elaborate mahogany hair-do had gone grey-black at the roots. But the most striking thing abut her was the look of concentrated hatred which she directed at Victor as he stood squirming with embarrassment on the platform.

The heckler himself was small and round, with a greyish goatee beard and a weak rosebud mouth. He had claimed to be the gardening correspondent of a national newspaper. But from her contacts at the Chelsea Flower Show and elsewhere, Celia knew most of them by sight. She had never seen this man before in her life.

Stratton watched the pair go in silence. Then he said: 'Now that nonsense is over, I'll go on with the lecture, shall I?'

But the interruption had broken his hold on the audience. As he took up the thread again, coughing and fidgeting began, making him lose his nerve. He was no longer putting his jokes over convincingly, and they fell flat. Abrupt transitions made Celia suspect that whole chunks of the lecture were being omitted. Presently he sat down amid thin applause, and when the chairman invited questions he had to step into the breach and ask one himself out of politeness. When no one else followed his lead he apologised for the interruption, 'not by a member of our society, none of us have seen him before', and wound up the meeting.

29

Maintaining his pretty-boy smile like a mask, Stratton gathered up his papers and made for the exit.

'Wait, Victor!' called Theo.

'What is it now?'

'Your slides.'

'Then get the damn slides and let's go.'

Theo took them out of the projector. Victor snatched them from him and swept out of the hall. Theo followed, and they waited in the porch for the Rolls-Royce to pick them up. After an ominous silence Victor said: 'You put that little pipsqueak up to rubbish me, didn't you?'

'Of course not, I've never seen him before. Why should I want to do a thing like that?'

'Because you're jealous, you want the limelight for yourself. Why the hell did you have to creep up to the edge of the platform like a rat out of a sewer and prompt me? To convince everyone that you knew more than I do, and make them think you'd written my lecture.'

'If you remember, I did write it.'

'No, I dictated a rough draft to Miss Foster and you put it into shape for me. My God, this is the last straw. Why don't you find yourself a job and clear out? I'm fed up with you cringing around the house looking apologetic, like a dog that's piddled on the carpet. Oh, where the hell's Anderson with the car?'

I did write the lecture for him and I don't cringe, Theo thought. Aloud he said: 'Why must we rush off like this? Shouldn't you have stayed a bit to socialise and show you didn't mind the heckler?'

'No, because I did mind, damn you.'

Theo murmured something mutinous under his breath.

'What was that? Speak up.'

'I said, I hope you turn into a pumpkin surrounded by white mice.'

'Talk sense, can't you?'

'I am talking sense. Balls to you, Cinderella.'

Celia left the hall in two minds about having anything more to do with Victor Stratton. He had gone off in a bad temper at the end, but that was understandable after what had happened. Her main worry was that he was a phoney, and phoneys were liable to dig their heels in stubbornly when crossed. If she agreed to lay out his garden and they differed, he would probably bare his fangs at her. But she had fangs too for use when necessary, and with the bank breathing down her neck she had to clutch at any profitable straw that offered. In short, she was prepared to do business with him, unless something very off-putting emerged when she met him over dinner at her uncle's.

Sitting beside him a week later at Sir Hugo's dinner table, she found nothing fresh to object to. On a closer view, he looked even more like a spoilt rich pretty boy gone to seed, but there was something disarming about his thinning hair. With no interruptions from a heckler, he talked agreeably without oozing undue quantities of charm, and told Celia about a soldier orchid that his uncle had found on the Downs near Worthing. This led to a discussion about the ethics of saving rare wild flowers by propagating them in cultivation, followed by one about the identity of the orchid in Ophelia's funeral garland. Which variety had Shakespeare meant? 'He may not have known himself, Mrs Grant, he wasn't altogether sound on botany. You probably remember his gaffe in *Cymbeline*, where he says there are crimson spots in a cowslip's throat.'

Yes, he is a phoney, Celia thought. But the week's takings at the nursery had been abysmal, and the bank's last letter had been peremptory to the point of barbarism. If he asked her to landscape his garden, she would have to accept.

When the party moved to the drawing room for coffee, Sir Hugo handed her her cup and said: 'I think Mr Stratton has something he wants to talk to you about.'

'Oh yes, that's right, I do,' said Stratton eagerly, and drew her away from the other guests to the far end of the room. 'Let me start by telling you about my house. It's called Clintbury and it was built in 1590.'

Two years after the defeat of the Spanish Armada, she thought. A rather vulgar period. When the style was resurrected in the 1920s, it was sneeringly dismissed by the pundits as Stockbrokers' Tudor.

He went on to describe the house. There was a projecting porch in the middle of the main front, and two wings jutting forward to enclose the entrance courtyard. 'That gives one quite an

31

interesting ground plan,' he said and cocked his head enquiringly, waiting for her reaction.

'In the form of a capital 'E' for Elizabeth,' she said, 'with the porch as the short cross-stroke in the middle.'

He nodded delightedly. 'Out of compliment to that marvellously cunning old harridan who was one of our cleverest monarchs. I adore the way she let a mass of flatterers write poems in praise of her youth and beauty and build themselves E-shaped houses in her honour, when all the time she knew she'd got them exactly where she wanted. She kept her wits about her and steered England through one of the most dangerous periods in its history. I know it was really the weather that defeated the Spanish Armada, but she got the credit, and morally she deserved it.'

He paused for breath, and produced the pretty-boy grin. 'Sorry, I get carried away. I used to live near Stratford-upon-Avon, and I got fascinated by Shakespeare, and now I'm mad about the whole late Elizabethan period with its belief in the magic of monarchy that no later monarch has inspired. This is where you come in.'

'Do I? How?'

'Clintbury must once have had a formal garden dating from the same period as the house. It was swept away ages ago, and what's replaced it is a rather pathetic muddle. I want you to make me an Elizabethan garden* that matches the house.'

'You mean, a knot garden and so on?'

'Oh dear. People put in a few square beds full of patterns in

---

* 'During Elizabeth's reign early Tudor royalist heraldry is transmuted into allegory of a kind related to the complex cult of the Virgin Queen. The Queen was, of course, always the Tudor Rose, the union of the white rose of York and the red of Lancaster. Through that rudimentary equation she was ever present in any garden in the kingdom. What is more significant is that that flower represented only a fraction of what came to be, as the reign progressed, an enormously diffuse horticultural image in which the Queen, the kingdom, the spring, the garden and flowers became inextricably intertwined . . . The garden under Elizabeth, therefore, becomes drawn into a network of symbolic royalist imagery . . . It is a phenomenon deeply related to the late sixteenth-century cult of monarchy which was expressed symbolically in imagery dwelling upon the almost magical powers of the sovereign over the physical universe'. (Roy Strong, *The Renaissance Garden in England*. Thames & Hudson, 1979.)

clipped box and different coloured sands, and they say, "Look, I've got a quaint old-world Elizabethan garden". They haven't. They've got what the ignorant nineteen-nineties think of as an Elizabethan garden. I don't want that, I want the sort of thing the Elizabethans laid out in honour of their queen, full of symbolic statutes and Tudor roses and so on.'

His face glowed with enthusiasm. Undoubtedly he was a little mad. Did he really want a replica of one of the great gardens laid out to flatter Gloriana towards the end of her reign, Nonsuch, for instance, or Theobalds? Theobalds in its heyday extended to thirty acres.

'You mean statues of Venus symbolising Gloriana's beauty, and Diana, symbolising her chastity? Surrounded by beds of flowers representing the twelve virtues, the three graces and the nine muses? And eglantine* everywhere.'

'Yes, masses of eglantine,' he agreed, 'growing up pillars with crowns on top, to cock a snook at Spain over the Armada. You will take it on, won't you? You'll lay out the garden properly for me?'

'I'm flattered. But why me?'

'Your book. After we met I realised why your name rang a bell. You and your husband wrote the standard work on the Renaissance garden.'

This was not strictly true. Roger had been struggling to finish the book during his last illness. She had done most of the research, and he had insisted that her name should be on it as well as his.

'You're the obvious person,' Stratton added. 'You know enough about the period to do a sympathetic job.'

I'm not the obvious person, Celia thought; as an expert on the period I'm as phoney as he is. If I read the book again to

---

* In Lord Burghley's garden and others the Queen was 'unequivocally presented as the single five-petalled eglantine rose, whose power was such that it could vanquish the might of Catholic Spain . . . A crowned pillar is a device of Elizabeth I, in one sense an adaptation of the famous *impresa* of the Emperor Charles V – the Pillars of Hercules with the motto *ne plus ultra* expressing the expansion of the Empire into the New World. After the defeat of the Armada the pillar appears with great frequency in relation to Elizabeth.' (Strong, op.cit.)

remind myself I can probably manage, and what with the bank acting up I shall have to. But oh dear, what a carry-on.

Suddenly a new danger hit her. What sort of household would she find when she arrived at Clintbury? A man as rich as this must have a houseful of assistants, secretaries and general hangers-on. Did they all regard him as a mad eccentric who had to be kept under control? Would they be hostile and obstructive when they knew what he proposed to do to the garden and how much it would cost? Stratton was wearing a wedding ring; there must be a wife. Would she be a sinister influence and why was she not here? And what about the gaunt, scrawny uncle who had been at the lecture; he was probably some kind of guru as well as a ghost writer. All these risks had to be faced. But what Stratton had in mind meant a six-figure contract. If she played her cards right, she would make an enormous profit and get the bank off her back for good.

She hesitated. 'It's a huge undertaking. Could I drive over one day next week and survey the scene, without obligation on either side?'

He agreed at once. But when they got out their diaries, fixing a date proved difficult.

'How about Tuesday?' Celia suggested at length.

'I've got something on Tuesday morning, but the afternoon seems to be free.'

'I could come over then. About three?'

'Very well, but we'll have an awful lot to discuss. So why don't you stay the night? Then we can go on putting our heads together on Wednesday morning.'

This suited Celia admirably. The longer she spent at Clintbury, the better her chance of getting to know the household. If it proved to be a zooful of people with power complexes or psychological hang-ups she could withdraw, and no harm done.

She accepted at once. 'I'm sure you realise, Mr Stratton, that what you're asking for will be pretty expensive. Can you afford it?'

His face hardened. The pretty-boy smile disappeared and she caught a glimpse of fangs.

'Yes, Mrs Grant,' he said softly. 'I can afford anything I want.'

34

THREE

Inspector Grainger was disappointed. The only heavily tattooed rapist known to the police computer turned out to be alive and safely in prison, and his hair was not red. Photographs of Alison Montgomery's assailant were being circulated to tattooists all over England, in the hope that one of them would claim responsibility for the decorative state of his torso. But Grainger suspected that this was a vain hope.

'I bet it was done abroad,' he remarked gloomily. 'That dragon looked like Hong Kong to me. What about the Lewisham angle? If he's been living there someone must recognise him.'

'They say the photos are the trouble. The post-mortem ones are very grim. You couldn't show them to sensitive old ladies. Most of the time they're having to use an artist's impression.'

Returning disgruntled to his office, he found a visitor waiting to see him, an alert-looking young man in a very new but cheap-looking suit, who produced a note from Harry Marshall of the regional crime squad. Superintendent Marshall wrote to introduce 'our latest recruit, Alan Porter, still wet behind the ears from his training course, but they say he's very bright. And I've bad news for you, John, we want the inquest on your rapist adjourned for further inquiries. He'll tell you why, but don't take it out on him, it's not his fault'.

Grainger was not pleased. Why had he not been given longer notice? The inquest had been fixed for ten next morning, witnesses had been summoned from far and wide, and now he was expected to inconvenience everyone by offering formal evidence only and asking for an adjournment. The coroner would complain of police incompetence and wipe egg all over his face before he let him out of the witness box.

35

He choked back his indignation and looked across his desk at Porter. To judge from his expression the poor young sod expected a furious reaction and was terrified. 'Okay, lad, what's the story?' he said quite gently.

Alan Porter breathed a sigh of relief. Grainger was twenty years his senior, and he had been dreading this confrontation all the way from headquarters in Reigate. He had been an inspector for less than a fortnight, and had never wanted to be one. When he was a raw detective constable, chance had handed him a key role in a long and complex undercover investigation. On that level he had been a keen and efficient officer, quickly picked out for promotion. When it came he could not refuse it, but he feared responsibility and knew he was bad at dealing with subordinates. As a spotty young man with long unwashed hair he had mingled confidently with drop-outs and proved efficient at uncovering iniquity. As an inspector in a neat suit with an expensive haircut and his acne well under control, he felt unhappy and insecure.

It had all begun because his life at school had been made miserable by a gang of bullies operating on the fringes of the drug culture. The experience had left him with a hatred of people who misbehaved and a firm belief that drugs, rather than money, were the root of all evil. That was why he had joined the police force. On the course he had just attended he had been assessed favourably as 'highly motivated'. Only the Home Office psychologist had thought it necessary to add: 'may prove over-zealous if not watched'.

Encouraged by Grainger's mild reception of him, he managed to put on a bold front, unaware that it made him sound arrogant. 'We thought we'd better run another check on your rapist,' he said firmly. 'We know who he is, but we don't want his identity made public for the moment.'

Typical, Grainger thought. The regional crime squad wasted a lot of time on long-term undercover operations with everyone's lips sealed. Most of them evaporated after months of effort without an end-result.

'Remember the Kahlberg brothers?' Porter asked.

'I do indeed,' said Grainger. He doubted if Porter did: he would have been in his teens when it happened. But if a tie-up with the Kahlbergs had emerged from the archives, the regional squad was really on to something.

'Your corpse was in on that. He was very minor and only got five years, he was just one of the crew. He was Polish-born, name of Krasinski, and we think he was up to his old tricks again. Anyway, we've put in a query on him to Interpol.'

'How did you get on to him?' Grainger asked.

'Ah, that's a long story. I'll tell you in a moment. Has the path lab reported on him?'

Grainger handed him the report, which took a whole paragraph of anatomical jargon to say that the deceased had died of a broken neck.

'There's one thing they didn't look at. Could they have another go at him?'

'I suppose so. What d'you want checked?'

When Porter told him, he looked at him as if he was mad. 'You can't be serious?'

Quailing inwardly, Porter heard himself sounding more arrogant than ever. 'Why not? I'm perfectly serious.'

There was a moment of tense silence. Then they both began to laugh.

It was just after nine in the morning when Alison Montgomery turned the corner from St. James's Square, and saw a policeman standing in the doorway of her shop. Coming closer, she saw why. The window had been shattered; there was glass all over the pavement. The burglar alarm was ringing wildly.

'What on earth . . . ?' she began.

'There's been an explosion, madam,' said the policeman, shouting over the noise of the burglar alarm. 'I'm sorry, it must be a nasty shock.'

An exquisite eighteenth-century serpentine chest which had been in the window was wrecked. The pair of Kiang-si vases which had been on either side of it seemed to have vanished without trace. Inside the shop there was ruin and chaos.

'Oh,' she said, as she turned off the burglar alarm. 'Oh, hell and damnation!'

The next few hours passed in nightmare activity. While explosives experts poked around for clues, and carpenters arrived to board up the shattered window, Alison and her assistant listed the damage to her stock and began drawing up an insurance claim. Presently detectives arrived to question her. What enemies did she have? What did she think was the motive behind the attack? Could there have been a political angle?

'God, no. If you ask me, all politicians are mad as cuckoos.'

'I was thinking of . . . Northern Ireland. Or perhaps . . . the Palestine question?'

'Well, I'm not Jewish, and I've never set foot in Northern Ireland.'

'In that case we're left with mistaken identity or a personal vendetta. Someone you'd clashed with over a business matter, perhaps.'

'I'm sorry, my mind's a blank.' She thought hard, then added: 'There's one vague possibility I can think of, an American who tried to sell me what he said was a Riesener escritoire. It was an obvious nineteenth-century fake and I told him so. He must have taken it elsewhere and been told the same thing, because a few days later he came back here and accused me of having done the dirty on him by spreading nasty stories about his escritoire around the trade. Now I come to think of it, he was pretty venomous, really abusive. I suppose it could have been him. What was his name now. Hallam? Hanson? Something like that.'

'He didn't leave you his business card?'

Picking her way among the wrecked antiques on the floor, she went to her desk and searched in a drawer. 'No, I'm sorry. If he gave me one, I must have thrown it away.'

Behind the wheel of Victor Stratton's Rolls-Royce Anderson, his chauffeur, chewed over his chronic grievance. He and his wife lived in the gate lodge and Ellen, who suffered painfully from arthritis, was required under the terms of their employment to hobble out of the lodge and open and shut the heavy iron gates whenever anyone wanted to go in or out of the park. Why could they not be left open, at least in the daytime?

The trouble was that the gates, flanked by great pillars with stone birds on top, were right in the village; in fact they blocked off the top end of the picturesque main street. Previous owners of Clintbury Park had allowed village people to walk through the grounds, but Mr Stratton was having none of that and wanted the gates kept shut to exclude trespassers. When Anderson hinted at Ellen's troubles, Stratton had put on his stone-wall face and made it clear that the subject must never be mentioned again.

The inquest was due to start in Worthing at ten. Enthroned beside Victor in the back of the car, Theo suffered pangs of nausea. He hated the prospect of giving evidence, and having Victor there would not help. Victor was behaving as if the whole thing was a squalid nuisance and entirely Theo's fault, but he had refused suggestions that he should stay away. He was 'not going to be seen failing to back up a member of his family in a tricky moment'.

When the car reached the outskirts of Worthing, Theo broke the silence. 'Victor, must we drive up to the courtroom? I'd be happier if we parked in the main car park and walked.'

Victor had intended the grand arrival in the Rolls to add emphasis to his generous gesture of support. 'Must we? I don't see why.'

'There'll be a lot of morbid excitement,' said Theo. 'The media pounce like vultures on anything to do with rape. There'll be reporters, television cameras, inquisitive sightseers gaping at the heroic old gentleman – that's me – who stopped a rapist in his tracks. I don't want to be photographed getting out of this ridiculous car with Anderson in his uniform looking po-faced as he holds open the door.'

Victor scowled at him in sulky silence.

'Please, Victor,' Theo begged in genuine distress.

Victor slid the glass partition aside crossly. 'Anderson, don't go to the court-house; find a car park near there and we'll walk.'

Anderson parked near the pedestrian shopping centre and held the door open for Theo and Victor to get out. As soon as they were out of sight round the corner, he locked the Rolls and went straight to the betting shop. He was coming up to sixty-five, and had no idea how much longer his job would last. When it ended, he and Ellen would have to leave the gate lodge to make room for his successor. Mr Stratton was not a generous employer, and could not be relied on to supplement the meagre pension provided by the state. A poverty-stricken future with no home to go to loomed ahead, hence the betting shop. He was not a gambler by temperament, but a few lucky days with the horses had encouraged him to think of the turf as a realistic way of cushioning himself and Ellen against the hardships of old age.

Theo's prediction of heavy media interest at the coroner's court proved correct. They approached the building on foot, and found a sizeable crowd round the entrance. Theo was recognised at once as the heroic rescuer of a rape victim. Microphones were thrust at him by reporters shouting questions, to which he replied with a firm 'no comment'. A group of Women Against Rape pressed him in vain to accept distasteful gifts of flowers. Deeply distressed, he had to be rescued from the buffetings of the mob by a policeman and escorted into the building with his glasses askew.

Once inside, he was separated from Victor and ushered into the well of the Court. Kevin and Samantha, the two teenage witnesses, were already there, waving to friends as if on a jolly holiday outing. Presently Alison Montgomery came in, looking disgruntled after having run the gauntlet outside. Theo beckoned her towards the vacant seat next to him, but she frowned and sat down some distance away.

The court came to order and the inquest began. The first witness was Inspector Grainger of the West Sussex police. He announced that he wished to apply for an adjournment pending further inquiries.

The coroner was not pleased. 'Why?'

'We have not succeeded in identifying the deceased.'

'If you haven't identified him yet, are you likely to do so ever?'

'We think so. There is evidence that he's been living in the Lewisham area of London, and we are making house-to-house inquiries.'

The coroner treated Inspector Grainger to thirty-seconds-worth of silent disapproval, before saying: 'These last-minute police requests for an adjournment put the court to great inconvenience, and are not fair to the witnesses who have been summoned to attend. However, I suppose I must grant your application. The inquest is adjourned till a date to be arranged.'

'Oh no!' cried Alison Montgomery loudly. 'You mean we've got to come down here and face the media circus all over again?'

'Silence in court,' shouted an usher severely.

40

Inspector Grainger left the court-house well satisfied. He had been very economical indeed with the truth, a thing he was always prepared to be in the witness box when he thought it necessary in the interests of justice. The coroner's rebuke did not distress him in the slightest. It was the sort of thing a policeman was expected to take in his stride.

Anderson transacted his business at the betting shop, then treated himself to a cup of coffee before strolling back to the car park. He reckoned he was in good time: the inquest would not be over for another hour at least. But as he turned the corner into the car park, he took alarm and quickened his pace. There was a sizeable crowd round the Rolls, larger than could be accounted for by admirers of an expensive car, and there were people milling around with TV cameras and microphone booms. He pushed his way through to the front and saw that someone had slashed all four tyres and written the word 'murderer' in huge letters along the side of the car in white paint.

Victor Stratton was standing beside the car, scarlet with rage. 'There you are, Anderson. Where the hell have you been?'

Anderson's head went giddy; he almost fainted. 'I . . . had to go to the toilet, sir,' he lied, saying the first thing that came into his head.

The crowd parted to admit the tall figure of Inspector Grainger. 'I'm sorry about this, Mr Stratton, very sorry.'

'And so you should be!' Stratton shouted, and switched his wrath to the inspector.

An hour later, Grainger telephoned regional headquarters to report. Porter was not there, so he talked to Superintendent Marshall.

'Things are hotting up. They've attacked Stratton's car.'

'Have they now? How did he take that?'

'About what you'd expect from a man like him. How dare the chauffeur go to the toilet and leave the car unguarded; he seems to think only the leisured classes are privileged to have attacks of the squitters. Why didn't we police the town properly so that people's tyres didn't get slashed? In the end I had to send him back to Clintbury in a police car. The media were in full cry after him, so I had to leave a man on the park gates to keep them out.'

'And what happened at the inquest, John?' asked the super-intendent.

'Oh, he grumbled a bit, as usual,' said Grainger. 'Then he adjourned it indefinitely, as per instructions. Afterwards Theo Stratton made quite a dignified little press statement, saying he wasn't a murderer and had always been against capital punishment, and although the deceased had been committing a horrible crime, he sincerely regretting having used so much force that he killed him.'

'Did he and the Montgomery woman get together at all?'

'No, she kept quite clear of him. Afterwards she lost her temper with the feminist circus and the media. I think she hated the whole business.'

'About the media, John. Were there any awkward questions?'

'No, thank God. Not so far. How long do we have to keep the lid on this thing?'

'As long as it takes, John. Sorry, but there it is.'

Ignorant of the day's dramatic developments, Celia drove over to Clintbury that afternoon to keep her date with Victor Stratton. The main street of the village was a picturesque jumble of fifteenth- to eighteenth-century houses, marred only by the garish shop-front of a general store with ambitions to become a mini-supermarket. At the top end of it she was confronted by the imposing wrought iron gates of Clintbury Park, flanked by aggressive stone eagles on top of pillars. The gates were shut. As instructed by Victor, she honked to be let in.

As she waited, two men in jeans and bomber jackets approached the driver's window. One of them levelled a video camera at her, and the other said, 'Member of the family, are you?'

'No, just calling on business.'

'What sort of business, dear?'

'Private business, of interest to no one but me.'

An elderly woman had hobbled out of the lodge, and called through the gate for Celia to identify herself. Celia said who she was and was let through, pursued by shouts from the journalists. Wondering what Victor Stratton had done to attract the attention of the media, she drove on through parkland dotted with trees till the house came in sight.

Though it was Elizabethan, there was no nonsense about exposed beams and walls leaning at odd angles. It was too large and grand for that. Its brick façade was tricked out with the over-rich ornament typical of an age which believed that wealth, much of it newly acquired, ought to be put on display. There were busts in niches, onion-dome turrets topped with fancy wind-vanes and tall chimneys with fantastic barley-sugar twists in carved brick. The jutting porch in the middle of the entrance front was a riot of little pillars and carved strapwork.

As she drove into the forecourt Victor Stratton came running out of the house to meet her, looking like an over-excited schoolboy. 'Welcome to Clintbury, Mrs Grant. Leave your keys in the car, my chauffeur will take it round to the stable yard. I can't wait to show you the garden.'

He hurried her into the house, through a Great Hall hung with heraldic banners and Elizabethan portraits, and on into a wide central corridor with a glazed door at the far end, which led out on to a raised terrace on the garden side of the house. 'Well, here you are, such as it is,' he said. 'My garden. Terrible, don't you think?'

Viewed from the terrace, it did not seem terrible to Celia. It was reasonably well kept, and its history was clear from the layout. Some Georgian enthusiast for landscape gardening had swept away whatever formal garden the original owners had left behind them, substituting nothing much except grass, which merged into rolling parkland with a lake and a few tastefully arranged clumps of trees in the middle distance.

Far more recently, some owner of Clintbury had found this empty flowerless landscape too austere. Abandoning the fashionable dictates of Capability Brown for those of Gertrude Jekyll, he had broken up the area below the terrace with irregularly shaped shrub and flower borders on either side of the lawn which overlooked the park. A herd of fallow deer, which had survived from an earlier stage in Clintbury's development, was grazing near the lake in fulfilment of its duty to look picturesque. Whatever I do, Celia thought, I must on no account block out this marvellous view.

A flight of steps led down from the terrace and Victor Stratton took her on a guided tour. As they inspected exhausted-looking

43

rosebeds, an overgrown fernery and a scummy lily pool, she tried to find out what he had in mind by way of an Elizabethan garden. He was only too eager to explain, and talked volubly of pleached alleys, fountains, mazes and knot parterres, though he seemed to have only vague ideas of how they were all to be fitted in. 'And I must have a privy garden, just for me. Elizabeth had to have one leading out of her private apartments wherever she went to stay on her progresses. I want one too.'

He led her on into a sunken garden sheltered by grim evergreens. In it was a deck chair containing the ghost writer of Victor's lecture, asleep with a book open on his lap. 'My Uncle Theo,' Victor explained.

Theo leapt to his feet, and bowed elaborately to Celia. 'Ah. The fairy queen Proserpina bids me awake.'

'No, she does nothing so bossy,' Celia protested. 'Do go back to sleep if you want to.'

'On no account. You and your garden project are a welcome distraction after a morning of shock-horror vicissitudes. Were you stopped at the gates and torn to pieces by the votaries of the goddess Media?'

'There were two newsmen there, but I escaped intact.'

'Only two? Then the main orgy must be over. When we arrived back from the inquest they were holding high revel, moved to Bacchic frenzy by the smell of blood.'

What have I walked into, Celia thought; what inquest, whose blood? But it took her only a moment to get her curiosity firmly under control. However lurid the details, she was too busy to bother. Her job here was to land a fat landscaping contract and rescue Archerscroft Nurseries from near-bankruptcy.

Victor Stratton too seemed anxious to avoid digressions from the business in hand. 'Never mind that now,' he said, quelling Theo with a look, and began explaining that there had to be arbours perched on high mounds, so that their occupants could feast their eyes on the geometrical patterns in the knots below.

'Francis Bacon took a poor view of knots,' remarked Theo with a twinkle of mischief. 'According to him "they be but toys: you may see as good sights many times in tarts".'

'Tarts?' Victor echoed coldly.

44

'Yes. Splendid affairs with elaborate patterns in pastry on top. The Elizabethans called them "Subtleties".'

'Bacon was writing in the next reign,' said Celia. 'Knots had gone out of fashion by then and the Frenchified *parterre de broderie* had come in.'

Victor's chubby face moulded itself into a sneer. 'Exactly, you've got your dates muddled up,' he said with malicious relish, and began sketching out plans for a series of enclosures surrounded by hedges, and containing fountains and statues galore. 'Venus and Diana, of course, all the usual Gloriana symbols, and the Nine Muses, the Twelve Worthies, and Old Uncle Tom Cobley and all.'

'And pelicans?' Theo added with a panic-stricken smirk, as if he knew he was suggesting something outrageous.

Victor glared. 'Certainly not, you must be out of your mind.'

Squashed by his rebuke, Theo subsided. Celia was puzzled. What was wrong with pelicans? They were a perfectly standard piece of Tudor religious symbolism, because of an unfounded belief that they fed their starving young sacrificially on blood from their own breast. They were a commonplace in Elizabethan gardens. Why was Victor so against them? Before she could think this out he was off again, this time about pillars entwined with eglantine, and his eyes glittered with enthusiasm. Decidedly, he was a little mad. She was prepared to lay out this labour-intensive nightmare for him, provided he paid her handsomely. But who was to maintain it afterwards?

At the other end of a long grass walk a young man was hoeing a flowerbed, none too vigorously. He was lanky and serious-looking, and his long brown hair was trapped into a queue at the back of his neck with an elastic band. 'Your gardener?' she asked Victor.

'Only a stopgap. I hired him to keep the weeds down till I could get this operation of ours organised. I'll get rid of him when you start work.'

'Oh, but you should keep him on,' Theo urged. 'Your Elizabethan garden won't be complete without a hermit in a grotto, to sing your praises in rhyming couplets whenever you come out to take the air. He'd be ideal for the job.'

'Is he a poet?' Celia asked. 'He looks as if he could be.'

'No, a budding novelist,' Theo told her. 'Heavily influenced by Robbe-Grillet and Raymond Queneau, I suspect. He adds a paragraph or two in the potting shed from time to time.'

Victor walked up to the young man. 'Hullo, Elton. Getting on with it, are you? Keeping the weeds down?'

'Yes, Mr Stratton.' His tone was neutral, but the cold dislike in his eyes astonished Celia. Any rhyming couplets he penned for his employer would be very sour.

'I'm told you do a bit of writing,' said Victor, suddenly becoming a patron of the arts. 'Experimental stuff, is it? I'm all for that. There's some fascinating writing in Robbe-Grillet.'

'Do you think so?' said Elton, with a malicious smile. 'I don't.'

'Oh, come,' bleated Victor weakly, finding himself wrong-footed.

'The *nouveau roman* is as dead as a dodo,' Elton proclaimed. 'I can't imagine why anyone back in the sixties fell for that ridiculous hype. And now, if you'll excuse me, it's time I knocked off.'

As he walked away, Celia wondered what Victor had done to Elton to make himself so hated. And on a more down-to-earth plane, what were the young man's working hours? Eight to four would be normal for a gardener, so why was he still around at ten to six?

Victor was looking daggers at Theo. 'Why the hell did you tell me he was a Robbe-Grillet fan?'

'I didn't say he was,' said Theo, looking frightened but delighted at Victor's discomfiture. 'I said I thought he might be, but I was wrong. The flavour of the month is probably someone in his twenties that we've never heard of.'

For some time Celia had suspected that Theo's feverish banter hid a loathing of Victor quite as deep as young Elton's. Her suspicion was confirmed when it emerged that Victor wanted the area below the terrace closed in with high hedges and banks which would shut out the view over the park. Celia's horror at this idea was nothing to the savage alarm with which Theo greeted it. 'You can't be serious, Victor. If you really intend to block out that marvellous view, you're – yes, I have to say it, a horticultural hooligan and a vandal.'

Victor's ageing pretty-boy face took on an obstinate look. 'Nonsense, all Elizabethan gardens were enclosed.'

'Not all of them.' Celia began citing exceptions, and hoped he would not notice that most of them dated from the next reign.

'Why stop at a few hedges if you want to be authentic?' wailed Theo. 'Have the lawns cut with scythes. The lawnmower was a new-fangled nineteenth-century invention.'

'Don't be ridiculous,' said Victor, red with anger. 'Come and look at the walled garden, Mrs Grant. I'm sure we could do something with that.'

It had once contained fruit and vegetables, but the fruit trees that had survived were wallowing in a sea of nettles and bind-weed. While Celia was deciding that several lengths of the wall were crumbling and would have to be rebuilt, Victor's imagination worked overtime. 'I thought we'd turn it into a sort of copse, with obelisks at intervals among the trees, like the ones in Pliny the Elder's garden.'

After they had spent some time pacing up and down and discussing possibilities, he decided it was time to go indoors. Their way back to the house took them through the stable yard. A Land-Rover pulling a trailer had just driven into it, and a strikingly beautiful young man with coal-black hair and very blue eyes was climbing out, looking pleased with himself and the world. 'Hi, Victor,' he called. 'I'm back.'

'Oh yes, you've been away,' said Victor, coldly. 'This is my half-brother, Mrs Grant. Nigel Burke.'

The newcomer smiled cheerfully, baring very white, very regular teeth. 'To amplify that a little, Mrs Grant, I'm the result of a last elderly spasm of our father's loins, and my surname isn't Stratton because he couldn't be bothered with wedding bells at his age.'

Victor looked disgusted and Theo said: 'Did you have a good trip?'

'Marvellous. Just look what I found in Hungary.'

The 'find' was in the trailer, covered with a tarpaulin which he pulled off. A vintage car was revealed, with chromium exhaust tubes sprouting out from under an enormously long bonnet, and coachwork in a dilapidated state.

'A beauty, don't you think?' he exclaimed. 'She's a 1927 twelve-cylinder Delage, very rare; they built less than twenty of them. I found it in the stables of a castle near Lake Balaton that had been turned into a workers' holiday home, and had

47

hell's delight getting it out, had to bribe everyone right left and centre. But fortunately they'd no idea what it was worth. When I've finished restoring it it'll sell for a million at least.'

Celia eyed the rusting body panels. 'Isn't it a bit far gone for that?'

'Oh, that's the cleverness of me. The coachwork's a mess, but the engine's okay, perfect condition in fact. Come and look in here.'

He opened the doors of one of the coach houses, revealing a twin of the car on the trailer. Its bodywork was in far better condition, and some restoration work had been done. 'I shall cannibalise them, combine the two. This one was mouldering in a barn in Andalucia, belonged to a mad old nobleman who gave it to me, just imagine! Luckily for me people don't realise how valuable these old wrecks are.'

Victor was fidgeting, as if he disliked being ousted from the centre of attention by his half-brother. 'Time to go in and change for dinner,' he announced.

'Oh, that reminds me, Victor,' said Nigel. 'I've been away a month, there's nothing in my fridge and I'm starving. Could I come down on you for some food?'

For some reason, his blue eyes were brimming over with mischief.

'I suppose so,' said Victor grudgingly. 'Go along to the kitchen and see what they can do for you.'

The mischief deepened into savage mockery. 'The kitchen?' Nigel exclaimed with exaggerated delight. 'May I really aspire to the kitchen? Shouldn't the crumbs from the rich man's table be eaten off the ground outside?'

Celia was astonished. Far from being a member of the Clintbury household, Nigel was evidently too much of a pariah to be invited to join it for dinner.

Being directed to the kitchen like a tramp seemed to amuse him. He treated Celia to a winning smile. 'You look gorgeous. I'm sorry I shan't be meeting you at dinner. As you've probably gathered, I'm not considered house-trained.'

'Shut up, you silly little gigolo,' snapped Victor. With an effort, he switched on a smile. 'Let's go indoors, Mrs Grant. I'll get someone to show you to your room.'

Summoned by vigorous tugs on a bell-rope in the Great Hall, a pretty young uniformed maid led Celia up an enormously grand stone staircase and along a corridor to a bedroom containing a sumptuous four-poster bed, a bathroom cunningly concealed behind linenfold panelling and a reproduction of Hilliard's portrait of Mary, Queen of Scots. She bathed and changed, and was on her way downstairs again when a door halfway along the corridor opened and Theo put his head out. 'Hullo, Mrs Grant. How about a tot of sherry?'

Celia hesitated. Whisky was really her tipple, but would it not be indecorous to drink even sherry in a man's bedroom?

'Come on, you won't get anything with dinner,' he urged. 'This is supposed to be a teetotal house.'

She accepted, and stepped into a pleasantly book-lined room with a bed in one corner. Looking conspiratorial, Theo produced a bottle of sherry and two glasses from the depths of a wardrobe. They settled down to drink, and Celia decided to improve her knowledge of the Clintbury set-up. 'Mr Stratton's half-brother doesn't live in the house?'

'No. He did, but he moved out last year into a flat over the stables. It's a better arrangement. As you probably gathered, Nigel and Victor don't get on.'

'I suppose relationships between half-brothers are always difficult, especially when there's a difference of age.'

'And of temperament,' said Theo. 'They've hated each other since they were children.'

'I'm surprised that they lived together under the same roof for so long.'

'Ah, that was because they had to, under their father's will. Nigel receives a small income under a trust, provided he lives under Victor's roof. It was stretching it a bit when he moved out into the stable block, but the trustees agreed in the end. It was obviously the sensible thing from both their points of view.'

It seemed to Celia that their father's testamentary arrangements were far from sensible. She was about to say so when a dinner gong sounded somewhere downstairs. Theo put away the glasses and bottle hastily. 'We'd better go down. There's hell to pay if you're late on parade.'

The grand staircase deposited them in one corner of the Great

Hall, where Victor Stratton was waiting near a long table laid for dinner. A youngish manservant and a sour-faced middle-aged maid in uniform stood against the wall, ready to serve. Two other members of the household were in attendance, ranged behind Victor like courtiers on parade. He introduced them as Frank and Helen Bradbury. The man was undersized, thin, and barely five feet tall, with an ugly but amusing face and sticking-out ears. His wife was a complete contrast, a generously built woman in her forties, so distinguished looking and elegantly groomed that Celia wondered what mad urge had made her marry her pint-sized husband.

'Helen very kindly helps to make the house run smoothly,' Victor explained, 'because my wife is much taken up with our baby boy who was born last December. Frank keeps my finances on the rails. He gave up a brilliant career in merchant banking to come and look after me.'

Bradbury's ugly features split into a broad grin. 'The firm was taken over and I was made redundant. Victor very kindly took me on.'

It came too pat. He is like a performing seal, Celia thought. He has been trained to bark out this tribute to his generous employer whenever Victor mentions his 'brilliant career'.

Victor rewarded him with an indulgent smile, then turned his attention to Celia. 'Has Theo been leading you astray?' he asked, in what seemed to be an oblique reference to the sherry bottle in the wardrobe.

'One can't be led far astray on a staircase,' she replied evasively.

Theo produced a nervous giggle. Victor glared at him coldly, then turned to face the staircase and glanced tetchily at his watch. Someone, presumably the hitherto invisible wife, was late for dinner. Under his displeasure an atmosphere of crisis began to develop.

'I'm sure dear Marcia will be with us in a moment,' Helen Bradbury murmured, to dispel the mounting tension.

After a few moments a young woman appeared at the top of the stairs and struck a theatrical attitude of contrition. 'Horrors! Are you all waiting for me? I do apologise.'

Under a mass of fair hair she was rather plain. Surprisingly, however, she was behaving as if she was a raving beauty. As she started down the staircase she took hold of the skirt of her day-length dress with both hands, raising it slightly as if it was a ball-gown or a stage costume. Her beatific smile suggested that she was not an ordinary young woman coming down late for dinner, but a celebrated actress making an entrance down a staircase amid thunderous applause from the audience.

Arriving at the bottom, she treated her husband to a deep, contrite curtsey. 'Oh Victor love, I grovel, am I very late? Henry was playing up, the little imp; he wouldn't go to sleep.'

'Babies are very sophisticated saboteurs,' said Helen Bradbury. 'They have no respect for timetables.'

'True,' said Victor, and treated Marcia to a forgiving smile. 'Mrs Grant, my wife Marcia. Before we married, she was an actress of great promise with the Royal Shakespeare Company at Stratford.'

Marcia produced a laugh of the sort which is often described as silvery. 'Don't take any notice of Victor's "hype", Mrs Grant. My "great promise" never got me beyond bit parts as third lady-in-waiting.'

The party was now complete and dinner began. The food, handed round by the manservant and the sullen-looking parlourmaid, was luxuriously French, but there was only bottled water or orange squash to drink. Celia took stock of her surroundings. A bust of Shakespeare, copied from the one in the church at Stratford, occupied the place of honour on a side table between the windows. Decayed looking banners hung from the balustrade of the minstrels' gallery. A dazzling array of Elizabethan portraits in sumptuous gilt frames ran round the walls, mostly of Elizabeth herself, but also of her favourites and prominent members of her court.

Frank, Celia's neighbour at table, turned to her with an engaging jug-eared smile. 'So you're the garden guru, Mrs Grant.'

'Not if that means a horticultural mystic in a sari. I'm very down-to-earth.'

'Good. I like people who are practical. How many gardeners will Victor need when you've finished?'

'It depends on how much he wants me to do. Two at least.'

'And I suppose statues of the Muses and so on could be quite expensive.'

Celia agreed, and reflected privately that the problem would be to find Elizabethan-style statues of the Muses at any price.

51

'Frank is my financial watchdog,' Victor explained. 'His mission in life is to stop me spending money.'

'Watchdog? Yes, I suppose so,' said Frank with comic ruefulness. 'I bark at him like a frantic Pekingese when I think he's spending too much, but he doesn't take much notice.'

'If you want to save money,' suggested Theo with one eye on Victor, 'pelicans would probably be less expensive than Muses.'

'That is not funny, Theo,' thundered Victor.

Theo's pelican joke seemed to be at Victor's expense. To judge from their reaction, the others had heard it before and were tired of it. Celia wondered again what its point was.

Evidently Marcia was as much in the dark as she was. 'Uncle Theo, I don't understand. Why have you got pelicans on the brain?'

Theo gave Victor a look full of secret meaning. 'Ah, that would be telling.'

'Penetrating Theo's mental processes is a task for a clairvoyant with a doctorate in abnormal psychology,' Helen Bradbury told her. 'Surely you know that by now?'

Victor decided to change the subject. 'Tomorrow morning, Mrs Grant, I shall have to leave you to your own devices for an hour or so. Something's come up unexpectedly, and Theo and I have to go into Mayhurst.'

This was welcome news. An hour in the garden without Victor babbling about statues and fountains would give her a chance to pull her ideas into shape. She assured him that she would put the time to good use.

'The police want to quiz us about the untoward events of this morning,' Theo explained.

'And I want to give them a piece of my mind,' said Victor, 'for letting a thing like that happen in the town centre in broad daylight.'

Theo told the story of the rapist's accidental death at his hands and the resulting inscription on Victor's car. 'We should have gone in my Ford, and let it take the brunt. If anyone deserves to be called a murderer I do, not Victor. Or did they really think the Rolls belongs to me?'

'The real question is who's behind this business?' Frank remarked.

'The rapist's girlfriend,' Helen suggested, 'wailing for her demon lover and hell-bent on revenge.'

'If a demon lover of mine went about raping people and somebody killed him,' proclaimed Marcia in tragic tones, 'I'd say good riddance and forget about revenge.'

'Let us hope,' said Helen with dignity, 'that you'll never find yourself in that predicament, Marcia dear.'

'Anyway,' said Victor heavily, 'the whole thing's a nuisance. In some ways I wish Theo had let the rapist get on with it. But we've probably heard the last of the whole affair, so can we please talk about something else.'

It was Helen who obliged, with well-bred enquiries about friends of hers who were neighbours of Celia's.

I have them taped now, Celia thought. Theo was the court jester, who sometimes went too far, then got frightened and insecure. Frank was the Chancellor of the Exchequer, anxious to curb the monarch's extravagance. His wife was a puzzle. Socially she was a cut above the others, including Victor and her husband. What went on behind that relaxed air of elegance and authority? But the biggest riddle was Marcia, the Queen Consort. She seemed to function at one remove from reality, a hostess-figure buoyed up by fantasies about herself. What was she like when she was not on parade? It was anyone's guess.

Looking round the magnificence of the Great Hall, Celia noticed suddenly that nothing was what it purported to be. The dazzling array of royal portraits in their carved and gilded frames were copies, or perhaps even photographic reproductions of pictures in public collections or famous houses; the one opposite Celia was a copy of the Rainbow portrait at Hatfield.* The moth-eaten banners hanging from the minstrels' gallery had probably been bought as a job lot at an auction. Were the people any more genuine than the furnishings? For a moment she was convinced that they were not: that everything said had a subtext, that a show was being put on for her benefit, that beneath the surface the relationships between Victor

---

* In which Elizabeth's bodice is embroidered symbolically with spring flowers, and a rainbow held in her hand tells of the peace she has brought to her kingdom after storms.

and his court were quite different from what they appeared to be.

Nonsense, she told herself, you are imagining things, you are light-headed. That could not be blamed on a single glass of Theo's surreptitious sherry. She was probably suffering from an almost fatal overdose of Elizabethan garden design.

FOUR

The servants passed round an over-rich pudding, then withdrew. Lena, the sour-faced parlourmaid, carried the coffee tray into the drawing room with the dark oak panelling and waited to hand round the cups that Marcia poured out. Then she joined the other servants round the television in the staff sitting room.

'Anyone at home?' called a voice outside in the passage, and Nigel Burke walked into the room. 'Hi, Briggs, hi, Jane, hi, Lena. I'm back.'

He was popular with the servants. To make him welcome they switched off the television and produced a bottle of cheap red wine.

'Now, tell me all the gossip,' he said. 'What's the delicious little number with the white hair doing here? Is she Victor's latest bit of fancy goods?'

'She's something to do with the garden,' said Steve Briggs, the hard-faced blond manservant. 'But I bet he fancies her, the dirty dog.'

'I think she's creepy,' added Lena. 'She reminds me of a cat. Tiny and neat and watchful and out for what she can get.'

'Her brushes and things are silver and her nightdress is lovely,' said Jane, the pretty young housemaid who was being courted by the village grocer's son.

'What else has gone on while I've been away?' Nigel prompted.

Briggs told him about Theo's heroic rescue of Alison Montgomery from rape, and the alarming consequences.

'Good for Uncle Theo,' commented Nigel. 'I didn't think he had it in him.'

'Yes, fancy him interfering,' said Briggs. 'He's a dirty dog too. You'd expect him to stand by and enjoy the spectacle.'

After more exchanges in the same scabrous vein, Nigel broached the object of his visit. 'Victor says I can have some food to tide me over till I can get to the shops. What is there?'

They adjourned to the kitchen, where Adolphe, the Belgian chef, was brooding over the contents of the refrigerator and drawing up the next day's shopping list. When Nigel departed to his quarters over the stables, he took with him bread, butter, milk, two lamb chops, most of a game pie, and the remains of the *profiteroles au chocolat* that had been served at dinner.

'Bugger,' lamented Briggs when he had gone. 'I was looking forward to that pudding. You're too soft with him, Adolphe.'

Lena thrust a finger round the edge of the empty pudding dish and licked it. 'He could charm the birds down from the trees, that's the trouble.'

Briggs grinned. 'I bet he has little Miss Muffet with the white hair before he's through.'

'He could have anyone he wanted, with his looks,' said Lena, gloomily. 'I'd open me legs for him any day, soon as he asked me.'

'You'd be lucky,' said Briggs.

Adolphe took no part in the conversation. As usual, he was worrying about the dietary habits of the Clintbury household. 'So they eat eggs *Florentine* and *Tournedos Rossini* and cheese and *profiteroles au chocolat*,' he lamented. 'But they drink no wine to cut the fat. So they die of cholesterol, isn't it?'

'I hope they do,' said Briggs and Lena merrily.

Next morning, Celia sat down fully dressed to peck at the massive breakfast which Jane, the pretty young housemaid, had brought to her in her room. She was still determined to make a lot of money out of Victor Stratton and his garden, but had no intention of pandering to his wider horticultural idiocies. The sort of garden he had in mind was not practical under modern conditions, and its cost would never get past undersized monkey-faced Frank Bradbury with his sharp accountant's eye. But she could probably make Victor accept a drastically scaled-down design which would satisfy him as Elizabethan, come within Bradbury's budget limits and allow her enough profit to keep the bank at bay.

Having breakfasted, she decided to go out, survey the scene

quietly and get her ideas together before Victor arrived back from Mayhurst to create mental chaos out of order. Cleaning women from the village were busy in the downstairs rooms, and Helen Bradbury was constructing a massive, depressingly professional-looking flower arrangement in the Great Hall. 'Ah, Mrs Grant,' she said. 'Can you amuse yourself till Victor gets back?'

'I need to take a lot of measurements in the garden, if you call that amusing.'

'Then shall I tell them you'll be here to lunch?' It was a question, not an invitation.

'That would be very kind,' said Celia, wondering about her faint undertone of hostility, and went out on to the terrace.

Her first task was to make a plan of the garden as it stood. Her long tape measure was in her car, and she went round to the stable yard to fetch it. The doors of one of the coach houses were open, and Nigel Burke was working in it on the vintage car which he had manoeuvred off its trailer. Cheerfully absorbed in his work, he gave her a friendly nod as she passed by.

She needed someone to hold the other end of her tape measure. Where was young Elton, the novelist-gardener? There was no sign of him among the flowerbeds, so she went to look for him in the potting shed, which stood among collapsing glass-houses along one wall of the vegetable garden. He was sitting inside it, writing away laboriously in what looked like a school exercise book.

'Hullo,' he said, looking up. 'I saw you in the garden yesterday with the Grand Panjandrum. I'm Jeremy Elton.'

'Busy with your novel?' she asked.

He shut the exercise book hastily.

'Don't worry, Jeremy. I won't sneak. How's it going?'

'Not bad. On fine days I hoe a few weeds, then come in here and write. When it's wet I sit in here and write all day.'

'Last night it was almost six before you left. Why do you work such irregular hours?'

'If I do he loses count and doesn't know how much time I've put in.'

Celia wondered what sort of novel he was writing. A sensitive account of his adolescent awakenings at school? Probably not, he looked too intelligent for that. Something unstructured and mini-malist, perhaps, with only one character and an endless stream of consciousness.

'Anyway, who are you?' he asked.

'My name's Celia Grant. I've been commissioned to redesign the garden.'

'Ah. I was afraid he'd start on that. He was out there a lot the other day, waving his arms about. Does he want it made more labour-intensive?'

'Yes. Lots of bedding out and plenty of hedges to clip. Your publishers will have to be patient, I'm afraid.'

He looked at her solemnly. 'All good things come to an end. I shall have to give notice and move on.'

'Not just yet. I need someone to hold the other end of my tape measure.'

After an hour she had managed with his help to make her ground plan of the garden. She thanked him, then said, 'Don't move on in too much of a hurry. Mr Stratton may not accept my estimate, and even if he does there's no knowing when the work will begin.'

He frowned. 'I'll probably stick around for a bit. I can always pick up another sinecure in the autumn.'

'Such as?'

'Attendants at all-night filling stations can manage an aston-ishing literary output,' he said earnestly.

'When they don't get mugged.'

'Oh, I can look after myself.'

Glancing at his sharp, determined face, Celia decided that he probably could.

Her next problem was the knot parterre. There would have to be one somewhere if the layout was to pass muster as Elizabethan. But where? Viewed from ground level, knots were a dead loss; they were intended to be looked down on from the apartments of the nobility and gentry on the first floor. Which first-floor rooms at Clintbury were in general use? It would be a pity to waste elaborate patterns in box and hyssop and thyme on the view from a guest bathroom.

Going upstairs, she worked out that the rooms on the opposite side of the house to her bedroom must be the ones overlooking the garden. But there were only two doors on that side of the passage, and from what she remembered from bedtime the previous night, one of them was Victor's room. Nevertheless she boldly tried the door. It was locked, and so was the only other door on that side of the corridor. Frustrated, she was about to go back to the garden when she detected sounds of a typewriter coming from round the corner at the end of the passage. She investigated and found an office, occupied by a middle-aged woman with wispy brown hair escaping from a bun.

She rose from the typewriter. 'Ah, you must be Mrs Grant. I'm Miss Foster, Mr Stratton's secretary. Can I help you at all?'

'Well, I've started replanning the garden and I wanted to see what the plot looks like from the first floor. But the doors of both the rooms on that side of the house seem to be locked.'

'Oh yes, Mrs Grant, they would be. Both those rooms are part of Mr Stratton's private suite. We none of us go in there, except on rare occasions when we're asked to.'

Surely it was very odd to keep one's bedroom locked in a private house? Prompted to explain, Miss Foster proved to be an enthusiastic member of the Victor Stratton fan club. He was a wonderful man, she said, teeming with ideas, and marvellously generous to his dependants. But there were times when he wanted to get away from them, and why shouldn't he have rooms which were forbidden territory to the rest of the household? The suite consisted of a bedroom and bathroom, and also a library in which to teem with ideas.

It soon became clear that being Victor Stratton's secretary was the most exciting thing that had happened to Miss Foster in her whole life. She lived in Clintbury village with her elderly widowed mother, who was marvellous for her age and had a wonderful memory. 'In fact, a very interesting foreign lady is writing a history of West Sussex, the old customs and so on, and she comes to see Mother once or twice a week to hear her talk about the old days. And Mother takes such an interest in all our doings here. It quite brightened up our lives when Mr Stratton bought Clintbury and I came to work for him.'

'When was that?' Celia asked.

'Let me see. He moved in at Christmas three years ago, and I started work here just after Whitsun.'

Celia was surprised. She had assumed that Stratton had been at Clintbury much longer. 'Where did he live before?'

'Ah, that was a beautiful house too, Mrs Grant. He showed me some photographs. Ashton Lacey, it was called. It's near Stratford-upon-Avon; that's where Mr Stratton got all his wonderful ideas about Shakespeare and Queen Elizabeth and all that. He knows a lot about flowers, wild ones as well as the garden kind, all their Latin names and so on. So does Theo. It's quite an education to hear them together.'

'When they write anything, a paper for a botanical society for instance, which of them does the actual drafting?'

'Theo,' replied Miss Foster, promptly. 'Mr Stratton has most of the ideas, and they're put into shape by Theo.'

On being offered mid-morning instant coffee, Celia accepted, and they settled down to a cosy gossip in which the household passed in review before Miss Foster's rose-tinted spectacles. Marcia, she said, was 'very artistic' but a wonderful mother. Mrs Bradbury was 'a real lady, though I sometimes wonder if she doesn't take too much on herself'. Her husband had a very good head for business and did his best to 'stop Mr Stratton from being too generous to people who don't deserve it'.

'There's one person you haven't mentioned,' Celia prompted. 'The half-brother, Nigel Burke.'

'Oh, him.' Miss Foster compressed her lips into a hen's bottom of disapproval. 'I'd better not start on *that* story, Mrs Grant. Mr Stratton has to let him live here, under the terms of the trust their father set up, but – oh dear, one really mustn't gossip.'

'Mustn't one?' said Celia.

Miss Foster yielded to temptation. 'Sex,' she hissed. 'He is insatiable.'

'Is that why he had to move out of the house?'

She nodded gravely. 'He made improper suggestions to Mrs Stratton.'

Had he? And had Marcia complained to her husband of his behaviour? Or was the whole story a figment of a gossipy spinster's imagination? Celia tried to find out more, but Miss Foster had become discreet, probably because she knew too little.

Thanking her for the coffee, Celia went downstairs and found that Victor had just arrived back from Mayhurst with Theo. 'Ah,

60

Mrs Grant, there you are. Come and have elevenses with us. There's some coffee in the business room.'

She refused more coffee, but went with them into a room just inside the garden door, which seemed to be Victor's office. 'Well?' he asked her. 'Have you reached any conclusions about the garden yet?'

She was held up, she said, because she could not decide where to put the knot garden, a key feature of any design. Knots were meant to be looked down on from above. She would have to view the garden from the upstairs rooms before she could advise.

'Which rooms upstairs d'you want to see?' he asked.

'Only the ones on the south front, overlooking the garden.'

His chubby face sagged. Her request seemed to be unwelcome. He thought for a moment, then said: 'Where's Helen?'

'Shopping in Mayhurst,' Frank told him.

A bad-tempered silence descended. Showing Celia into his private suite seemed to present Victor with a problem that only Helen could solve. There were overtones for the others too. Theo had let out a chuckle of savage amusement at whatever the problem was. Frank Bradbury's face was grim with embarrassed distaste and his hands shook a little.

After a lot more thought, Victor seemed to decide that he must solve the problem himself. Muttering an excuse, he hurried off to make arrangements for getting rid of whatever it was in his suite that amused Theo and made Bradbury uncomfortable, and which Celia must not see.

Frank Bradbury watched him go, then said: 'Mrs Grant, you won't let this Elizabethan thing get out of hand, will you? Victor's very impulsive and his purse isn't bottomless.'

'Oh, I realise that. A lot of the ideas he throws out are quite impractical. I shall design something quite modest in scale, and if necessary it can be presented to him as the first phase of a much more ambitious project.'

'Only an intoxicated Visigoth would want to block out the view over the park,' Theo put in. 'You won't let him do that, will you?'

'No, it would be a crime. That was the first decision I reached.'

'And you will supply us with an estimate?' said Frank. 'Itemised so we can omit anything we think we can't afford?'

'Of course. You won't find me unbusinesslike, Mr Bradbury.'

He treated her to a wide grin of approval. 'Thank you. I'm sorry to seem miserly, but I have to try to keep his finances on the rails.'

Celia's own finances were about to be derailed with disastrous consequences unless she took great care. She would have to fight Frank tooth and nail if he tried to cut costs to a point that made the job unprofitable. It sounded as if Victor was less wealthy than he pretended; she must not allow him to run up a massive debt. She would insist on stage payments for every phase of the work.

In due course Victor returned, having made his private quarters fit for inspection, and took her upstairs. He showed her first into his library, an imposing state room stretching halfway along the garden front. The oak bookcases were decorated with swags of carved flowers and fruit, and the bosses in the elaborately patterned plaster ceiling were picked out in gold leaf. The furniture was equally rich. A copy of Gerard's *Herbal* lay open on a library table. Two Knole settees flanked the huge fireplace, and an antique globe of the world occupied a window bay. What was it that had to be hidden from her? The room offered no clue.

She opened one of the windows to look down over the garden and saw Jeremy Elton on the lawn below. He had no gardening tools with him, and she wondered what he was doing. He was standing there very still, and seemed to be in the grip of some strong emotion. His fists were clenched and he had fixed his eyes on something on the terrace under the window. When he saw her at the window he relaxed his rigid pose and moved away. She leaned out further, trying to see what he had been looking at. But a projecting tangle of Wistaria on the wall below her cut off the view.

'Have you decided where to put the knot?' asked Victor from behind her.

'Not yet. Can I have a look from the windows of the other rooms?'

The next two rooms of the suite were a dressing room and bathroom. To put a knot garden under their windows would be an idiotic waste of labour-intensive horticulture, so she passed on to a large and beautifully panelled bedroom at the other end of the garden front. It contained an imposing four-poster bed with appropriate hangings and some good furniture. There was nothing in the room to suggest that he shared it with Marcia. Everything on the dressing-table conveyed the message that the sole occupant was male.

She crossed the room to a door in the linenfold panelling. 'Where are you going?' Victor asked sharply, then added in a gentler tone: 'It's a hanging cupboard, there's only my suits in there.'

What had caught Celia's interest was not the door, but a sampler hanging on the wall beside it. Four areas of pattern, with ribbon-like tracery interwoven in a variety of stitches, were separated by sand-coloured areas like garden paths, with a circular feature where they crossed in the middle. 'Did you bring this with you from Ashton Lacey,' she asked eagerly, 'or has it always been in the house?'

'It was here when we came, as far as I remember. Why?'

'You realise what it is? A plan for a knot garden, four square knots with a space in the middle for a statue or vase. People often made a sampler for the gardener to work to, or else the daughters copied the design of an existing knot garden to show how well they could sew.'

He became very excited. 'You mean, we may be looking at the design of a garden that existed somewhere down there, four centuries ago?'

'It's a possibility.'

He took it off its hook and handed it to her. 'Borrow it. Make me a knot garden like that.'

An inner voice of caution made her hesitate and she handed it back. 'I'd love to, later. There's a lot of groundwork to be done first.'

Why had he panicked when she approached the cupboard allegedly containing his suits? Whatever he had hidden away before bringing her upstairs must be in there.

But there was something in the room which no amount of tidying could hide: the faint but pervasive smell of an expensive sandal-wood scent. The message of the all-male dressing-table was misleading. It had been wiped hastily, but traces of face powder on one corner had been overlooked. Anything lying about in the way of feminine fripperies had been thrust away in drawers, or into the forbidden cupboard. It was not Victor's scent, he used none. It was not Marcia's. It was Helen Bradbury's, she wore it all the time.

Celia pretended to study the view from the window while she digested this new insight into relations within the household. No wonder Frank Bradbury had been uncomfortable, his wife's unconventional bedtime arrangements were about to be exposed for a stranger's inspection. And Theo, who was not really a pleasant person, had been amused. Poor Marcia; no wonder she had to fantasise about herself to make life bearable. She put up a brave show as Victor's consort and the hostess of a great house, but the pretence was very hollow.

'Have you found that smashing naughty magazine yet, Mr Briggs?' asked Lena.

'No such luck, I've looked everywhere.'

'It could be up in Victor's love nest. I bet he has to take a peek on the sly before he can get it up with Helen.'

'Theo probably has a peek too,' Briggs suggested. 'He's past doing anything but pinching bottoms, but he's a dirty old man all right.'

'It's not in Theo's room. I had a good look this morning when they were out.'

'I still think it must be somewhere downstairs,' said Briggs.

'Oh, do let's have another look for it. There's men with king-size willies in some of the pictures, they really turn me on.'

Celia spent the rest of the morning scampering after Victor as he strode up and down in the garden throwing out ideas. The subject also dominated lunch, eaten less formally than dinner in a dark little dining room with stained-glass windows.

'Victor dear, you're getting to be a crashing bore about your garden,' Helen Bradbury interrupted suddenly. 'Can't we talk about something else?'

As Victor's official consort, Marcia felt entitled to stamp on this subversive talk by his mistress. 'You should speak for yourself, Helen dear.'

'I'm glad the subject fascinates you, Marcia. But then you always were easily amused.'

Everyone looked at Victor, caught in crossfire between his women, and wondered which of them would win.

He plumped for Marcia, and babbled on. 'I've been thinking that we ought to fit in a bowling alley somewhere.'

Frank let out a grim chuckle, delighted by the implied rebuff to his unfaithful wife.

'"A bowling alley",' Theo quoted, '"is the place where there are three things thrown away besides bowls, to wit, time, money and curses".'

'What's that from?' Frank asked.

'John Earle, writing in 1628. The book's called *Microcosmographie*. He survived the Commonwealth and became Bishop of Salisbury under Charles II.'

Celia had decided that she would go home to work out a design for the garden on the lines they had discussed. But Victor would have none of this. 'If you do the rough sketches here,' he said in a fever of eagerness, 'we can look at them together and decide on any changes before you do the final drawings.'

This meant that she would not get back to the nursery before closing time. She rang Bill Wilkins to tell him this, and warn him about a delivery she had scheduled for next day. But he came out gloomily with his own news before she could say anything. 'Fordham's been round.'

Fordham was the manager of the garden centre on the main road, whose competition was ruining Archerscroft. 'Really? What did he want?'

'Oh, Celia, he made a takeover offer, a disgusting one. I won't even tell you the figure. The sort you'd make to a bankrupt, buying up his stock.'

'Oh Bill, what damn cheek. I hope you sent him away with a flea in his ear?'

'I made a face like he was covered in fleas and said we weren't interested, but he'll not have been taken in and I'm dead worried. He'll have heard we're in trouble from one of the firms you tried to sell the alpines to. We're done for if the word's got round: we'll have our suppliers wanting cash with order next. Celia, we got to sell them alpines.'

'We will when we get a reasonable offer.'

'Oh no, Celia, it's panic stations now. We got to sell them

for what they'll fetch, and their glasshouse too, and cut down on staff till the books balance again. You better be back here quick as you can; we got to put our thinking caps on.'

This was all very well, but if the Clintbury deal came off it would give them a breathing space. She could not afford to offend Victor by rushing off home. She went out on to the terrace with her sketch-book and settled down on a seat to design a garden layout she could sell to Victor.

At the other end of the terrace, Marcia came out of a side door pushing her infant in a pram. 'Henry's asleep,' she told Celia in a conspiratorial whisper. 'I'll be inside, call me if he wakes up.'

After half an hour's hard work Celia lifted her head from her sketch-book to see Jeremy Elton standing stock still on the lawn below the terrace. He had no gardening tools with him. It was a repeat of the strange carry-on she had seen from the library window that morning.

'Hullo there,' she called. 'D'you want something?'

He shook his head, and walked away.

When her design was finished she was rather proud of it. The knot parterre was to be at one end of the garden front, where it could be looked down on from the library windows. In the middle of it a statue of Diana, the chaste huntress, would symbolise the great queen's virginity and perhaps also her tendency to ensnare handsome men whose ardours she did not intend to satisfy. The maze that Victor insisted on would balance this feature at the other end. At its heart would be a statue of Venus, the goddess of love, symbolising the queen's alleged beauty, while the surrounding defensive labyrinth symbolised the frustrations of ambitious courtiers who pressed their attentions on her in vain. A garden house at each end of the composition, on a mound overlooking the maze and the knot garden respectively, would complete the picture.

Whatever Victor said, the space in the middle of the front, between the two features, was going to be left open, apart from a pair of pillars representing England's ambitions in the New World, entwined with the obligatory eglantine. The pleached alley and orchard and herb garden could be fitted in round the side of the building, and if Victor Stratton insisted on his privy garden, part of the walled vegetable garden could be pressed into service. She would bring in earth-moving equipment to produce changes of level, and specify decorative wrought iron gates at various points. The whole design would look much more expensive than it was, thus justifying a hefty bill. Normally she disliked overcharging. But the crisis at Archerscroft had made her more unscrupulous than usual. Besides, Victor Stratton deserved to be ripped off, and was rich enough to afford it.

She was making detailed drawings of some of the features when a shadow fell across her sketch-book. She looked up and saw Victor smiling down on her. 'May I see?'

But at that moment the baby, who had been making small distressed noises for some time, began to yell blue murder. 'Oh, damn the little nuisance,' Victor snapped.

Celia rose to see what she could do, but Victor pulled her down again on to the seat and seized her sketch-book. 'Don't bother, that's Marcia's job. Where the hell is she?'

Marcia came rushing out of the house and picked up her child. 'I'm sorry, Victor,' she cried above its screams.

'Okay, but take it away, I'm busy,' he said, and began to examine Celia's sketches. 'How d'you propose to enclose the garden on the park side? With a hedge, or with a wall?'

This was the crunch, and she prepared to do battle. 'Does it have to be enclosed?'

'Of course. A sense of protection against the outside world was an essential feature of the Elizabethan garden.'

'Not necessarily,' said Celia, lying through her teeth. 'That was a hangover from the mediaeval *hortus conclusus*; it was on its way out. Anyway, I think we should look at the garden and front of the house from the park before we decide.'

Theo had been hovering further along the terrace. 'What a good idea,' he said, rallying to her support.

Victor made no objection and they set off through a wicket gate which gave access to the park. Its long grass was a mass of wild flowers and Theo, lingering behind Victor, called Celia back to admire a spotted orchid. 'Well done, Mrs Grant. D'you think you can swing it?'

'I hope so. Even he can't want the hard line of a hedge halfway up the ground floor windows.'

But she was wrong: Victor proved impervious to reason. Come hell or high water, all Tudor gardens had to be enclosed on all sides.

As they stood there arguing, a tiny drama was being played out on the lawn by the house. Jeremy Elton had taken up his vigil there and Marcia, emerging from the side door, advanced to the edge of the terrace and spoke to him as he stood below. At such a distance nothing could be heard, but to judge from her gestures she was very angry. After a while Jeremy climbed up on to the terrace and began answering her back. But whatever the argument was, he lost it, retreating with a hangdog air in the direction of the potting shed.

Victor, still preoccupied with the argument over enclosing the garden, had noticed nothing. Theo, meanwhile, had lifted his nose to sniff the air. 'There is what Shakespeare calls "a very ancient and fish-like smell",' he complained.

Celia had noticed it too. It was the foul stench of rotting flesh. Following the smell to windward they spread out, searching for its source. It was Victor who found it, gave a shout of anger and disgust, and backed away from it with his handkerchief over his nose and mouth. Joining him, Celia saw something lumpy, lying in the shade of a spreading beech tree. It was a magnificent stag from the herd in the park, with flies buzzing obscenely round its eyes and mouth. The sight was as shocking as the stench was appalling, but that was not the worst shock. Propped against the splendid animal's flank was a rough board with a single word on it in white paint: 'murderer'.

'This is the best lead we've had yet, Porter,' said Superintendent Marshall, Porter's chief at the regional crime squad. 'But it needs very careful handling.'

'Yes, sir.'

'Krasinski's only important if he leads us to the people behind him. What do we know about him?'

'Only that he was Polish by birth and a French national, and comes from a criminal family based in Marseilles. His first name's Konrad, and he was the eldest of three brothers; the other two are Jan and Stash, which is short for Stanislaus. All of them with form of one kind or another. Pimping, mostly, and we know what that can lead to. Quite a lot of nasty violence too.'

'Can't the French turn up anything more on them? They must be in league with one or other of the Marseilles mafias.'

'I'll get on to them again,' said Porter. 'The only other thing we know is their father used to be quite a well-known international jewel thief. His speciality was breaking in through upstairs windows, apparently.'

Marshall nodded. 'That was before your time. They used to be known as cat burglars. They were put out of business when women stopped leaving their jewellery lying about in their bedrooms. He's dead, is he, their dad?'

'No, in a wheel-chair. He fell off a Belgian banker's roof with a diamond necklace in his pocket.'

The telephone rang on the superintendent's desk. Inspector Grainger from Mayhurst wanted him.

'Stratton's been creating again, Harry,' Grainger began. 'These jokers of yours have killed a stag in his park, and I've just had an earful on the phone for not having foreseen this and prevented it.'

'John, you're sure it's the same people? Could it be copycat?'

'Possibly, he's not popular in the village. But there was 'murderer' written in white paint again, on a piece of board. Anyway, Stratton wanted me to come and view the remains of the stag, which he says are ponging something frightful. I had to tell him that the police weren't responsible for removing dead and decaying livestock from private property.'

'Sorry about all this, John. I hate having to make you put up a front for us, but it can't be helped.'

When the call was over, the superintendent passed on the news to Porter, who leaped in rashly with a suggestion. 'Perhaps I should go and see Mr Stratton, calm him down?'

'Good heavens, no, Porter. With things as they are, the more you keep in the background the better.'

'Yes, sir,' said Porter, cringing inwardly at his gaffe.

The household at Clintbury had assembled in the drawing room, where an elaborate afternoon tea with sandwiches and cake had been laid at a table in the window. After the shock of the dead stag's discovery no one had much appetite. But the unnecessary

69

meal seemed to be part of a fixed ritual which no disaster could disrupt.

'The rapist's loved one is getting very vicious,' remarked Helen Bradbury as they settled round the table.

'Only a heftily built woman could kill a stag with a knife,' said Frank.

Helen shrugged. 'Herne the Hunter then, avenging a comrade-in-arms.'

'They can say what they like, I am not a murderer,' lamented Theo.

'Of course you aren't, Theo dear,' Marcia assured him.

'But you're a damn nuisance,' said Victor crossly. 'Why did you have to interfere and land us in all this mess? What made you decide it was rape? For all you knew, they were both enjoying themselves.'

'She was screaming,' protested Theo.

'Some women scream with pleasure,' said Helen, pouring from a silver teapot, 'like cats when they copulate.'

The fair-haired manservant sidled into the room and hovered.

'Yes, Briggs, what is it?' Victor asked.

'A telephone call for you, sir.'

'Who from?'

'They wouldn't give a name or state their business.'

'Then I won't talk to them, you know that. Get Miss Foster to find out who it is and what they want.'

'She tried, sir. They used a lot of foul language and said they'd go on ringing till she put them through to you.'

Tension spread round the tea-table. Marcia broke the shocked silence. 'Who can it be?'

'Think for a minute, dear,' said Helen acidly, 'and you will realise that it must be Herne the Hunter who has now decided to make a social call.'

Theo choked, and spilt some tea.

'We may as well know what they want,' said Frank, in a scared-to-death voice. 'I'll talk to them, Victor, shall I?'

'They asked particularly to speak to Mr Stratton himself,' said Briggs.

'Oh very well,' said Victor angrily, and went to take the call. The others watched him go in frozen silence.

70

After some minutes it was broken by Frank Bradbury, who began to say something, then thought better of it.

'What?' Theo asked.

'Oh, nothing.'

It became clear that whatever Frank had intended to say could not be said in front of Celia, a fact which registered with Helen. 'I'm sure you realise, Mrs Grant, that this is hardly the moment for you to start fiddling with the garden.'

Celia had to agree. 'I'll have a word with Mr Stratton when he comes back,' she promised.

When Victor came back, his face was like thunder. The others held their breath, avoiding the slightest movement that might provoke him. Celia wondered if they knew from past experience that he became violent under stress.

He went to the fireplace and pulled on the bell-rope. When Briggs reappeared, he said: 'Tell Miss Foster I want to see her at once.'

While he waited for her, he stood on the hearth-rug facing the group round the tea-table, directing a lunatic glare at each of them in turn. No one spoke.

Miss Foster hurried in fussily, and Victor attacked her at once. 'Where do you keep my engagement book?'

'On my desk, Mr Stratton.'

'You don't lock it up when you leave at night?'

'Why no, Mr Stratton.'

'In future it's to be locked up whenever you leave the room.'

'Very well, Mr Stratton. Oh dear, is something wrong?'

'Some unauthorised person has had access to it. You have no idea who it might be?'

'Why no, Mr Stratton.'

'You're sure? Quite sure?'

She thought for a moment. 'Yes, Mr Stratton.'

'Then . . . thank you, Miss Foster. You may go.'

'Victor, what is all this?' asked Helen urgently when she had gone.

'That phone call was from a lunatic with a foreign accent. He accused me of killing someone called Conrad, which seems to be the first name of Theo's rapist. I told him he'd got the wrong person, he'd mistaken me for Theo, and anyway it was

71

an accident, but he wouldn't listen. Believe it or not, he asked for blood money: two million pounds.'

Everyone gasped in horror.

'He also says the stag's only a beginning; he's going to make my life a misery, follow me about and wreck my social life.'

'Oh, no!' cried Marcia.

'He knows what my engagements are for the next week or so. Someone in this house must have told him.'

'Not necessarily,' said Frank.

'Yes. He knew we'd found the dead stag in the park. That happened an hour ago. Only someone in the house could have told him.'

He glared round accusingly at his wife, his mistress, her husband whom he had cuckolded, and his much-bullied uncle. There was a long silence, broken in the end by Marcia, who strode across the room to him and struck a suppliant attitude, as if pleading for the lives of the Burghers of Calais. 'Victor dear, how can you suspect anyone in this room, even for a moment? We all love you, we're your friends, we'd never let you down.' She turned to the others. 'Would we?'

'Unfortunately,' said Helen, to no one in particular, 'this sort of problem can't be disposed of by smothering it in synthetic honey.'

Celia wondered if she should go. The Elizabethanising of the garden would obviously have to be put off till the crisis was over, but would it be revived then? She was not sure she wanted it revived: this zooful of psychopaths was proving too much for her. But she needed some decision from Victor, and this was not the moment to ask him for it.

'What about Nigel?' Theo suggested in a frightened voice.

'Do talk sense, Theo,' Helen retorted icily. 'How would he get a look at Victor's engagement book? If he went anywhere near that sex-mad virgin's office she'd clap on her chastity belt and jump on a chair and scream.'

'What about Miss Foster herself?' said Marcia urgently.

'The silly woman has a schoolgirl crush on Victor,' Helen pointed out. 'She'd never let him down, a fact that would be obvious to anyone who wasn't too busy dramatising herself to notice what goes on.'

72

'I'm afraid this isn't the moment to make plans for your garden, Mr Stratton,' Celia broke in. Helen, Frank and Theo agreed in eager chorus that it was indeed not the moment. After some thought, Victor said: 'I suppose you're right. But I'm not giving up the idea, Mrs Grant. Do work out a finished design and let me have an estimate. When this silly business is all settled we'll see what we can do.'

I am well out of this, Celia thought, as she drove out of the park gates and down the village street. Victor would have been an impossibly difficult customer, changing his mind from one minute to the next about what he wanted. His courtiers were firmly set against the project and uttered cries of woe whenever the garden was mentioned. Clintbury was not going to rescue her from the bank's clutches with a fat contract. Other, more drastic solutions must be adopted to keep Archerscroft afloat.

Halfway through the village she noticed an elderly yellow Mini parked outside one of the pretty eighteenth-century cottages. She recognised it from a badly buckled wing as Miss Foster's: it had been parked next to her own car in the Clintbury stable yard. Instinct told her to stop, and she pulled in to the kerb. Analysing the instinct, she tracked it down to a vague hunch, arising from something Miss Foster had said over coffee that morning. Clintbury's affairs had only an academic interest for her now, but unsatisfied curiosity was a torment to her and her orderly mind did not tolerate a loose end. She walked back up the street and knocked on the door of the cottage.

When Miss Foster appeared, she produced her excuse for calling. What was the name of the woman Miss Foster had mentioned to her, who was writing a book about old customs in West Sussex? A Swiss friend of Celia's sister was doing just that; was it perhaps the same person?

Miss Foster said her friend's name was Mrs Lamont. The very same, Celia exclaimed, and they agreed that this was an extraordinary coincidence.

'Do come in for a moment and meet my mother,' Miss Foster urged. 'She sees so few people, and she does so love a chat.'

Celia accepted at once. The front door opened straight into a tiny living room, containing a very large old lady asleep in the only comfortable chair.

'Mother, here's someone to see you!' shrieked Miss Foster in the forceful tone required for communication with the very deaf.

The old lady roused herself, like a dog shaking off sleep because something is happening at last.

'It's Mrs Grant,' yelled Miss Foster, as if announcing an unheard-of treat.

As alert as a dog that has caught sight of its dinner, the old lady beamed at Celia. 'Ah,' she croaked. 'Agnes has told me all about you.'

Miss Foster vanished into the back premises to fetch sherry, and her mother began asking questions, causing Celia to bellow most of her life-history into the old lady's good ear. It soon became clear that she had a voracious appetite for gossip. She had already extracted from her daughter a detailed account of the day's dramatic events at Clintbury, and was commenting on them in detail to Celia when Miss Foster returned with the sherry and biscuits, and served up another titbit to her mother: 'That dreadful Nigel Burke is back.'

'Telegraphic address "Tomcat",' cackled the old lady.

'Hush, Mother, we mustn't gossip,' shouted Miss Foster.

But she was ignored. 'Mr Stratton caught him trying to rape Marcia,' the old lady croaked. 'At least, that was what poor little Marcia said was happening.'

'Oh, Mother, you are naughty,' cried Miss Foster delightedly.

When Celia brought up the subject of Mrs Lamont again, an explosion of enthusiasm resulted. She seemed to have done a thorough job of charming them, bringing them 'wonderful presents', entertaining them to Sunday lunch at a rather up-market pub, and in general brightening up their lives. She was a most fascinating person, they said, who had travelled widely and had known a lot of distinguished people, but she was ever so simple and natural; it was amazing what an interest she had taken in the humble details of their daily affairs.

Celia did her best to make them tell her what Mrs Lamont looked like, but got only vague answers, interrupted by further outbursts of enthusiastic praise. 'But if you can stay for a bit,' said Miss Foster suddenly, 'you might meet her. She sometimes calls in about now.'

Celia's curiosity about Mrs Lamont was now at fever pitch, and she was prepared to sit there till doomsday if necessary in the hope of meeting her. After she had listened to a lot more boring gossip and forced down a second glass of disgustingly sweet sherry, her patience was rewarded by a knock at the door.

'That'll be her!' cried Miss Foster and opened it. Mrs Lamont walked into the room, ready to go on exploiting the Foster grapevine and learn more about the contents of Victor's engagement book. She was the woman with mahogany hair who had disrupted Victor's lecture, and at this Celia was not surprised.

FIVE

'Dear friends!' cried Mrs Lamont. With a predatory smile on her face she advanced with both hands outstretched and kissed the old lady and Miss Foster, who introduced her to Celia.

'Aha, I am knowink all about you,' she commented. 'The dear friends tell me you will arrange the garden at the Park, isn't it so?'

Miss Foster went to pour sherry for the new arrival, and Celia faced the fact that an awkward situation would arise at any moment. Miss Foster would start exclaiming about the 'extraordinary coincidence' concerning the mythical sister of Celia's who was supposed to be a friend of Mrs Lamont's, and some fast talking would be needed. But for the moment all was well: the old lady was monopolising the visitor. 'Such excitement up at the house today, dear,' she began, and embarked on the saga of the dead stag.

Celia saw with alarm that Miss Foster, rigid with horror, was pouring sticky sherry over the brim of an overfull glass on to the tray. She had made the connection at last. On the pretext of helping to staunch the flood of sherry, Celia went close to her and murmured: 'Don't say anything. Keep her here while I fetch the police.'

But Miss Foster, trembling from head to foot, was too indignant to take notice. 'Mrs Lamont, you are a spy and an impostor and a false friend,' she shouted, near to tears. 'Please leave this house at once.'

'No!' said Celia, blocking the way to the door. 'Not till she's answered some questions.'

But Mrs Lamont was twice Celia's size and heavily built. She advanced like a steam-roller and knocked her aside. 'I am not answerink any questions, but I tell you this. Victor Stratton is murderer. In that house all are murderers.' In the doorway she turned to Miss Foster. 'Tomorrow you tell him you don't go there any more, you don't work for murderers. If you go, we cut your face open. And you, Mrs Grant. You don't fix his garden. If you do, we burn your nursery down. You are what terrorists call legitimate target. Anyone who work for Strattons is legitimate target because they kill my Konrad.'

With a rude two-fingered gesture she strode along the pavement to her car. Celia followed, and managed to note down the number as Mrs Lamont drove away.

Miss Foster ran out into the street too and began exclaiming weepily. Celia sent her back in to look after her mother, and decided after a moment's perplexity that it was her civic duty to go straight back to Clintbury and report her discovery. The sooner the number of Mrs Lamont's car was in the hands of the police, the better.

Fuming at the delay when the lame old woman at the lodge took her time opening the gates, she roared up the drive to the house.

'They're all having their baths before dinner,' said Briggs, who admitted her.

'Then go and shout through Mr Stratton's bathroom door. Tell him it's urgent. I've found out who's leaked what's in his engagement book.'

'Oh, thank God for that, madam. He's been accusing me and Lena and Jane, bellowing at us fit to bust. I'll get you a gin from the bottle we keep in the kitchen, if you promise to drink it before his teetotal nibs comes down. You deserve it.'

'No, thank you. Tell him to be quick. I noted down the number of the person's car; if he tells the police at once, they can get after it.'

Victor appeared almost at once, looking plumper than usual in a towelling bathrobe. Helen and Frank, also in a state of undress, were with him, and Theo, fully dressed but still in his day clothes, followed almost at once. Celia told her story, and produced the registration number of Mrs Lamont's car.

'Frank. Phone Grainger at Mayhurst police station,' Victor

ordered. 'Give him that registration number and tell him to get on with it.'

Frank looked startled. 'But the police can't touch her. She hasn't committed any offence, not yet.'

'What about slashing the tyres on the Rolls? And killing the stag?'

'But Victor, we can't prove it was her.'

'Stop nit-picking, damn you,' Victor thundered. 'Go and phone at once.'

He went, and Victor rounded on Celia. 'Now, Mrs Grant. I'm very grateful for what you've found out, but why on earth did you let Miss Foster frighten the woman away? If you'd kept your head, we could have confronted her and put a stop to her nonsense.'

'I kept my head, but unfortunately Miss Foster lost hers.'

'So now we don't know who this Mrs Lamont is. It may not be her real name.'

'Probably not, but it all links up,' Celia told him, and explained that the Fosters' visitor was also the woman who had organised the rubbishing of his lecture. 'I was there. I recognised her at once when she came into the room just now.'

'You were at the lecture?' he echoed, suspicious and displeased. 'Why?'

'The subject interested me, and I like to know as much as I can about anyone I'm going to do business with.' Choosing her words diplomatically she added: 'I suppose some remark by Miss Foster led Mrs Lamont to believe that your uncle ghosted the lecture for you to deliver— '

'There, Victor!' interrupted Theo triumphantly. 'What did I tell you? That heckler was nothing to do with me.'

'Shut up, Theo,' said Victor. 'I could kill that gossiping cow Foster. I did a rough draft and Theo tidied it up. That's right, Theo?'

'Oh yes, of course, Victor. Absolutely right,' said Theo in a resigned voice which conveyed that it was absolutely wrong.

When Frank Bradbury came back from the telephone and was given an update, he looked alarmed and said, 'I don't understand this at all.'

The three men made eye contact. Helen Bradbury adjusted

the folds of her dressing-gown and cleared her throat. Constraint descended. Once more, things which could not be said in front of Celia hung in the air.

'Theo killed the damn man, I didn't,' Victor complained. 'Why are these mad blackmailers gunning at me?'

No one answered and the constraint deepened.

'Frank,' said Victor suddenly. 'Tell Anderson I want the car. I shall go into the village and tell that idiotic babbling bitch what I think of her.'

Theo and Frank exchanged another set of mute signals, to the effect that Victor must be kept away from Miss Foster. In his present state he was capable of kicking her to death. They objected that the Rolls was still out of action, having the outrage to its paintwork repaired, but were told that Anderson would have to drive him in one of the other cars. 'You must think me very stupid, Mrs Grant, but I'm absurdly unmechanical, I've never learnt to drive. You'll stay to dinner, of course?'

Celia was filled with horror at the prospect of another grim feast with nothing to drink and Victor glowering at his panic-stricken court. She declined.

'Oh, very well,' said Victor, 'I'm sorry about all this. When it's over we'll really get down to the garden.'

Celia replied non-committally. Clintbury was a quagmire of uncertainties; she had given up hope of doing profitable business there. If Victor propositioned her again later, she would say she was too busy.

'Well, at least all that shouting and blasting has stopped,' said Briggs when he returned to the kitchen after letting Celia out.

'Thanks to the creepy garden woman,' Lena added.

'Creepy? No, I wouldn't call her that,' Briggs decided. 'She's very sexy for her age. It would be quite an experience.'

'What are they up to now?' asked Lena.

'Sitting in there having the glooms, like they've been doing ever since tea,' Briggs told her. 'They're in the cart this time, and no mistake.'

'So I cook them *Coulibiac de Saumon* and *Soufflé Grand Marnier*,' muttered Adolphe, 'and I hope they get bilious in their cart.'

'You found that nice filthy magazine yet, Mr Briggs?' asked Lena.

'No such luck.'

'I'm sure it's somewhere in the drawing room. Could there be a secret drawer in that bureau?'

'Have a look-see tomorrow, will we?' said Briggs.

On her way through Clintbury village Celia decided that she was hungry and that the Blacksmith's Arms looked inviting. After enjoying a steak and salad in its saloon bar, she started home. She took no particular notice of the car with two men in it which pulled out of a parking space behind her as she left, and followed her out of the village. Though dusk was falling the car was still without lights. But they were on when it turned left behind her at the next crossroads and right at the fork which would point her away from Mayhurst and towards home.

Her route to the main road took her through a maze of lanes, and the other car was following all her twists and turns. Suddenly she remembered Mrs Lamont's threat: she would be punished if she went on working for Victor Stratton. She had defied the warning at once by driving straight back to Clintbury Park. This was frightening, she was alone in the car and it was almost dark. What if her pursuers overtook her, blocked the road in front and made her stop? She sped on, hoping it was only her nerves playing tricks.

At the main road the other car turned back towards Mayhurst instead of following her eastwards. Why? If it was going in the Mayhurst direction it would have turned away west much earlier, its route through the lanes made no sense. Worrying about this, she kept an eye on the traffic behind her – three cars travelling at roughly the same speed. She slowed down and let them pass. Two vanished into the darkness ahead, but the third overtook, then slowed down to her speed and kept station with her fifty yards ahead. She had read enough about surveillance techniques to know that a shadower often travelled ahead of the quarry to avoid attracting attention. But surely that method was fallible? By way of experiment she turned off abruptly into a side road to see what would happen. No one followed, and she sighed with relief. But she had gone barely half a mile when headlights appeared again behind her. Coincidence? To make sure she began twisting and turning at random among side roads. Twice she thought she had shaken off the pursuit, but each time the headlights caught up with her again.

What alarmed her most was the scale of the operation. This was no personal feud: Mrs Lamont had an organisation behind her which could produce a whole fleet of cars and crews to man them. Such forces could only be mustered in the battlefield of major crime.

She was in an area she did not know. Speeding towards a fork in the road she had to make a lightning decision, right or left? She took the left fork, and found herself in a speculator's development of four or five largish houses with no way out, except the way she had come in. She was trapped.

There was no sign of her pursuers. But they had seen her come in; they must have parked somewhere near and switched off their lights. For the next phase of the operation they would be on foot. There was only one thing do to. One of the houses still had lights on downstairs. She drove up to it, banged on the knocker and pressed the buzzer of the entryphone.

After a long wait a man's voice answered. 'Who is it?'

'You don't know me. Some men are chasing me in a car, I'm terrified. Would you please let me in and lock the door.'

There was no reply and the entryphone cut off. She buzzed again. 'Please, I really am in danger.'

'Go away,' shouted the man in a panic. 'I'm not opening the door for anyone at this time of night.'

I must hide, Celia thought. At the side of the house a shrubbery screened the back garden. She crept behind a *Viburnum tinus* and peered out, but for several minutes nothing happened. Then two men appeared in the entrance to the development, dim figures in the light of a quarter moon. On seeing the car, they made for her hiding place and she shrank back. But instead of searching for her, they stopped in front of the car. One of them brought out a small flashlamp and bent down. Straining on tiptoe to see, she decided that he was checking the registration number. The other man crept up to the front door and noted down the name of the house; after which, with an air of satisfaction at a job well done, the pair turned and went away.

81

They think this is my house, Celia realised with relief, and if they burn it down, it will serve that coward right.

'Oh Celia, hiding in the bushes at your age!' said Bill Wilkins reproachfully when they met next morning.

'You'd have done the same, with all those cars chasing you.'

'Not me.'

'Why not?'

'I'd never have gone near a house where they killed the wrong person and got themselves done over for making such a shocking error.'

'I didn't know that when I went there, and why is killing a tattooed rapist with red hair a shocking error?'

'It upset this Mrs Lamont,' Bill suggested. 'He was her boy-friend, she goes for tattooed rapists with red hair.'

'In that case, one could understand her "doing over" Theo. She doesn't. She rubbishes Victor Stratton's lecture and she starts an all-out campaign against the whole Clintbury set-up, including hangers-on like me. Why does she want to know where I live, and how can she afford to put all those cars on to the job of finding out? She must have a huge criminal organisation behind her. It doesn't make sense.'

'She and lover-boy are master-criminals: drug-pushing, bank robberies and that. But he used to do a bit of rape on the side.'

'That still doesn't answer my question. If they're out for revenge, why don't they concentrate on Theo and leave the others alone? There must be an explanation, and I think they know it at Clintbury. But they're not saying.'

'Not saying what?'

She thought for a moment. 'The man who made the threatening phone call to Victor said he wanted two million pounds, apparently as blood money. You'd think they'd fasten on that as the most alarming thing about the phone call. They didn't, not while I was there. They skirted round it and talked about everything else.'

'So?'

'I don't think it was a demand for blood-money. I think they're being blackmailed, and they know why.'

The collapse of the hopes she had based on the Clintbury

contract left them two months in arrears with the interest on the bank loan. They decided to hold out for a few more days in the hope of getting a better offer for the alpines, then went on to discuss the day's business. A batch of *Encarsia* must be ordered to control an outbreak of red spider in one of the greenhouses. One of the Saturday girls had resigned: with the fall in business it would be madness to replace her. 'And one other thing, Celia. A man rang while you was at lunch, name of Grainger, wanting an appointment.'

That name meant nothing to her. 'What about?'

'He wouldn't tell. Said it was personal.'

She was panic-stricken. 'Some bully-boy of Mrs Lamont's, do you think? Or could it be the bank, putting on the thumbscrews! That would almost be worse.'

'Some sort of sneaky salesman more likely, creeping up on you and not letting on. Anyway, he's coming at twelve. I put it in your book.'

Promptly at twelve, not one man but two appeared in the frame yard asking for her. One of them was solidly built, middle-aged, and looked faintly familiar. But she could not place him till he produced an official card which jogged her memory: Inspector John Grainger, West Sussex Police.

'Of course! I remember now. We met at Glyndebourne.'

He laughed. '"We met at Glyndebourne", that's the understatement of the century, Mrs Grant. I told you about that, Alan.'

His companion was in his twenties, with brown hair trendily cut and the wide-awake look of a clever, alert fox-terrier. Grainger, by contrast, was very wide-awake and clever, but managed not to look it.

'What with a terrorist taking pot-shots at the audience and that jewellery being stolen, and you as cool as a cucumber putting us all to rights,' Grainger reminisced. 'And then you fainted from that bullet wound. Cor, what a night, I shall never forget it.'*

'Nor shall I, Inspector. It put me off opera for life.'

---

*See *Flowers of Evil*, Gollancz, 1987.

Porter studied Mrs Grant and wondered whether to feel threatened by her. Back in the office he had happened to mention her name to Grainger, who said 'What's her address?' When told, he had shouted, 'It's her! Alan boy, this is the first lucky break you've had.'

Grainger had made her sound rather formidable, with a brain that was well worth picking. But he had not mentioned her delicate prettiness, which struck Porter as sinister. He had hang-ups about women, and found them easier to deal with if there were no discernible resonances of allure.

After reminiscing for a few minutes about the alarms and excursions of that hectic evening at Glyndebourne, Grainger got down to business. 'Anyway, you're looking as spry as ever, Mrs Grant, and I bet you're just as sharp-witted and observant. Which is why I've brought Alan Porter to see you. Or if we're being formal, Inspector Porter from the Regional Crime Squad. Alan's hoping you can give him a bit of help.'

'I'm flattered, Inspector, but how can I help you?'

'It's about the situation at Clintbury Park,' said Porter. 'I'm hoping you can help me to make sense of it.'

'I doubt if I can, so don't look at me like that. I can't make head or tail of it and I'm terrified of the whole carry-on.'

There was something about him that she found unlikeable. In his effort to ingratiate himself he was looking at her with dog-like adoring eyes, but she was not deceived. Dogs were self-centred creatures. When they rolled over on their backs and begged one to scratch their stomachs it was always because they wanted something.

'Mrs Grant gets mixed up in the damnedest things,' Grainger murmured.

'You're investigating the business of the rapist with the broken neck,' she ventured. 'Is that it?'

'That's right,' said Porter, but not amplifying. He did not want Grainger to hear what he was going to say and wished he would go.

Grainger misinterpreted his silence. 'Don't know where to begin, do you, Alan boy?'

'I shall probably think of something.'

This time Grainger took the hint. 'I'm off now I've brought

you two together. In your place I'd start by explaining why you've eliminated Mr and Mrs Peter Reynolds from your inquiries.'

Porter was furious. The bungle over the Reynoldses was his fault: that was why he wanted Grainger away while he discussed it with Celia. And Grainger was right. It would have to be dealt with first.

'Who are Mr and Mrs Peter Reynolds?' she asked.

'They live near Petworth,' said Porter, covering his embarrassment with a fox-like grin. 'You banged on their door late last night.'

She was astonished. 'How did you find out about that?'

He broadened the grin. 'The report was on my desk first thing this morning. I feel bad about the way we scared you. All three crews have been reprimanded for what the thriller writers call sloppy tradecraft.'

Celia did not think this at all funny. 'You mean, those were police cars? How dare they! They frightened me out of my wits!'

'It was very incompetent of them. You weren't meant to notice. They should have kept their distance and followed you on the radio beacon.'

'What radio beacon, Inspector?'

'They'd fitted one to your car while you were in the pub. It gives off a signal they can follow from over a mile away.'

'Oh, really! I'll thank you to remove your radio beacon from my car at once.'

'They've attended to that already, Mrs Grant, while it was parked outside the Reynoldses'.'

Celia knew she looked ridiculous when she lost her temper: she was too small to do it impressively. But she was past caring. 'Damn you, Inspector, how dare you sit there like a self-satisfied Buddha after what you've done? If I hadn't thought they were checking my registration number, I'd have decided they were putting a bomb under the car and had seventeen fits.'

Porter was frightened of angry women. 'I do apologise,' he bleated.

'If you wanted to talk to me, why didn't you come straight here?' she stormed. 'You could have traced my address from my car registration number. There was no need for that James Bond carry-on, chasing me all over West Sussex to find out.'

Unfortunately, she was quite right. He had decided that the six detective constables working on the case were getting lazy, and had ordered a shadowing exercise which was quite unnecessary. But he had rubbed them up the wrong way, and they had taken their revenge by being too obvious and frightening their quarry.

But he was not going to tell her that. 'The point is, I had to treat you as a suspect.'

'A suspect? Me!' she cried indignantly. 'Why, for heaven's sake?'

'Because you'd been to Clintbury Park. We note all the car numbers of people going in and out of there, and yes, of course we get the owners' names and addresses from the computer in Swansea. Unless they're local tradespeople and so on, we follow them to see where they go.'

'But that's a silly waste of time, if you know where they live.'

'Not really,' said Porter, hoping the next bit would sound credible. 'This is a wicked world, Mrs Grant. People who come away from places like Clintbury don't always drive straight home to their permanent addresses: they get up to mischief instead. We've been shadowing cars that come out of there for almost a week. So when you started turning up there, I put you through our computer, but you hadn't committed any crimes as far as it knew so you didn't show up.'

'I should hope not, indeed!'

'But you could still have done something frightful that the computer didn't know about. So you were still a suspect till I happened to mention your name to Inspector Grainger, who isn't involved in this investigation any more. I'm very glad I did. An inside view of the household at Clintbury is just what I need.'

Celia was bewildered. 'But why are you so interested in them? They're supposed to be on the receiving end of crime, not committing it.'

'They're on both ends.'

'What d'you mean? What have they done?'

'They're drug traffickers. Another lot have got it in for them. You've stumbled into a war between rival drug mafias.'

SIX

'Victor Stratton is a big-time criminal: he's been laundering drug money for at least two years,' said Porter in a voice harsh with indignation. By his reckoning, drug-taking was not just a filthy habit which threatened the whole fabric of society with a vast explosion of drug-related crime. What offended him most was that the people who pocketed the laundered drug money could live a life of ease as respectable members of society. At the thought of Clintbury's opulent life style a little muscle twitched furiously in his cheek.

Celia too was appalled, but for a different reason. Any mention of the drug scene made her numb with shock, because it brought back the memory of her niece Sarah, who had lived with her and Roger at Kew when she came over from Canada to attend drama school; Sarah, once so pretty and clever, who had lied and cheated and stolen and promised over and over again to break the habit; who had run away and lived rough, and reappeared only when she was desperate for money; who had been picked up dead from a public lavatory in Hammersmith and lain for three months in a freezer compartment at the mortuary before she and Roger were asked to join the queue of people trying to identify her. To Celia, the drug scene meant looking down on the barely recognisable thing that had once been Sarah.

She tried to banish the memory and think straight. Where did the truth lie? She had viewed the Clintbury household as a collection of tiresome people whose parlour games had been interrupted by a menace from outside which they did not understand. But her mind went back to those moments when she had felt that nothing was what it seemed, that issues were in the air which could not be mentioned in front of her. Was this unlikeable young inspector right? If so, the reality behind the Clintbury carry-on was frightening beyond belief. She had been wandering barefoot in a snake pit.

Misreading her expression of horror, Porter decided that she was still aggrieved about the bungled car chase, and panicked himself into apologising abjectly. 'Mrs Grant, I throw myself on your mercy. We get overstretched on a big investigation like this, and the crews of those cars were very inexperienced. And to be honest I'm not very experienced myself. I need all the help I can get and Inspector Grainger says you're very clever. Please don't turn me down.'

Celia decided that this was play-acting. The spectacle of a cocky young inspector from the regional crime squad pretending to be in need of a mother-figure drew from her a faint smile. Porter saw it, and misunderstood the reason.

'Farcical, wasn't it, Mrs Grant, us chasing after you like the Keystone cops on the rampage? Am I forgiven?'

'Oh yes, I suppose so.'

'Then let me make amends by taking you out to lunch. The one thing that's right about this job is the fat expense account.'

Even on an expense account, she was not going to take lunch off a man she disliked. 'How kind of you, but there's nothing round here but fish and chips in sordid surroundings or decorative platefuls of nothing much at astronomical prices. So why don't you save the expense account for your *louche* underworld contacts and come to the cottage for bread and cheese with me?'

'May I? I'd love to.'

It was a sunny day, and when they reached her Georgian doll's-house cottage just up the lane, she settled him down with a beer on the patio while she assembled the lunch. He sipped his beer, well content with progress so far. In a way he would have preferred to host the lunch on his new credit card: it would have put her, not him, under obligation. But her offer of bread and cheese meant that his gaffe over the car chase was well and truly buried, putting them on terms of intimate collaboration. With her as his eyes and ears at Clintbury, he stood a good chance of seeing Stratton and his accomplices in jail and emerging with credit from the case.

When Celia came out with the lunch she found that he had

88

taken off his jacket and tie. It made him look even younger; much too immature to be so arrogant and artful.

'Now, tell me all,' she began. 'If these people are so wicked, why haven't they been arrested?'

'Good question. That's because they're part of a big under-cover investigation that's been going on for two years in half a dozen countries. When it's finished several hundred people will be arrested, but none of them must suspect that they're being watched till we're ready to scoop them all in.'

'I see. And all these people are drug-pushers?'

'Oh no, it's much higher-level than that. Huge sums of money have been whizzing round the globe in bank computers, and we're sure it's drug money being laundered.'

'Tell me, Inspector, how does one launder drug money?'

'Unlaundered drug money is cash, paid to pushers by addicts. Somewhere in the world, it has to be put into a bank, the sort of bank that doesn't ask awkward questions. From there it's moved round the world electronically till its origins are lost and it looks respectable. Luckily the international banking system does what it can to help us, and reports anything suspicious.'

'And they reported something suspicious about Clintbury?'

'Yes, about two years ago. We've been keeping an eye on them since then, but we had nothing hard to go on till the other day, when something happened to alert us.'

'Ah. By "something" you mean the tattooed corpse that no one can identify?'

'Bang on, Mrs Grant. The first point about him is, the pathologists say he wasn't trying to rape Mrs Montgomery.'

'Pathologists have been known to make idiotic mistakes,' she objected.

'Not in this case, I'm afraid.' He swallowed, turned bright red and spoke over-emphatically. 'This isn't the sort of thing you mention to a lady, certainly not over lunch, but if you're going to rape someone, you . . . empty your bladder first.'

'Oh, I suppose you would. Had he not done that?'

'According to the pathologists, no.'

'But if it wasn't rape, what was he trying to do to her?'

'Nothing. He was already dead. He was arranged to make it look like rape, but it was a put-up job.'

She thought for a moment. 'But if he was killed earlier, he couldn't have been passed off as a freshly killed rapist. He'd have gone cold, the police surgeon wouldn't have like that.'

'Ah, but he'd only been dead a few minutes. Before that he'd been drugged to keep him quiet. The pathologist thinks he'd been chloroformed. We reckon that the murderer and Mrs Montgomery drove him to the scene alive but unconscious in the boot of her car. She must have had someone with her: a woman couldn't have handled the dead weight of a man by herself. They make sure there's no one in sight up and down the lane, then lug him out of the car boot into the wood and the murderer kills him by breaking his neck. After arranging him suitably, he withdraws from the scene, leaving Mrs Montgomery to raise the alarm. Needless to say, she has connections with the drug scene. Her husband was an addict and drug pusher who committed suicide in prison, but they couldn't charge her for lack of evidence.'

'I can't make head or tail of this,' said Celia scornfully. 'She reckons on someone coming along and hearing her shouting that she's being raped, but she couldn't have foreseen that it would be an old gentleman who put his walking-stick round the corpse's neck and thought he'd killed it.'

'Ah, but she didn't have to trust to luck. Theodore Stratton was an accomplice too.'

'But he and Mrs Montgomery were total strangers to each other.'

'That's what we're meant to think, but it's wrong.'

Her doubts showed in her face, and he reacted fiercely. 'Don't look at me like that, I can prove it. You'd recognise Theodore Stratton's voice?'

'Of course.'

He opened his brief-case and took out a small cassette recorder. 'We've been taping the Clintbury telephone for over a week, and I brought this for you to listen to. It's a call he made to Mrs Montgomery after the inquest the day before yesterday.' He snapped a cassette into the machine and switched it on. After a few bursts of the ringing tone, a woman's voice answered.

'King Street Antiques.'

'Alison? It's Theo.'

'Oh. Should you be ringing me?'

'No, but this is an emergency. It turns out that our problem wasn't just a piece of individual enterprise by Konrad. He had backers. They've just written "murderer" on Victor's car and slashed the tyres. I had to warn you, in case they come your way.'

'They already have, the shop was wrecked by a bomb early this morning.'

'Oh dear, I am sorry. Much damage, is there?'

'Yes, and I realised at once that Konrad's friends must be behind it. I told the police a fairy story about a business rival with a grudge, but they'll probably connect it with what's happened at your end.'

'I don't think it matters if they do. They're quite happy to believe that some mad friend of an unidentified rapist is taking it out on us because I caused a fatal accident. Your bomb fits neatly into the same pattern.'

'Well, thanks for the warning, Theo. Can you still keep things under control?'

'We hope so. Frank thinks they want to resume negotiations, and this is their way of softening us up.'

'Good. Don't phone again unless you have to, there's always the danger of being overheard on a crossed line.'

The recording ended with a click. 'I still don't understand,' said Celia. 'What on earth happened up there on the Downs?'

'The scenario runs something like this,' Porter explained. 'Theodore Stratton has arrived on the scene, on the pretext of looking at a rare orchid he'd found growing in a wood farther up the hill. He mentioned that in his statement, on the understanding that it wouldn't be brought out in evidence because he's afraid of people stealing the plant.'

'And the orchid was where he said it was?'

'Yes, we checked. Either they selected the murder scene because the orchid was there, or he planted the orchid to fit a murder scene which had already been selected. The next problem is timing. Mrs Montgomery and the murderer arrange

91

a convincing tableau of rape, but they need an independent witness or two. They're at the bottom of a bank and can't be seen from the lane, so they can afford to wait till someone suitable comes along. Choosing the right moment is Theodore Stratton's responsibility. He fiddles about on the edge of the wood till two likely customers, a pair of teenagers, come in sight climbing up the hill. Incidentally, they confirmed in their statements that he stopped fiddling about and started down towards them as soon as he saw them. Anyway, Stratton reaches the murder spot a few minutes before they do, and by the time they peer down over the fence to see what's happened, there's a woman with half her clothes ripped off, a trouserless corpse lying on its face, and the lady's heroic rescuer in a state of dither because he didn't mean to kill the corpse. And meanwhile the real murderer has slipped away quietly and become an innocent party enjoying a ramble.'

And if the dead man's avengers knew that the 'rape' was a put-up job, Celia thought, no wonder they were venting their anger on the entire party at Clintbury, instead of concentrating on Theo.

But the rest of the story baffled her. 'This is all very elaborate,' she complained. 'Why was it necessary? They could have killed him quietly at Clintbury and buried him in the park.'

'Risky, unless the whole household, including the servants, are in the know.'

'Then kill him somewhere else and dump him in a ditch.'

Porter decided to regurgitate the key passages of a lecture he had heard on his training course. 'D'you know what the political scientists mean when they talk about "Noise"?'

'Schoolboy misbehaviour in the House of Commons?'

'Not exactly. "Noise" is when everyone from the media down agree that something is so self-evident that it doesn't have to be discussed, though in reality it isn't self-evident at all and has only become so because all concerned have been repeating it over and over again like an incantation. Now: the "noise" about our corpse is that he's a rapist, and it's been deliberately created to deceive.'

'Ah!' cried Celia as light dawned.

'Got there have you, Mrs Grant?'

'His tattoos. The red hair. Am I right?'

'Bang on. If you dump a heavily tattooed red-haired man in a ditch, he's going to be identified sooner or later. His background will be investigated. If you're part of his background the police will get round to you presently and ask awkward questions. So what do you do? You kill him in a way that doesn't look like foul play, you put some misleading clues in his pockets, some hard porn photos and some receipts from a supermarket checkout in Lewisham, and you create "noise" to the effect that he's a rapist. Result: Inspector Grainger checks the computer for red-haired tattooed rapists, possible living in South London. He doesn't find any, so he starts house-to-house inquiries in Lewisham. No one is looking for a red-haired tattooed member of the drug scene who doesn't live in Lewisham, so you're home and dry.'

'Clever,' Celia commented, thinking: too clever by half.

Pleased with the effect he had created, Porter went on: 'It was a brilliant piece of planning, and wouldn't have come unstuck if Clintbury hadn't been in the computer under the "query drugs" heading because of the money-laundering. That means anything odd they get up to is reported to us automatically by the local force. We weren't at all happy with the rape theory and we knew Mrs Montgomery had a past drug connection, so we asked their pathologist to check on the deceased's bladder as well as his neck.'

'And killing your tattooed corpse links the Strattons with the drug scene,' she guessed.

'Yes, we know exactly who he is. Konrad Krasinski, born of Polish refugee parents in Marseilles on 12 April 1956. Profession, merchant seaman, hence the tattoos which were probably done in Hong Kong. You won't remember, but back in the seventies two brothers called Kahlberg were caught by Customs and Excise bringing a yacht stuffed full of heroin into the yacht marina at Littlehampton; it was one of the biggest hauls we'd had up to then. Krasinski was crewing for them and got five years. When he came out the international drug agencies kept track of him for obvious reasons. According to them he's been living in Narbonne and making regular trips across the Spanish frontier, and as he seems to have had plenty of money but no job, they assume that he was up to no good.'

He took a swig of his beer and continued: 'According to Interpol, crime seems to run in the family. Krasinski senior was a jewel thief. His wife used to get herself hired as a domestic so she could tell him how to break in and where the worthwhile jewellery was.'

Celia made a quick calculation. Mrs Lamont was well into her sixties. She had a strong central European accent. Konrad Krasinski, born in 1956, was the right age to be her son. 'I think I've met your tattooed corpse's mother,' she said.

When she told Porter about the dramatic confrontation at Miss Foster's, he was genuinely delighted. He made her describe Mrs Lamont's appearance down to the last detail.

'In my innocence,' she added, 'I gave Victor Stratton her car number to pass on to you.'

'Yes, it turned out to belong to a Birmingham midwife's Ford Fiesta.'

'You mean they actually passed it on? How odd. What number did they give you?'

Porter produced his notebook. 'F687 KKP.'

She fished her diary out of her handbag and searched through the tangle of scribbled notes on the endpaper. 'Here we are: the number I gave them was E876 KKP. Near enough for them to say I'd misread it if there was a comeback.'

Porter's heart leapt. His intense expression looked to Celia like a grotesque parody of love at first sight. 'Mrs Grant, you are a marvel, let me write that down. A car number, that's terrific.'

'I'm sure it's right.'

'Now at last we've got a real lead to follow up. These people are nearer the supply side of the business than the Clintbury lot; you may have led us into an area that we know nothing about.'

But Celia was reflecting that a lot of this made no sense. Why had Frank Bradbury phoned the police at all with a number, albeit the wrong one, instead of pretending to have done so for her benefit? And why did they think killing Krasinski would get them off the hook? To kill one member of a gang made the others turn even nastier. This is awful, Celia thought; where the drug scene's involved I get so choked up about poor Sarah that I can't think straight.

But she could and did provide Porter with character sketches of all the inhabitants of Clintbury: Victor, the half-mad bully; Marcia, the wife in name only, fantasising as she put a brave face on her status as a nursery drudge; Theo, the frightened jester; Jeremy Elton, the gardener who worked irregular hours so that he could loiter on the lawn and argue with Marcia; Frank, the dried-up, undersized accountant, and his wife Helen, the reigning mistress who ruled the roost. 'I don't think her husband gets much of a look in,' she said.

'My dear Mrs Grant, Bradbury wouldn't want one,' Porter told her with prurient relish. 'He's homosexual. I'm told he has a weekly date in Mayhurst with the assistant manager of a furniture store that shuts on Wednesday afternoons. The local police are worried because lately they've been joined by various young men, and some of them look as if they're under-age.'

She was astonished by this fresh insight into the Clintbury psychodrama. 'But if he's on that side of the fence, why on earth did Helen marry him?'

'Goodness knows, women do the damnedest things.'

After marking her disapproval of this remark with a chilly silence, she said: 'In this case the damnedest things seem to have been done by men.'

Porter collapsed into self-pity. 'Oh God, what have I said? I'm sorry, I'm not a male chauvinist pig, really I'm not.'

'Let's say it just slipped out.'

'I apologise.'

'So you should. I'm not sure if I want to tell you any more.'

Porter took refuge from her rebuke in arrogance. 'Perhaps there isn't any more to tell.'

But Celia had a lot more to ask. 'I can't see Victor Stratton as an international drug baron. He's not efficient enough.'

'He has a history of addiction. Did you know that?'

'To drink, surely?' said Celia. 'He's teetotal and doesn't even let the others have wine at dinner in case he's tempted. The others tried not to look disgusted when he told me he was unmechanical and had never learnt to drive, so I assumed that he'd lost his licence and gone to Alcoholics Anonymous.'

This woman is too clever by half, Porter thought. 'It was drink and drugs,' he corrected severely.

'Goodness me. Do people really make pigs of themselves with both at once?'

'He did. He got blind drunk and killed some people with his car and went to prison for manslaughter. And when he started serving his sentence the prison doctor had to treat him for symptoms of heroin withdrawal.'

She was still far from satisfied. 'But how did he graduate from being an addict to being a drug baron?'

'It was being in prison got him into the big league. Most prisons are universities offering an advanced course in crime, but Winchester when he was there was a bit special. The drug barons weren't the usual small fry: they were two big-time pushers serving long sentences, with high-level contacts outside. Stratton probably wasn't a customer: the prison records suggest that he did a good job on his addiction problem and got himself clean. But he was in big trouble over money. Bradbury, who looks after his finances, did his best while Stratton was in prison, but Stratton had been running a non-stop orgy at Ashton Lacey Manor which must have cost him a packet, and he was in prison when the stock market crashed in October 1987. He must have taken the hell of a pasting then, because his house in Warwickshire was on the market unsold and Bradbury was having trouble paying the outstanding bills. Just before Stratton was released on parole Bradbury managed to sell the manor, and we think Stratton must have arranged with the drug barons to buy his way into a syndicate with the proceeds when he got out.'

'A syndicate? That means he put up the money but didn't have to handle the stuff himself.'

'Correct.'

She thought for a moment, frowning. Porter noted her expression with annoyance. 'What's worrying you?' he asked sharply.

'My difficulty is that Victor Stratton's half mad, and not very clever. I don't think he's capable of masterminding anything as elaborate as a drug ring.'

'You forget, he's got a tame financier on tap who knows the ropes. Bradbury got slung out of a very respectable city firm for being too clever with the firm's money. Stratton can leave the details of the money-laundering to him.'

'It's not just that, it's Stratton's whole attitude to what's been happening: the attack on his car, the dead stag, and so on. I was there when that threatening phone call came through. He was obviously bewildered by the whole carry-on.'

'An act,' Porter said firmly, 'put on for your benefit.'

No, Celia thought. Victor was the only person at Clintbury who had not been putting on an act. 'You must have recorded that call too. Could we listen to it?'

'I haven't got it here. But – wait, I think I've got a transcript.'

He produced a sheaf of typescript from his brief-case and ruffled through it till he found the place. 'Oh dear, this is the bit where the caller uses filthy language to the secretary, to make her put him through to Stratton. I don't think you'd want to see that. Ah, here we are.' He handed her a typewritten sheet. 'The typists who transcribe the tapes don't know the speakers' names, so they just put letters. Stratton's "A" and the blackmailer is "B".'

A. 'Hullo. Stratton speaking. Who the hell are you?'

B. 'Never mind who I am. So at last you find the stag we killed. It is dead since many days, perhaps it smell unpleasant?'

A. 'Look here, what's this all about?'

B. 'It is about, you have sold things which are not yours. We want our share.'

A. 'Oh really, your share of what? We can't converse intelligently unless you tell me what you mean.'

B. 'You know very well. We talk about this to your woman calling herself Montgomery, but she takes no notice, therefore we talk directly to you.'

A. 'Well, to start with, Mrs Montgomery's not "my woman". Apart from seeing her across the court at the inquest, I've never met her. Do talk sense.'

B. 'I talk sense, you tell lies. Listen, you think you end your troubles by killing one of us, you do not. On the contrary, your troubles get worse.'

A. 'If you're accusing me of murder, you must be even madder than I think you are.'

B. 'We accuse you of murder, yes. Because you kill Konrad, we ask more money and we give you hell till we get it.'

A. 'I don't know anyone called Conrad, I haven't killed anyone and I don't owe you any money.'

B. 'You do, and I tell you, we give you real hell. Do not go on Tuesday to the dinner of Lord and Lady Arundel. If

you go we smash their windows and we cut the tyres of all the cars, and afterwards we ring them and tell them we do the same to anyone who receives the murderer Stratton in his house. We do the same at the cocktail with Williamses on Saturday, and anywhere else you go till you pay us. Two million pounds we want, one million for what you owe us, and one million more because you killed Konrad. Get ready the money, because today week we collect.'

'You see?' said Porter. 'It's Stratton himself that they're black-mailing. He had Konrad Krasinski killed to avoid paying him a million, and now he's being dunned for two.'

'But he didn't seem to know what they were talking about.'

'A negotiating tactic, don't you think? To gain time.'

I must forget that this is about drugs, Celia told herself, and try to think clearly. 'Let me ask you a question. Why did Frank Bradbury phone the wrong car number through to the police?'

'In case you checked and found he hadn't called them?'

'Why would I do that? No, it was in case Victor checked. Frank didn't want to ring them at all, but Victor made him, so he gave the wrong number. Victor isn't in on this plot. It's going on all round him, but he doesn't know a thing.'

'Impossible, he's up to the neck in it,' said Porter firmly.

'So you say, but is he? With the possible exception of Helen Bradbury, every one of the hangers-on at Clintbury has good reason to hate Victor Stratton, but they're all dependent on him financially. Isn't it much more likely that they're lining their pockets with laundered money because they want to break free?'

'No. Stratton gets the money that's being laundered: it goes straight into his bank account. He's the king-pin of the whole thing. Besides, he's the link with the drug barons, he was in Winchester prison with them. Now let me ask you a question. Krasinski was a big, heavy man, thirteen or fourteen stone at least. Who lugged him out of the boot of Mrs Montgomery's car and broke his neck? Not Bradbury, he's five feet tall and as thin as a rake, a weakling. Not Burke, he was in Hungary when it happened. So who is there left?'

98

Celia could not see Victor in this rôle, and her doubtful expression registered with Porter. 'Look, Mrs Grant, he may have had karate lessons. A lot of very rich people do, if they don't want to bother with bodyguards. If it wasn't him, who else could it have been?'

Not the mysterious Jeremy Elton, he was a marginal figure without close links to the household. 'Could Nigel have come back on the quiet from Hungary?'

'Very far-fetched, Mrs Grant.'

'But he's definitely involved. He says he bought those vintage cars dirt cheap, but everyone knows what they fetch nowadays. He's obviously lying.'

'Of course, they must have cost him half a million each. Buying valuables like that and bringing them into the country is one of the simplest ways of laundering money.'

'My trouble is, I can't see Victor Stratton and Nigel as part of the same conspiracy. They hate each other's guts. If Nigel's in, Victor's out.'

'No, Mrs Grant,' he said fiercely. 'They're all in it together, the whole lot of them.'

He's got it all wrong, Celia thought. He hasn't seen them at close quarters, he doesn't think of them as a set of individuals all at odds with each other. He had a fixed picture of them in his mind as a set of wicked, like-minded exploiters of the drug scene. He's wrong, but what's the answer? Damn the drug scene, why can't I think straight about this?

When she came to, Porter was saying 'next time you go to Clintbury', and she decided to call a halt. 'I'm sorry, but I can't help you. I'm not going back there.'

SEVEN

Porter was so shocked that he knocked over his empty beer glass. 'Not go back to Clintbury? But you must.'

'No. I've decided to have nothing more to do with them.'

'Because Mrs Krasinski threatened you with reprisals if you worked for Stratton?'

'Not just that. Anything to do with drugs terrifies me.'

'They terrify everyone,' he retorted. 'But some people face up to it and do their duty.'

Confused and driven into a corner, she cast round for excuses. 'Besides, the thing isn't a commercial proposition. Victor has this vision of an Elizabethan garden but he's half mad and doesn't know what he really wants, so he'll probably change his mind halfway through and let me in for extra costs. All the hangers-on are against the idea and Frank Bradbury's terrified about how much Victor's going to spend. If I start on the job they'll probably get it stopped halfway through and I won't get paid. I'm a business woman, I can't afford to spend time on anything loss-making.'

Why am I saying this, she wondered. It's not true; if I handled it carefully I could have made a profit. I'm pulling out because I'm a coward about drugs, anything to do with them makes me go weak at the knees.

Porter's private thoughts were quite different. When she says she's a business woman, he argued, she's telling me she'll play if we offer her enough money. Well, he would have to see about that.

He thanked her for the lunch and they parted coldly. Back at regional headquarters he reported to his chief that Mrs Grant was making excuses and threatening to pull out. 'But I happen to know, sir, that her business is going bust. Her number two was on

100

about it in a phone call to her at Clintbury that we intercepted, and they sounded pretty desperate. I was wondering if you'd consider bailing her out from the special account?'

'That might cost us a lot,' Marshall objected.

'I was only thinking of enough to give her a breathing space.'

'Hm. How useful d'you think she'd be?'

Porter wanted desperately to have clever Mrs Grant available as a brain to pick. But he hated having to admit as much to his superior. 'Having someone on the inside would be a big help,' he managed.

The superintendent promised to think about fending off bankruptcy at Archerscroft with his slush fund. Porter went back to his office and fed the car registration number that Celia had given him into the computer. It proved to be a Maestro belonging to a car rental firm in Worthing, and on hire to a Mrs Krasinski. The clerk who had taken the booking could provide only a vague description of her, but it corresponded roughly with Celia's description of Mrs Lamont. The address she had given the car hire firm proved to be false, but she had paid by credit card, and her bank was in Aix-en-Provence. A telex to the police there produced no interesting information, except that her cat-burglar husband had indulged in no criminal activity, as far as they knew, since his confinement to a wheel-chair with a broken spine.

Next day Grainger rang regional headquarters from Mayhurst. Marshall would be interested to know, he said, that some unauthorised person had been up in the tower of Clintbury church, having forced the lock on the door of the turret staircase. On discovering this, the vicar had investigated and smelt stale tobacco smoke in the bell chamber. Alarmed at the danger of fire, he had arranged to have the lock repaired. He also mentioned the matter casually to the local constable, who included it in his routine report to Grainger at Mayhurst.

The superintendent saw the point at once. 'A good view over the park, is there?'

'Marvellous, Harry. With binoculars you can see all the comings and goings at the house: who's working in the stable yard, the lot. Your jokers must have known everything that goes on there. We asked the vicar not to have the lock repaired for the present, in case your jokers come back for another look.'

'Fine, I'll get Porter on to it. What d'you make of him, by the way?'

'A bit too anxious to please.'

But Porter was efficient, the superintendent had to admit that. In no time at all he had arranged for relays of detective constables to keep watch on the door to the turret staircase from behind a barricade of cassocks and surplices hanging on pegs. And after three days, patience was rewarded. A man in his thirties wearing jeans, a sweatshirt and what looked like designer stubble was seen mounting the tower shortly before midday. He stayed there till dusk. No fewer than six cars were detailed to follow him to his home base, and Porter read the Riot Act to their crews. He was determined that there should be no slip-up this time.

Celia, meanwhile, wrestled with the realities of Archerscroft's poor receipts. Pelargoniums that had failed to sell in the end-of-May rush cluttered up the frame yard, and Hilburys had made a miserable offer for her alpines that she knew she must accept. Half in tears, she rang them and arranged to have them collected.

'It's better than letting the business go bust,' said Bill when she went for a last look at them.

'It will probably go bust anyway. They're so beautiful and what we're getting will only give us a few weeks' respite.'

Though she had washed her hands of Porter and the whole Clintbury carry-on, an unsolved problem still irked her. Could the household at Clintbury be taken seriously as members of a drug mafia? Yes, if they had really committed murder they must be ruthless. But why had they mounted this elaborate carry-on about rape? Why had they not given the servants the day off, invited Krasinski in for a drink and buried him in some quiet corner of the park? Answer, because some members of the household were not in the know and would ask awkward questions if they noticed a murder taking place or a corpse being disposed of. She could not go along with Porter's black-and-white picture of the whole household locked together in a wicked drug conspiracy. Unlike her, Porter had not seen them reacting to each other. He had failed to grasp that they were all at each other's throats and couldn't have got together to run a children's birthday party, let alone an elaborate murder plot. Instinct told her that Stratton was a bewildered innocent fallen among criminals. But logic said no: it

102

was his money that was being laundered. What other able-bodied male was there who could have lugged Krasinski out of the boot of Mrs Montgomery's car and broken his neck?

Damn, she muttered, I'm being stupid about this, I can't think clearly about it because drugs are involved and they frighten me.

She had a bad dream that night. It started off as her standard nightmare, to the effect that she was a saxifrage, and pot-bound. Presently, however, she grew human but remained rooted to the spot, while Sarah sat up on her mortuary slab and begged her for help. She woke up in a cold sweat with her conscience nagging her. Why are you being so damn feeble about this? it scolded. You're asked to help the police with an important case and you say no because you have a thing about drugs. Why the hell are you refusing to help stamp out the horror that killed poor little Sarah? Ring that odious young policeman in the morning and tell him you'll co-operate.

But next morning it was Porter who rang her and made an appointment 'to tie up some loose ends'. He arrived bringing with him an older and obviously very senior policeman. Unlike Porter in his badly cut, too-new business suit, he had put on what looked like his full-dress uniform to impress her and soften her up.

Porter introduced him as Superintendent Marshall, in overall charge of the undercover operation against the drug ring, and the softening up process began. Drug abuse, Marshall said, was a terrifying problem which could lead to the break-up of whole societies and bring misery to millions of individuals. The police needed every bit of help they could get from the general public and from people like herself who came in normal business or social contact with the criminals involved.

Celia was about to say she agreed with him, and would co-operate, but he swept on. The Clintbury investigation was specially important. While the two mafias were quarrelling they were at their most vulnerable to penetration and detection. 'But of course people like yourself with a business to run can't be expected to take time off from it and work for us for nothing. We'd be very happy to come to a financial arrangement.'

Damn, thought Celia. Now that money had been mentioned it was too late to make a noble gesture. She could still say she had changed her mind and was willing to help, but the gesture would not be noble unless she turned down the money. Could she afford to? Not unless it was chicken-feed.

'How far had the negotiations with Clintbury got?' the superintendent asked.

'I'm supposed to submit drawings and an estimate, for Mr Stratton to consider if and when the Krasinski crisis is over. Goodness knows when that will be.'

'Don't worry, Mrs Grant. This is a long-term investigation. It may be years before we pull these people in. If we can get you working there in two or three months' time, it will still be worth it, so do please submit your plans to Stratton.' He produced a bundle of crisp, clean bank-notes from his brief case. 'There's four thousand pounds there towards the cost of producing detailed drawings and estimates that may turn out to be a waste of effort.'

Celia was staggered. It was a huge sum. Were the police always so generous? But of course, she was a special case. They were tapping the Clintbury phone, they had intercepted Bill's despairing call to her there and knew what a dire state Archerscroft was in. Four thousand pounds was what they believed was enough to keep her in business.

'If a contract with Clintbury results,' said the Superintendent, 'please get in touch with Inspector Porter on this number, and we'll come to some more formal arrangement about your remuneration while you're working in their garden.'

They went, leaving Celia speechless. When Bill Wilkins came into her office he found her still staring at the bundle of notes on her desk, as if trying to convince herself that they were real.

'What's that, then?' he asked.

'The arrears of interest on the bank loan and a bit over to help with next week's wage bill.'

'Oh Celia, how come?'

'I have been co-opted as a sleazy police stool-pigeon and this tainted money is my reward.'

When she explained he was horrified. 'Oh no, Celia, you mustn't. What about that nasty woman who says you're not to work for Stratton or she'll do you over?'

'I shan't be working for him. They're all too busy being terrorised and blackmailed to bother with the garden.'

'Good thing we sold the alpines, then.'

'Oh yes, I suppose so. What with that money and my bribe, we've got a bit of breathing space.'

Over the next few days she drew up the designs for the transformation of Clintbury. In all probability they would never be carried out, but she could not bring herself, even on paper, to block out the view over the park. The problem, therefore, was how to cope with Victor's demand for a closed-in garden, and in the end she solved in quite neatly. There would be a sunken feature in the middle of the garden front, filled with statues and topiary. On the park side of this sunken feature she would plant a low hedge along the boundary. Anyone standing down in the sunken area would have the illusion of being in an enclosed Tudor-style garden. Anyone looking out from the terrace along the garden front of the house would have an uninterrupted view of the park.

For good measure she threw in a herb garden and a pleached alley leading from the house to the walled kitchen garden, which could be laid out later as a Grove of the Muses if he thought he could afford it. Having no idea how much statues cost or where they were to be found, she left them out of the schedule of works and concentrated on the basic layout. She could not be bothered to cost the various items accurately, but put an absurdly stiff price against each of them. If she ever had to do the work her profit would be huge.

She was about to put it in the post when the telephone rang. 'Mrs Grant? It's Victor Stratton. Have you worked out your ideas for the garden?'

'Yes,' she said, recovering from her shocked surprise. 'I was just going to send off the plans and the estimate.'

'The thing is, I've had one or two more ideas. I do think we need a bowling alley, and I'm rather taken with the idea of a monster symbolising the might of Catholic Spain being dunked in a pool by Neptune. Could you come over some time soon, and we'll have another talk?'

'Yes, of course. But are you sure you want to be bothered, with all this trouble going on at Clintbury?'

'Oh, that. Of course it's very worrying, but I need something cheerful to think about, to take my mind off it. How are you fixed tomorrow?'

Celia said she would be busy, but agreed to go the next day. And I shall be busy, she reflected, being briefed before I go by that odious little policeman.

Still reeling with surprise and shock, she rang Porter's number.

'Oh, fabulous, we're in luck!' he burst out.

You may be, Celia thought, but I'm not. She was more or less committing herself to constructing a fake Elizabethan garden in the worst of taste for a half-mad client she disliked, having been warned by a member of a sinister drug mafia that she would do no such thing if she valued her skin.

When she reminded Porter that Mrs Krasinski had threatened to burn Archerscroft to the ground if she worked at Clintbury, he assumed that she was trying to put her price up, and said coldly: 'Surely you're insured against arson?'

'Of course,' she replied even more coldly, 'but it could be accompanied by violence. You mustn't take offence if I find the prospect a trifle daunting.'

He backed down at once. 'I do understand your feelings, Mrs Grant. But don't worry, we'll give you lots of support. Meet me at Welstead police station an hour from now and I'll fill you in on the details.'

By the time they met in a bleak little interviewing room at the local police station she was wild with panic. 'I'm still very worried. Am I walking into some trap? Why do they want me there with all this mayhem going on?'

'To make it look like business as usual,' Porter suggested. 'Remember, they're still putting it across that they're being persecuted to avenge the death of a rapist that Theodore Stratton killed by accident.'

Dissatisfied with this explanation, Celia returned to her theory that Victor was an innocent party among the plotters. 'They know he's obsessed with the garden, perhaps they've encouraged him to get on with it to keep him happy and out of the way.'

But this explanation did not really satisfy her, and it infuriated Porter. In his book the hateful Stratton deserved the death penalty for making millions out of the sufferings of miserable addicts.

106

But he swallowed his anger. There was no point in arguing with women who were frightened; they were impervious to logic. He would give her reassurance, if that was what she wanted.

He went to the door and opened it. 'Come in, will you, Johnson.'

A sad-looking middle-aged man carrying what looked like a very small cordless telephone joined them in the stuffy little room.

'Sergeant Johnson is our electronics expert,' Porter explained. 'When he's shown you how to work this gadget you can put it in your handbag. It's tuned to the frequency of the CID room at Mayhurst police station where they can always put you through to me.'

'But doesn't the whole criminal underworld eavesdrop on police frequencies?' she objected.

'Not on this one, the speech is scrambled automatically.'

Johnson handed over the cellphone and showed her how to work it. Porter waited impatiently for him to finish, then swept on to the next item on his agenda. 'It would be very helpful if you could smuggle Johnson into Clintbury disguised as a member of your staff.'

No way, Celia thought. Johnson looked and spoke like a butler or family solicitor. There was no hope of passing him off as an earthy Archerscroft employee.

'You see, we want him to bug the place,' Porter added.

'You mean, I dress him up as a gardener and take him into the house to plant microphones in holes in the walls?'

'Oh, dear me no, madam, nothing so crude,' said Johnson. 'Only an inconspicuous little device that I shall attach to a telegraph pole or a tree somewhere in the garden. I shan't enter the house; if I may I'll leave that to you.' He produced a round metal object the size of a ten-penny piece. 'The inspector will be very obliged if you would hide a few of these behind pictures and so on in rooms where the family meet and converse.'

Celia eyed the pellet-like objects with distaste. 'What are they?'

'They're microphones,' said Porter eagerly, 'with UHF transmitters attached. But of course they can only transmit on very low power. The signal's received by the device in the tree and amplified and rebroadcast, and we pick it up at the police station in Mayhurst.'

Celia could think of no credible excuse for taking a gardener with her on what was supposed to be a preliminary consultation. But Porter waved her objections aside. 'We thought Johnson could bring a theodolite with him and pretend to survey the garden. You could say you were killing two birds with one stone by having it surveyed now.'

On thinking it over, Celia agreed. Having a policeman with her, even one with more technical know-how than muscle, would do wonders for her morale.

'Very well, madam,' said Johnson. 'I'll go and get the equipment ready while you settle the details with the inspector.'

When he had gone Porter said: 'You'd better know what I've been up to,' and repeated to her what the French police had told him about Mrs Krasinski. 'Moreover,' he added, 'we know where she's hiding out, in a holiday camp on the coast between Rustington and Bognor. We kept observation there and sure enough, one of the caravans is occupied by a woman corresponding to your description of Mrs Lamont.'

'You're sure it's her and not a lookalike?'

'Certain.' He went on to explain about the observer post in the tower of Clintbury church. A man had been seen leaving it, and had been traced back to the holiday camp by a small army of police cars. 'Mrs Krasinski has two men living there with her, and we assume that they're her sons, and brothers of the deceased. According to the police records she and her cat-burgling husband had three sons in all.'

Celia reflected that a minor problem was solved. The observer on the tower had been on watch when the horrified party from Clintbury discovered the dead stag in the park. The knowledge had been used to great effect in the threatening phone call to Victor. She congratulated Porter on his discoveries and asked what he wanted her to do when she got to Clintbury, apart from smuggling Sergeant Johnson in and scattering microphones about the place.

'One very important thing. Please keep your ears open for any mention of the words "sunflower" or "harlequin".'

'Very well, but may I have a bit of background?'

'Certainly.' He put the cassette recorder on the table and switched it on.

'Police. Please, I must speak to Mr Stratton. Concerning the damage to his car.'

'Mr Stratton's not here, this is Frank Bradbury. You can talk to me.'

'Listen, we know that Stratton is in the house. I think you are an intelligent man who wishes to avoid unpleasantness, therefore you will put me through.'

'Ah. I thought it was you. Your accent's too outlandish for a policeman. What d'you want?'

'To be connected with the murderer Stratton at once.'

'There's no point in your talking to him. Thanks to you he's having a nervous breakdown. You'll get no sense out of him. I'm doing the negotiating, so say what you want to say, and get on with it.'

'No. I speak only to Stratton. His nervous breakdown is a lie.'

'If you choose not to believe me I can't force you. But we're wasting each other's time, I shall put the phone down.'

A click in the recording was followed almost at once by the ringing tone.

'Clintbury Park, Bradbury speaking. Is it you again?'

'Listen, you tell Stratton again what we told him before. He owed us already one million, that was our share. To punish him for killing Konrad, another million, so two million we want now. Not any more excuses, we want money now.'

'He hasn't got two million. It's all tied up in a trust.'

'That's a lie, it isn't,' Porter put in. 'Stratton could raise two million tomorrow.'

'Then you must pay us instead in goods.'

'What on earth d'you mean?'

'You must hand over to us the two lots you still have.'

'Which lots are you talking about?'

'The harlequins and the sunflowers. And fifty per cent of the other lots.'

109

'That's nonsense. You take the harlequins, we keep the sunflowers.'

'And fifty per cent of what you made from the other lots.'

'Ten per cent if you're lucky.'

'No.'

'Listen, let me talk about this to Victor and ring me again tomorrow.'

'You see?' said Porter. 'He's negotiating on Stratton's behalf.'

'Or pretending to,' Celia argued, 'because Stratton's an innocent party and mustn't know anything about it.'

'We'll have to agree to disagree about that, Mrs Grant. The point for you to keep in mind is that "harlequins" and "sunflowers" seem to be code-words for drug consignments.'

'I don't think they'll be mentioned in front of me.' She thought for a moment. 'If Nigel Burke came back from Hungary on the quiet to break Krasinski's neck, would there be extra stamps in his passport?'

'Possibly,' Porter admitted coldly, 'but how are you going to get sight of his passport? We don't want you taking extra risks in an attempt to prove your, if I may say so, very way-out theory. But you say he and Stratton appear to be at daggers drawn. Could you try to find out if this is a blind?'

Celia was convinced that it was not a blind. 'Does Nigel have a separate telephone in his flat over the stables?' she asked.

'Yes, and of course we're tapping it. But all we've got so far is calls to several women he seems to have sexual relations with.'

The gossiping Fosters were right, then, about Nigel's promiscuous appetites. Their allegation of improper goings-on with Marcia Stratton might even be true.

'What else do you want me to look out for,' she asked, 'apart from keeping my eyes open generally?'

'We're still very puzzled about that drop-out you mentioned who's posing as a gardener. What was his name?'

'Jeremy Elton,' she reminded him.

'That's right. Is he really writing a novel? What's he up to?'

'Goodness knows. He must have some reason for haunting the place.'

There seemed to be nothing more to discuss, so she left the

110

police station and suddenly had cold feet. What could happen to her if they found out at Clintbury that she was a police spy?

Bill Wilkins was profoundly shocked when she told him what she had agreed to do. 'Oh no, Celia, you can't go mixing with them druggy people, they could get very naughty.'

'I must, Bill. We've used the four thousand pounds they gave me to pay off the arrears on the loan interest.'

'But they could do you over proper, like they did the man with the tattoos.'

'Goodness, why would they want to do that?'

'I dunno. Because you know something they don't want you to know.'

'Do I?'

'It could be that. But look, Celia, he's still in a load of trouble with his stags being done over proper and what not. So why does he want you there?'

That was the big question, and she brooded on it as she drove towards Clintbury next day. Panic mounted as she thought of all the things that might go wrong, and among these the immediate problem was Sergeant Johnson, whom she had picked up at his house in the outskirts of Petworth with his theodolite. He wore a sweatshirt and jeans, but anyone who heard him speak would spot that he was in fancy dress. 'What's your first name?' she asked him.

'Kenneth, madam.'

'Well I shall call you Ken, and I'm Celia.'

'Very well, madam.'

'No, not 'madam'. You'd better practise calling me Celia, in case the other thing slips out when we get there.'

'It won't, madam. You can rely on that, but when we're by ourselves the other mode of address comes more naturally. You see, I was in domestic service for many years, as manservant to an elderly gentleman who left me five thousand pounds when he died. I've always had an interest in science, so I spent the money getting trained as a telecommunications engineer. But I've always kept my respect for the gentry; I can't help it.'

'Well I'm not gentry, I'm a shopkeeper,' said Celia.

'Oh no, madam. A lady is always a lady, whatever circumstances have forced her into.'

111

They were within a mile of Clintbury, and about to pass a horrendously ugly Edwardian villa standing by itself amid fields. It looked uninhabited, for its garden was a neglected mess and its blinds were down. But today there seemed to be movement. The house stood at the top of a bank and something, half seen through the straggly hedge, was rushing down the drive which sloped steeply to the road. She braked hard, expecting that a large dog would rush out in front of her wheels, but did not swerve into the middle of the road to avoid it for fear of colliding with a small delivery van coming the opposite way.

As she expected, the thing came out of the drive at breakneck speed. It was not a dog, but a heavy garden roller. It shot across the road within inches of her front wheels. The delivery van, about to pass her in the opposite direction, caught the full force of the impact, and was lifted into the hedge as if tossed there by a bull.

Twenty yards further on she braked to a panic-stricken halt. She had been warned: Mrs Krasinski had told her to have nothing to do with Clintbury. She had ignored the threat, and this was the result.

'Horrors,' she said, 'somebody's just tried to kill us.'

'Yes, madam.'

'They're probably still there.'

'Yes, madam.'

'Do we go back and investigate?'

'I think we should leave that to Inspector Porter's people. You have the cellphone in your handbag, I believe.'

She took it out and handed it to him. But it was indecent not to stop after an accident. She got out of the car and looked back. The van was lying on its side half in the hedge. Whoever was in it would need help if they were not dead.

Taking with her the small first-aid kit she always carried in the car, she ran back along the lane. Writing on the rear doors of the van proclaimed that it belonged to a firm which serviced domestic appliances. To her relief, there were signs of vigorous life within. The driver's door was open, and the head and shoulders of a middle-aged, fat, and very angry man protruded from it.

'Bugger them bloody kids, if I catch them I'll kill them. Sorry love, excuse my language.' Evidently he thought the roller had

112

been launched on its destructive career by children perpetrating a malicious prank. 'Help me out of here, and I'll go after them.'

There was a cut on his right cheek and blood was trickling down his face. She helped him to scramble out and prepared to administer first aid. But he brushed past her to go in search of the culprits, leaving her no time to tell him that they were not mischievous children.

Having searched at the back of the house, he reported that there was no one to be seen round there. 'Try the front door, will we?' he said, and wrenched at the bell-pull, which set up a faint tinkling somewhere inside. There was no answer, and he bent down to peer through the letter-box. 'Looks like the place is empty, but they could be hiding in there.'

'They couldn't be, unless they broke in,' said Celia nervously. If the house contained a murderous member of a drug mafia, it would be better for all concerned if he remained undiscovered.

Johnson had joined them and made his own inspection of the premises. 'There's no sign of a break in, Celia.'

'But Ken, where did the garden roller come from?'

'It was kept in a shed round at the back. The padlock on the door has been forced.'

Celia turned to the repair man. 'You're dripping blood all over the place. Let me clean you up.'

She brought out antiseptic and sticking plaster from her first-aid kit. But the wound was deep, and there were the beginnings of an enormous bruise. There was little she could do. 'This really needs stitches,' she told him. 'We'd better drive you to the hospital.'

'Thanks, love. Then I can phone the office from there and get the recovery people to collect the van. But I'll need your name and address as a witness, for the insurance. And yours, mate,' he added to Johnson.

Johnson wrote down his name and address, but not his police rank. Celia produced her business card.

As the repair man collected his personal possessions from his van, a dilapidated little hatchback with a youngish couple in it appeared round the corner and braked to a sharp halt when they saw the van in the hedge. The man, who was driving, leaned out. 'Cor, what happened?'

The van driver explained, with much abusive detail. Voicing

113

their concern and sympathy, the couple agreed that children nowadays were a menace.

'We're going into Mayhurst,' said the woman. 'We could drop you at the hospital. Okay?'

'Sure, hop in,' the man echoed. 'We go right past it.'

The repair man fell in at once with this admirable arrangement, leaving Celia and Sergeant Johnson free to pursue their mission at Clintbury.

'Very satisfactory, madam,' Johnson commented. 'We can leave everything to Detective Sergeant Jones and his colleague and proceed to Clintbury.'

'The couple in the car? Is that who they were?'

'Of course. There's usually a plain-clothes patrol on stand-by to cover unexpected developments at Clintbury. They'll inform the traffic police and tell them not to make any searching inquiries because the drug squad had it in hand.'

'That's fine and dandy,' she said tartly, 'but how did the Krasinskis know we'd be driving along this road at that precise moment? Someone ought to make searching inquiries into that.'

When they returned to the car, the cellphone was ringing. 'Good,' she said. 'We'll have a word with Inspector Porter about it.'

But the caller was not Porter. It was his chief, Superintendent Marshall, who was very apologetic. 'I'm very sorry about this, Mrs Grant. You're not hurt?'

'No, just puzzled and frightened. How did the Kraskinskis know where and when to strike?'

'I'm sorry, this will be rather alarming news for you. The Krasinskis weren't responsible. It was Frank Bradbury. Our patrol saw him leave his car in a lane behind that empty house and strike across the fields towards it. But of course they had no idea what he planned to do.'

Celia thought rapidly. Frank Bradbury didn't want any strangers around while he was at grips with a ruthless blackmailer. Victor's innocent invitation to her was an embarrassment, and he had acted accordingly.

'We're in your hands, Mrs Grant,' Marshall went on. 'They've failed to put you out of action, but they may try again. It's entirely up to you whether you go on to Clintbury, or decide that you can't

114

take the risk. But of course it would help us enormously if you felt you could go, and at least stay there long enough for Sergeant Johnson to install his equipment.'

She knew that if she gave herself time to think she would say 'no'. Taking a firm grip on herself, she said: 'I'm on my way there now.'

EIGHT

'You're late,' said Briggs when Celia arrived at Clintbury with Johnson in tow. 'His nibs is out in the garden, waiting for you.' He hurried them through the house and out on to the terrace, where Marcia was rocking her baby to sleep in its pram. Her smile of welcome shaded off into a look of concern. 'He's rather cross with you for being late,' she confided. 'He was expecting you at eleven.'

Clearly Celia's unpunctuality had set the whole household in turmoil. 'I'm sorry,' she said. 'We had a car accident just outside the village.'

With an exaggerated expression of dismay, Marcia demanded details. 'A garden roller? How utterly beastly. Who could have done such a thing?'

Did she know the answer perfectly well? Perhaps it was only her drama-school manner: she would have sounded insincere reading out extracts from the telephone directory. Celia recoiled from her instinctively. Everything and everyone at Clintbury was tainted by what Porter had told her about their involvement in the drug scene.

'Where is he?' she asked.

'In the walled garden, Mrs Grant, dear, and not in the best of tempers.'

She found him in the doorway of the potting shed, berating Jeremy Elton. 'You're bone idle, aren't you? Oh yes you are, there are weeds everywhere. The garden's a disgrace.'

Jeremy rushed furiously out of the shed, driving him back from the doorway. 'If you wanted the garden cleared of all vegetable matter you don't approve of, why did you make me spend three days digging an enormous hole to bury that stinking stag in?'

'Why did it take you three days to dig a hole?' yelled Victor. He turned, saw Celia and spoke crossly. 'Ah, there you are, Mrs Grant, you're late.'

'I'm sorry, we had a car accident on the way here.'

He frowned, but did not ask for details. 'Who's this you've brought with you?' he asked, shooting a suspicious look at Sergeant Johnson.

She explained about Johnson and his theodolite, and the need for a proper survey if her drawings were to be accurate.

'Then Elton can hold the sighting rod for Mr Johnson,' he decided. 'Come on, Elton, do a little work for once.'

Jeremy shot him a look of deep hatred, then followed Johnson out of the walled garden. Victor watched them go in silence, then gripped her arm fiercely. 'That's got rid of them. Now, Mrs Grant. To business.'

'Yes, I've got the plans and estimates here.'

'No, no, forget about the garden, we can't bother with that now. They're plotting against me, something's going on that I don't understand. I want you to find out what it is.'

'Me?' Celia echoed.

'Yes, you. You're supposed to be a detective, aren't you?'

Light dawned. She knew now why she had been summoned. 'Oh dear, who has given away my secret?'

'I met Lady Arundel in the village street. She'd heard from your uncle that you were going to work for me, and when I said I'd better not come to dinner because of the threats from the rapist that Theo killed, she said why didn't I get you to look into it, because the local police aren't too bright.'

Celia wondered what he would say if he knew that Porter had hired her to investigate him.

'Not a word to anyone, Mrs Grant. The others think you're here to work on the garden, let them damn well think it.'

Bewildered, Celia tried to get her bearings. 'What is it that you suspect?'

'Everything. Everybody. They get in corners and whisper behind my back. I know they're talking about me.'

This sounded more like paranoia than matter for investigation. She tried to extract more details.

'These phone calls from the blackmailers,' he said. 'Frank

117

won't let me take them. Now Miss Foster's gone he's moved into her office where the switchboard is, and he won't put the calls through. He says it's better if I let him do the negotiating. Why am I being blackmailed, what's he negotiating about?'

'You've no idea?'

'No. But they're all in it together: Frank, who has his fingers in the moneybags, and that fool Theo who despises me, and Nigel who's always hated my guts, the lot of them. I don't even trust Helen.'

If this was not outright paranoia, it was on the fringes of it. 'Why do you say Mr Bradbury has his fingers in the money-bags?'

'Something funny's happening to do with my money. I'm going to London tomorrow to see my stockbroker and find out what's what.'

'And meanwhile, you can't give me anything more definite to go on?'

No. Just keep your eyes open. When I get back from London I'll know more.'

'Oh dear, it's all very vague. For the present, I don't see what I can do.'

He came close, gave her a nudge and whispered in her ear. 'Elton. The gardener. He has funny staring eyes. He's got some reason for haunting the place, and I don't know what it is. And he's writing something: he goes and does it in the potting shed when he's meant to be working. I had a look, but it makes no sense, it's in some sort of secret code. Go and see what you think. Now, while he's busy with the theodolite.'

He strode away purposefully. Reflecting that the question of divided loyalties did not arise, since both her would-be employers wanted Jeremy's creative activities investigated, Celia went into the potting shed. Jeremy's exercise book was hidden under a seed tray, with its cover earthy and rather the worse for wear. Skimming through the contents, she decided that his opus was not a coded message, but a chaotic post-modern novel dealing fashionably with the occult. There was much talk of pentagrams and rosicrucians and medieval secret societies specialising in obscene rituals, some of them involving alarmingly explicit descriptions of perverse sex. A recurrent theme was the narrator's attempt to foil brutal guards and get into a mysterious castle which contained a secret so deep and ill defined that she doubted if Jeremy himself knew what it was.

Turning to the pages he had been working on last, she found a description of elaborate funeral ceremonies. The putrefying corpse of a monstrous animal was being buried in an enormous hole. Was this an autobiographical echo, related to Jeremy's laborious burial of the decaying stag? If so, the attempt to get into the castle might be autobiographical too. Was he haunting Clintbury because he hoped to establish a foothold in the house? And what secret did he expect to find inside?

Giving up the puzzle as too obscure to be worth bothering with, she went back to the garden, which Johnson, attended by Jeremy Elton, was pretending to triangulate. When he saw her he threw her an appealing look. He could hardly install bugging equipment with Jeremy looking on.

'I'll take over now, Jeremy,' she offered, 'so that you can get back to your weeds.'

He nodded crossly, and went to fetch his tools. 'Now, madam,' said Johnson. 'I've been looking round and that telephone pole in the park would be ideal: there's a clear visual path to the house for the UHF signal.'

'How about the visual path the other way?' Celia objected. 'Anyone looking out of a window could see you fastening your sinister little box to the pole.'

'Leave it to me, madam, there's no problem.'

Out in the park, he set up the theodolite at the foot of the pole and made her look through it at nothing in particular. Then, revealing a surprising athleticism, he shinned a few feet up the pole and waved an arm, as if directing her towards some object not visible from ground level. 'You'd be surprised, madam,' he panted, as he buckled on the device ten feet from the ground, 'at people's ignorance about the use of a theodolite. The ordinary person wouldn't know this wasn't a perfectly normal procedure.'

In the kitchen Adolphe was in a rage with Helen Bradbury. 'She is a monster, she is a barbarian, she is a peasant,' he roared. 'My *petites marmites de champignons au coriandre* are to be served cold, she says. Why? Because it is a hot day, she says, but it is not a hot day. They will be ruined. A *marmite de champignons au coriandre* is nothing if it is not freshly cooked. Left to cool, it is *fade*, it is a disaster. She is a boor, she is totally without gastronomic culture, I could kill her.'

'So could we all,' said Lena.

'You're too right,' Briggs agreed.

They fell silent as someone entered the servant's hall. Helen, with her unerring nose for social nuances, had decided that this was where Johnson should eat his lunch.

Celia, meanwhile, had been hiding Johnson's microphones behind pictures in the Great Hall, in the drawing room and, finding it empty for a moment, the business room. She was lodging one of them on top of the mirror over its fireplace when Victor walked into the room.

'Ah, getting on with your researches, Mrs Grant?' he said. 'You won't find much in here. Frank keeps everything connected with money locked up in his desk upstairs. What about the stuff Elton's writing, eh?'

'It really is a novel. One of the modern ones that aren't expected to make sense.'

'It's not got a hidden meaning that only initiates can decipher?'

'No. The point is to get people arguing about what it means, when in fact it doesn't mean a thing.'

'You're sure? Very well then, carry on detecting.'

But the gong summoning them to lunch had just echoed through the house. Going out into the passage, they almost collided with Marcia. Victor gripped her by the arm. 'You little fiend, you've been eavesdropping again.'

She lifted imploring, innocent eyes, like little orphan Annie. 'No, Victor, how can you say such a thing? I've just put Henry in the garden, and I was coming in to lunch.'

Victor gave a dissatisfied grunt and led the way into the Great Hall.

Long before lunch time Celia had realised with a shiver that a hefty dose of salmonella or botulism could be pressed into service to accomplish what the garden roller had failed to achieve. Having decided to eat only what was handed round in a communal dish that could not be tampered with, she was disconcerted, on approaching the lunch table, to see small earthenware potfuls

120

of something already laid in front of each place, including the one to which she was firmly directed by Helen Bradbury.

'It looks delicious,' she said on inspecting the contents of her pot, 'but unfortunately I'm allergic to mushrooms.'

Mushrooms had been on the Clintbury menu before, and she had eaten them. Had Helen remembered? She showed no sign of it, but behaved as a good hostess should. 'Oh, I'm so sorry. I'll get Adolphe to make you an omelette.'

Celia told her not to bother; she would wait for the next course.

'Do you know about the terrible thing that happened to poor Mrs Grant on the way here?' said Marcia. Exhibiting the whites of her eyes dramatically, she made the most of the horror-story of the garden roller. Frank and Helen produced expressions of sympathy and dismay which could hardly be sincere, and Theo said: 'The vengeful Mrs Lamont, I suppose.'

'Surely she must have stopped her nonsense by now,' Helen commented. 'That van driver was probably right, it was a malicious prank by children, like glue-sniffing and bank robbery.'

Victor was clearly not himself. Eating away steadily at the head of the table, he darted suspicious glances round him and said nothing. His gloom cast a blight over the company. Helen bickered for a time with Marcia, who wanted Anderson to drive her somewhere in the Rolls that afternoon, to Helen's enormous inconvenience. But the subject was soon exhausted and they ate a succulent *filet de boeuf en croûte* in a tense silence which Celia, unnerved by her escape from the mushrooms, was unable to break.

After strawberries doused in *crème chantilly*, they moved into the panelled drawing room for coffee. Victor lay slumped in his chair with a glazed look. The silence was still thunderous.

Suddenly Victor stood up and glared at Theo. 'Get out,' he shouted.

'What d'you mean, Victor?'

'Get out of this house. Now. For good.'

'No, Victor. You don't mean it, you're not well.'

'Oh yes I do, the sight of you makes me sick. Get out.'

Theo was cringing in his chair. As Victor confronted him, Celia thought for a moment that he was going to hit him. Then suddenly he was swaying on his feet with his eyes shut and a

121

pained look. 'Oh God, what's wrong with me, I feel so damn dizzy,' he moaned, and slumped to the floor.

'One of his migraines, I suppose,' commented Helen calmly as she rang for Briggs. 'He should be more careful what he eats.'

He should indeed, Celia thought. She had been right to suspect Borgia-style activities at the lunch table, but wrong in identifying the victim.

'Well, we know now why the starter at lunch had to be cold,' said Lena. 'Laid him out proper this time, she has.'

'What's she up to then?' asked Briggs.

'Vic fancies creepy little Miss Muffet with the white hair-do. So Madam slips him a knock-out powder to keep him from goosing her.'

'Would Mrs Grant let him?' Jane asked innocently.

Briggs considered. 'I doubt it. Too schoolmistressy.'

'He'd love it if she bent him over and took her cane to him,' said Lena, screaming with laughter.

Briggs was not amused. 'I don't like it. Something nasty and underhand's going on. Them funny phone calls are weird, I think I shall give in me notice.'

'Adolphe's the one should,' Lena argued. 'If Madam poisons Victor with her knock-out drops, she'll make sure Adolphe gets the blame for doctoring the food.'

Anderson, meanwhile, was humming cheerfully to himself as he eased the Rolls out of the stable yard and round to the front entrance. He was due to drive Marcia and her little boy to the mother-and-baby clinic in Mayhurst for his monthly check-up. He liked Marcia. She always chatted with him on the journey about homely things he understood and sometimes asked him to put a pound on a horse for her. She was the only member of the Clintbury household that he could relax with.

· When she came out of the house with Henry in her arms, the moment had arrived for a little ceremony which he always enjoyed. Instead of holding the car door open for Marcia in a correct parade-ground attitude, he took Henry from her and played with him for a moment, lifting him above his head and making him chuckle delightedly, till Marcia was settled in the car and could take him back.

'Thanks, Tom. What d'you fancy for the two-thirty at Epsom?' she said as they set off for Mayhurst.

On being told by Helen, in tones creamy with venom, that there was no point in her staying at Clintbury any longer, Celia was happy to agree. She collected Johnson from the servants' quarters, delivered him to Mayhurst police station, and reported to Inspector Porter on the morning's events.

'Yes, we know most of the story, thanks to you,' he told her. 'The system you and Johnson installed is working perfectly.'

'But there's one thing you don't know, because it happened in the garden out of earshot of your microphones. Victor has found out about my Miss Marple tendencies. He's asked me to do some detecting and find out what's going on behind his back.'

'A normal sympton, Mrs Grant. It's obvious now that Stratton is manic-depressive. He was on a high when he was planning his Elizabethan garden, and now he's on a low, suspecting everyone of plotting against him. All imagination, of course.'

'Not quite,' she corrected. 'I'm pretty sure Helen Bradbury's been doping him with Valium or something to make the depression worse.'

'Oh really! Why would she want to do that?'

'To stop him asking awkward questions about what they're doing behind his back.'

Porter made an impatient movement. 'Nonsense, Mrs Grant, he's not an innocent among thieves, he's a party to this whole thing. As I keep reminding you, the money goes into his bank account.'

'What if it does? It's easy to devise a scenario to cover that. Remind me: when did Victor go to prison for drunken driving?'

'April 86.'

'Very well, then. The whole household has hated his guts for years. They longed to get away, but they were all dependent on him financially. Suddenly he's in prison, stoned out of his mind, and this is their chance to make some money and be rid of him. The stock-market boom's still on, you can't lose, so they borrow a few of his millions, intending to pay them back when they've pocketed a nice speculative profit. Disaster. In October 87 the stock-market crashes, they're wiped out. But they're still his dependants: if they want to stay on the payroll they have to get the money back into his investment portfolio without letting him know what they've done. So they go into the drug scene to recoup the money.'

'Mrs Grant, I'm not a complete fool. I did consider that possibility, but there's a snag. How did a small-time swindler like Bradbury and a broken-down ex-schoolmaster like Theo Stratton get into the big-time drug scene? It just isn't credible. The link has to be Victor Stratton's high-level contacts in Winchester prison.'

Hell and damnation, Celia thought. I know he's wrong. There must be an answer, if only I could think straight.

'And you've forgotten about the other problem,' Porter went on triumphantly. 'Who lugged Krasinski out of Mrs Montgomery's car if Stratton didn't? Not weedy little Frank Bradbury.'

'Nigel Burke, back from Hungary on the quiet.'

'Oh Mrs Grant, don't talk such nonsense.'

Privately he was puzzled about Nigel Burke. The tap on his phone had yielded nothing but evidence of a lot of womanising. He was running three women at once, all of whom sounded besotted, and he had spent the previous afternoon in bed with one of them, the wife of an oil executive who was in Antwerp for the day. But he had to be up to the neck in the drug scene. He had bought two expensive vintage cars with laundered money.

Silence fell. The awkward questions remained unanswered. 'Well, thank you for your help, Mrs Grant,' said Porter. 'You needn't go on taking risks at Clintbury. Now that we've got the microphones installed we can rely on them.'

They parted coldly. He was glad to be rid of her, for reasons he refrained from analysing. If he had faced them honestly, he would have said that although she had no answer of her own to the Clintbury riddle, her insistent questioning was making him feel increasingly uneasy about his own solution. But he clung to it because he could see no alternative, and did not mention his doubts at his next conference with Superintendent Marshall.

Disaster struck the Rolls halfway to Mayhurst. Anderson was following a big delivery van down a narrow lane when it stopped, blocking the road completely, and a man in a stocking mask leapt out. Anderson tried to reverse away, then saw that another van had come up behind him and cut off his retreat. Another stocking-masked figure leaped out of it, brandishing a sawn-off shotgun. The two closed on the Rolls fore and aft, and the man without the shotgun snatched at Henry.

'No!' screamed Marcia and clutched Henry to her.

Anderson jumped out of the driving seat, and attacked the man with the shotgun. But he was coming up to sixty-five and no athlete. Kneed in the groin and punched in the stomach, he watched helplessly while the man on the other side of the car struggled to get Henry out of Marcia's clutches. 'Let go, you silly bitch,' he shouted over Henry's screams. 'D'you want the kid pulled in half?'

Terrified and furious, she let him go.

'Tell them we want the money now,' yelled the kidnapper. 'And say we'll kill the kid if you go to the police.'

The two vans shot off down the road in opposite directions. Anderson climbed painfully back behind the wheel and started the engine.

Marcia was distracted. 'What shall we do? Where are you going?'

'Mayhurst police station.'

'No! They said they'd kill Henry if we told the police.'

'They always say that to frighten you.'

'Oh, what are we to do?' Marcia lamented.

'Better tell Mr Stratton what's happened. Let him decide.'

'Home, then, as quick as you can.'

He turned the Rolls and started back to Clintbury.

'Henry's all I've got,' Marcia sobbed. 'I'm only Victor's wife in name. He treats me like dirt.'

'You're worth ten of him, love,' said Anderson from behind the wheel.

'He only married me because he wanted a child, God knows why but he did. I'd have left him, except that a child needs a proper home, not a cot in the chorus dressing room while I try to scrape a living on the stage.'

Victor would have to be told. She dreaded it, he would be furious. He was not fond of Henry; what would matter to him was the theft of his property and the affront to his dignity.

Back at Clintbury, she dashed upstairs and knocked on the

door of Victor's suite. Helen answered her knock, blocking the doorway. 'Oh, it's you, Marcia. What d'you want?'

'I must talk to Victor.'

'You can't. He's in bed, not at all well.'

'I must. Henry's been kidnapped.'

Helen's face froze with shock. But it was not the shock of sympathy for Marcia in her loss. It was cold and calculating, as she worked out the consequences for herself.

From somewhere behind her in the room Victor said weakly: 'Who's there, Helen love? What is it?'

'Nothing. I'll be with you in a minute,' said Helen and shut the door of the room behind her. 'Now, Marcia. Kidnapped, you say? What happened?'

Marcia told her, and added: 'Victor's got to decide whether we tell the police or not.'

'He can't. He's too ill,' shouted Helen, tense with nerves.

On the verge of hysteria, Marcia shouted back, 'If you've stuffed him too full of Valium or something you can dose him with black coffee. For heaven's sake, he's Henry's father.'

'Supposed to be. We all know who his real father is.'

'No, we do not, you slandering harlot,' Marcia hissed.

Helen glared. 'A woman who stands in the queue for the attentions of Nigel Burke, like a cow waiting for the bull, should be careful who she calls a harlot.'

Being slapped very hard across the face by Marcia made her grasp that she had gone too far. 'I'm sorry, Marcia, let's try to keep calm and be practical. You know as well as I do that Victor's a manic-depressive. The depressive phase usually starts with a migraine, and he's just gone into one that's almost suicidal. We must keep this news from him. If he's told about Henry, it will tip him right over the edge. Of course we must decide whether to tell the police. Why don't you ask Frank for his advice?'

Marcia ran downstairs to the business room, but Frank was not there. In the drawing room she found Briggs and Lena making elaborate preparations for afternoon tea. 'He's just gone out to the stable yard to get his car,' said Briggs.

'Oh no!'

'Want me to catch him for you before he goes off?'

126

'Yes please! I must talk to him. Henry's been kidnapped.'

'Oh, you poor thing,' cried Briggs, sincerely distressed, and ran from the room. He caught up with Frank Bradbury in the stable yard as he was starting his engine. Marcia followed, and told her story through the driver's window. 'They say they'll kill Henry if we go to the police. But if we don't, will we ever get him back?'

For almost a minute he was speechless, gripped by the same cold, calculating concern that Helen had shown. Then he said: 'Who knows about this?'

'Only Anderson.'

'No witnesses in the lane?'

'No. I didn't see anyone.'

'Then the police won't know unless we tell them and I don't see why we should.'

'Then what do we do?'

'Nothing, till they ring and demand a ransom.'

'Who will?'

Frank hesitated. 'The people who want blood money because Theo killed the rapist.'

'And when they ring and demand a ransom, what happens?'

'We pay it.'

'Can Victor afford it?'

'He'll have to,' Frank assured her earnestly. 'He can't let these people get away with his son.'

'Suppose they kill Henry anyway,' cried Marcia, 'and then collect the ransom?'

'They won't. They know we won't pay it till we have evidence that he's alive.'

'Oh, I can't bear it!'

Her cry brought Nigel Burke out from his work-bench in the coach house to discover what was going on. Frank explained, fixed Nigel with a meaningful stare, and said: 'I'm for keeping the police out of it.'

Nigel too seemed to be coldly weighing the pros and cons. 'I agree,' he said.

'Henry's safe,' Frank assured her. 'It's just a matter of time. Come in and have some tea, you'll feel better.'

She followed him indoors, but had no intention of joining

him over the senselessly elaborate afternoon tea set out in the drawing room. 'I'll be with you in a moment,' she told him and went straight to the telephone.

As Celia arrived back at Archerscroft and parked her car, the outside bell of the office telephone set up its clamour. She hurried inside to answer it. The caller was Marcia. She spoke in a furtive whisper, as if afraid of being overheard. 'Mrs Grant? Thank goodness you're back. I need your help.'

'Oh? What's the trouble?'

'My baby's been kidnapped, and they all say I mustn't tell the police. I suppose they don't want them poking their noses into whatever they're up to, but I'm desperate, I want my baby back.'

Celia expressed her sympathy, and waited.

'I happened to hear Victor say that you were doing some detection for him,' Marcia confessed. 'But you're not a police-woman, are you?'

'No.'

'Good, then you can tell me what to do.'

'I'll do my best,' said Celia, reflecting that Marcia would be the third client who had invited her to unravel the complications of Clintbury. 'When can we meet?'

'Oh dear, I'll have to slip out latish when they think I'm in bed. Let me think . . . I know! The gate lodge, it's where the Andersons live. He's a sweetie, we can meet there. Half past ten tonight, okay?'

After only a few moments' thought, Celia knew what to do next. She rang Porter, and told him about the kidnapping.

'Actually, I knew about that already,' he replied. 'Bradbury and Theo were discussing it over tea.'

A long silence followed. 'Well?' she asked. 'What are you waiting for?'

'I'm in a cleft stick, Mrs Grant. I'm sorry for Mrs Stratton, but there it is.'

'What d'you mean? You don't intend to let her go on agonising when in fact you know perfectly well where they've taken her little boy?'

'A policeman's lot is not a happy one,' he said in an offensively jokey tone.

128

'What on earth is that bit of facetiousness supposed to mean?'

'I've talked to Superintendent Marshall about this and he quite agrees with me. The Krasinskis are our only hope of linking up with the main supplier. If we charge into that holiday camp to search for the child, and the Krasinskis realise that they've been under police surveillance, a key operation against an international drug ring will be blown sky high.'

'Surely you can invent some excuse for searching the place, stolen goods for instance, and find Henry by an extraordinary coincidence?'

'We aren't even sure that the baby's there. If we went in now to look for him, so soon after the kidnapping, they'd know it wasn't a coincidence. In a fortnight or so we might try to dream up something like that.'

'And meanwhile,' said Celia, 'poor Marcia has to sweat it out. People who kidnap babies sometimes kill them before they start negotiating the ransom. Do you want that on your conscience?'

'It's the old argument. One life against the sufferings and deaths of thousands of heroin addicts.'

'If people get involved with heroin they have only themselves to blame. We're balancing them against an innocent baby. What did Theo and Frank say to each other about the kidnapping?'

There was another long pause. 'Mrs Grant, I'm very grateful to you for the help you've given us, but there's really no need for you to concern yourself with this business any further. It's the sort of situation that's best left to the professionals.'

There was a click on the line, and the phone went dead.

Celia was still in a state of frustrated fury when she arrived to keep her appointment with Marcia. Promptly at ten-thirty, she parked in the village street and knocked on the door of the Clintbury gate lodge. Anderson let her in, full of concern. 'Bless you for coming, Mrs Grant. She's in the front room, crying her eyes out, poor lamb.'

His wife was hovering in the background. 'I've taken her in some tea. Would you like some?'

Celia declined, and let herself be ushered into a tiny front parlour cluttered with knick-knacks. Marcia rose, and greeted her with arms spread out tragically in a gesture which habit had made unconscious since she first used it in a workshop production of the *Medea*.

'Oh, bless you for coming, Mrs Grant, dear. I'm half out of my mind. What am I to do?'

'Tell me a little more first. Who advised you not to tell the police about Henry?'

'Frank and Nigel. They've done something illegal, and Henry's part of it somehow. That's why they don't want the police poking their noses in.'

'What sort of an illegal thing?' Celia asked.

'I've no idea, except that they're being blackmailed. I'm sure of that because . . . well, Victor was quite right, I do eavesdrop a lot, it's the only way I can find out what goes on. There's a seat on the terrace, quite near the window of the business room, and when the window's open you sometimes hear things. That's why I go there with Henry's pram.'

She made a face, and corrected herself. 'Why I used to go there with it. And I had a bit of luck when Victor sacked Miss Foster, because Frank moved into her office so that he could take the calls from the blackmailers at the switchboard and stop Victor from getting them. Miss Foster's office is quite near the nursery, so I managed to hear quite a bit. But of course I only caught one end of these rather odd conversations and you can't make sense of them because they're partly in a sort of code.'

'What sort of code?'

'He seemed to be arguing about which of them owned something he called "Sunflowers", and there was another code-word that came into it, what was it? Pierrots? No, "Harlequins", that was it, and something about splitting fifty-fifty. And apparently what they're quarrelling about is connected somehow with Victor's father's will.'

Celia was astonished. 'What makes you think that?'

'Something I overheard yesterday, actually. Frank was taking one of the blackmailing calls and there was the usual talk about sunflowers and harlequins and something that sounded like a Gorgon. And Frank got very impatient and started shouting that they'd got it wrong, it was nothing to do with Victor, that wasn't the way things were left in his father's will. He was still arguing about it when Victor came upstairs and caught me listening in the passage. He gave me a very dirty look. Then he went in and caught Frank talking to the blackmailers. He started roaring at him in a black rage, like King Lear in the storm scene, for dealing with the blackmailers behind his back, so I didn't hear any more about the will.'

This made no sense at all to Celia. 'What on earth had the blackmailers to do with Victor's father's will?'

'I think they must have found out about some fiddle of Frank's, something illegal he'd done with Victor's money. And Henry comes into it somehow, that's why he's been kidnapped. You see, Victor wanted a child, and Nigel hates Victor. If Victor wants anything, Nigel wants to take it away.'

This seemed to Celia to make even less sense, and she said so.

'You don't understand,' said Marcia. 'Victor dislikes children, he's never taken the slightest interest in Henry, but there's something about it in his father's will, something about him suffering financially if he doesn't have a child, so I suppose Nigel benefits.'

'You mean, he inherits if Victor dies childless?'

'I suppose so. All I've been told is that there would be financial penalties if he didn't have a child, and producing an heir is my only function in the household.'

'Oh, really!' cried Celia, genuinely indignant. 'Who broke this charming tit-bit of news to you?'

'Helen, in one of her less charitable moments. Did you know that Victor used to be married to her, and divorced her to marry me?'

'No!'

'Nor did I, till she told me. I imagine he'd been screwing her like grim death for years with no result. He's infertile, I realise that now, but he was much too macho to admit it or even have tests done. He simply assumed that it was Helen's fault and hoped for better luck with me.'

'Then why is Helen still around?'

'That was always part of the plan. It was very stupid of me, but Victor can be very convincing when he wants to put on a show and I thought I was being swept off my feet by this rich, amusing man who knew a lot about Shakespeare. When we got back from our honeymoon Helen was already installed in the house, married to Frank Bradbury and describing herself as the housekeeper. But she soon started behaving as if she was Victor's wife and I was

131

some sort of low-grade concubine, and presently it dawned on me that Frank, who's a resident lame duck on Victor's payroll, is homo and had been made to marry Helen for the sake of appearances.'

'Goodness me, what a carry-on. How long have you and Victor been married?'

'Three years. When Victor was living at Ashton Lacey he was a friend of the management at Stratford and always in and out of the theatre, and he'd made a few lust-ridden passes at me on the grounds that bit-part actresses ought to be easy meat. But I saw him off, I was very much in love with someone else. Then when he came out of prison Helen looked over the field and remembered me and decided I'd do because I'm not clever: I'd lose out if there was a battle between us for the first place with Victor. So she sent him back to Stratford to woo me and I fell for it. I suppose he thought it would turn out all right because I'd had a child already, a lovely little boy . . . ' She broke off. 'Oh hell, why did I let him go?'

'Tell me about him,' said Celia gently.

'He's with my ex, Giles Gascoigne, and his new wife. You've probably seen him on the telly. He divorced me when he started getting juvenile leads, and, oh dear, I suppose it was best to let him have custody, but if Henry's gone for good . . . '

'I'm sure you'll get him back.'

'Are you? I'm not, and . . . oh, Mrs Grant, what if I don't? I can't bear it, he's all I've got. I'm sure Nigel's behind all this somehow. He was dead against me having a child.'

'Really? Has he said so?'

Marcia sighed. 'It was a matter of deeds not words. Oh dear, this is very embarrassing, but you'd better know. When I realised that Victor wasn't fertile I propositioned Nigel to stand in for him. Don't you see, I was twenty-nine and my stage career was a disaster. Victor was my meal ticket and I thought he'd treat me better if I had a child, even if he wasn't the real father. When I asked Nigel, he gave me a nasty grin and said, "Oh, so you've found out, have you? Victor's gun's loaded with blanks." Then he thought for a while and said, "Okay, then, get undressed and I'll see what I can do." So we got down to business, but he was being very cold-blooded about it, not like a lover at all, and halfway through I realised that the hellish man was wearing a condom. So I said what the blazes was going on, and he said he was damned if he'd set

Victor up to get away with fraud and cash in under the will on the strength of a child that wasn't his. And why didn't I let him divorce me for being barren and live happily ever after on the alimony? In the end all that happened between me and Nigel was a lot of quarrelling and hardly any sex.'

'So he isn't Henry's father?'

'No, and you're dying to ask who is,' said Marcia with a faint giggle, 'so I'll tell you. I'd been planning a dirty weekend with someone I knew at Stratford, but getting away was a problem and then Jeremy Elton turned up looking fierce and young and interesting at some evening classes I went to in Mayhurst. I decided that he'd do. My God, what a mistake. He's been a millstone round my neck ever since.'

'You didn't foresee that he'd hang around?' said Celia.

'No! It was all right at first, he rang a few times and I managed to choke him off. But later on, when I was as pregnant as a balloon, I ran into him in Mayhurst. He got very possessive and wrote to say I must elope with him and that I was to bring whatever I produced by way of a child. Of course I said no, but last month he came down here and waited till my back was turned and got Victor to take him on as a gardener. Of course I couldn't object.'

'And has he been making a nuisance of himself?'

Marcia considered. 'Only in a quiet way. He thought he could wear me down in the end and make me go off with him, and nothing I could say would make him see it was no use. Oh dear, I feel terrible about him, really guilty, and the worst of it was, having Henry didn't do me a bit of good with Victor, because darling Helen told him Nigel was Henry's real father.'

'Knowing you'd been to bed with him but not about the condom?'

'No! She didn't even know he'd had it off with me, she just guessed. When I got pregnant she twigged that there had to be somebody else because by then she'd realised that Victor's equipment isn't in working order. She picked on Nigel because she knew that would do me the most damage with Victor.'

'And Victor believed her?'

'He'd believe anything bad he was told about Nigel.'

'And Nigel didn't deny it?'

'Of course not, he was over the moon! What could be more

delightful than telling your half-brother that you'd slept with his wife and got her pregnant, something Victor had never managed to do. He even had the gall to tell Helen I wasn't very amusing in bed, a remark which darling Helen repeated to me. Oh, dear Mrs Grant, what's going to happen to Henry?'

'I don't know.'

'Don't you think we should tell the police?'

Celia had a nightmare vision of the local police and Porter's merry men running round in circles after each other and setting the cat among the pigeons at Clintbury. 'There's something I'd like to do first,' she decided.

'Oh, what?'

'Go up to London at the crack of dawn tomorrow to look up old Mr Stratton's will in the Probate Registry at Somerset House.'

NINE

When Celia phoned Bill Wilkins at seven next morning to say she would be spending the day in London, he grunted gloomily. 'Oh Celia, you ought to be here making decisions. The takings is down again this week.'

'I know, but there's enough to cover the wage bill on Friday.'

'Only because there's a bit left of your police money. How much longer can you go on milking the bluebottles?'

'That's stopped.'

'If they're finished with you, why are you off to London?'

'Marcia Stratton's baby's been kidnapped and the bluebottles won't do anything about it. So I have to.'

'On your own?' he asked, sounding alarmed. 'Oh, Celia, that's dangerous. Them druggy bastards will have the toenails off of you. Take care.'

'I will,' she promised. 'And I'll be back as soon as I can.'

Feeling very guilty, she cut him off before he could protest.

Her first task on arriving in London was to find out the date of Mr Stratton senior's death, without which information the Probate Registry would be unable to turn up his will. This entailed a long trawl through the records of the Registry of Births, Marriages and Deaths in the Aldwych. Assuming 1970 as the earliest possible year, she searched through every volume until she struck lucky in the one for February 1979. Donald Fergus Stratton, of Ashton Lacey Manor, Ashton Lacey, Warwickshire, had died on the 21st of that month.

On the far side of the Strand an imposing archway led into the beautiful courtyard of Somerset House. Threading her way among the parked cars to the door on the far side, she found Donald Fergus Stratton without difficulty in the index, paid her fee and after a short wait was studying a photocopy of the will.

The executors and trustees were a firm of solicitors in Stratford-upon-Avon, and this was one of the few provisions in it that did not amaze her. The main beneficiary was 'my said son, Victor, in the unhappy expectation that inheriting a fortune will be the ruin of him.' Nigel, surprisingly, was referred to as 'Amos Boswell, my son by Kenza Boswell, otherwise known as Nigel Burke.' In view of his dark, romantic appearance Celia was not wholly surprised to discover that he lived under an alias, probably concealing foreign origins on his mother's side, but what sort of name was Kenza? A trust fund was to be set up for him with a capital of £100,000, the income of which was to be used for his education and support, 'until he reaches the age of twenty-five years. His enjoyment of this income is conditional on his residing, except when absent for educational reasons, at the home of my said son, Victor'. If he failed to comply and went to live elsewhere, an arbitrator appointed by the Law Society was to decide whether he had gone voluntarily or whether Victor had turned him out. If the fault was Nigel's, his income from the trust would cease, but if the blame lay with Victor, the hundred thousand pounds would become Nigel's absolutely.

The will also laid down what was to happen to the trust fund when Nigel, alias Amos, reached the age of twenty-five and his income from it ceased. That depended on whether or not Victor had children. If he did, the trust would lapse and the capital would revert to him. If he was still without issue at that stage, the capital would be used to set up a charity which would ensure comfort for seaside donkeys in their declining years. Victor was to be its sole organiser and only paid official, with a salary of two hundred pounds a year.

To judge from his will, the testator was a mischievous old gentleman, determined to annoy and inconvenience his heirs as much as possible. Nigel and Victor, who hated each other, were condemned to live together. If they failed to do so they would face an arbitration process which might cost more than the sum under dispute. Victor and Helen were condemned to heroic exertions of procreation. The will had probably been drawn up at a time when their marriage had been childless for long enough to convince the wicked old man that their efforts would be in vain, and that Nigel would have the malicious satisfaction of seeing his half-brother deprived of a hundred thousand pounds and obliged to preside over an under-funded charity for the benefit of decrepit donkeys. No wonder Helen had been vague when Marcia asked her about the provision in the will, which, if implemented, would have forced Victor to cut an embarrassing figure as sole organiser of an unnecessary and rather ridiculous charity. And no wonder Nigel had refused to save Victor from ridicule by cuckolding him.

At the end of the will came rather mean legacies to two servants and a lavish one to 'my doctor and old friend Arthur Joseph Dixon'. He had also left 'my pictures to my brother, Theodore Michael Stratton'.

Was this another of the old man's malicious leg-pulls at the expense of posterity? What sort of pictures were they? Worthless ones, to cock a snook at a ne'er-do-well brother with no gift for making money? An embarrassing collection of obscenities? Did the pictures lie behind the blackmail of Frank and Theo? If so, why was Frank involved? There was only one way of finding out. By midday she was back in her car, heading north-west out of London. The answer to her question lay in Warwickshire, at Ashton Lacey.

'Ashton Lacey Manor,' she read on the huge notice-board at the gates. 'The historic home of the Laceys. Bowling alley, boating lake, amusement park, pizza parlour, civil war museum, zoo. An outing for all the family. Entrance £3.50. Children and Senior Citizens half-price'. The ancient home of the Laceys, and for a time the home of the Strattons, had fallen into the hands of an entrepreneur and become a theme park.

The house, at the end of a long drive, was a medieval manor house with later additions, surrounded by a moat, in a setting which must once have been peaceful but was now cluttered up with the strident commercial attractions listed on the notice-board at the gates. She parked, and found her way past roundabouts, ice-cream kiosks and cages containing moth-eaten birds of prey to the drawbridge over the moat, where she paid another stiff entrance fee, bought a guide book and studied it before embarking on a tour of the house.

The Laceys had kept to the old faith at the Reformation,

and had suffered as Catholics under Elizabeth. They were in even worse trouble under the Commonwealth, when Catholic priests had a price on their heads, and anyone who harboured a priest at the very least risked losing all his property. Ashton Lacey had been one of the safe houses for priests travelling the country to administer the sacraments to the persecuted faithful. An elaborate system of cunningly hidden 'priests' holes' had ensured their safety, and in spite of constant searches by Cromwell's soldiers none of the priests passing through was ever found.

The Laceys had achieved nothing remarkable in the centuries which followed, and were finally driven out of their home by the loss of what remained of their fortune during and after the Second World War. Celia scanned the subsequent history of the house eagerly, hoping to find some mention of its ownership by the Strattons. But the guide-book merely said that after passing through the hands of 'a number of owners', the house had been bought by Leisure Enterprises plc, and turned into a 'centre for the enjoyment of all, old and young, combining entertainment with a historical experience which no one who has seen it will ever forget'.

Celia found the 'historical experience' inside the house. The ground-floor rooms had been arranged in a series of tableaux illustrating the chief episodes in the history of Ashton Lacey under the Commonwealth. Waxwork Roundheads in full armour brandished spears at waxwork members of the Lacey family, dressed cavalier-fashion with lace collars and cuffs. Evil-faced informers, attracted by the reward for denouncing anyone harbouring a priest, pointed accusing waxen fingers. Saintly-looking priests prayed fervently in no less than three priests' holes. Celia had to admit that though this was not her cup of tea, it was an effective way of teaching history to a square-eyed, semi-literate generation of children willing to absorb information only if it was presented on a television screen.

But she was here to find out more about the Strattons. She tried their name on several of the attendants but drew a blank, for they were mostly youngish, and one or two were in the uniform of a security firm. But an elderly cleaning woman who was dusting down the waxwork cook in the reconstructed antique kitchen overheard her enquiry and came up to her. 'Why do you want to know about them, dear?' she asked grimly. 'They was nasty, filthy people, both of them, father and son. We all hated them round here.'

'Why? What was wrong with them?'

The old woman turned away. 'Look, dear, I've my work to do,' she muttered, and began dusting the plastic food on the kitchen table.

In one of the bedrooms upstairs she found a more promising informant, one of those upper-class village ladies who volunteer as guides and sit on chairs in the rooms of stately homes to answer queries about the antique furnishings and, more important, guard them against theft.

'The Strattons?' she said. 'I knew them slightly, yes. We came to one or two parties here when my husband was alive. But we didn't keep up with them. Their friends weren't our kind of people.'

'Too jet-setty?'

'Oh, I wouldn't say that. Second-rate. New-rich people who drank too much. Helen Stratton was all right, she was quite well connected. One of the Lazenby girls, quite a good county family. But he was difficult, even at the beginning no one in the village liked him. One day he was all over you, your best friend, then before you knew where you were he'd bite your head off.'

She broke off to answer a query from an American woman about the embroidered bed hangings. When this was over Celia approached the key question obliquely. 'I suppose the house looked very different in the Strattons' day? Did they have lovely pictures and so on?'

'Oh no. Pretentious Knole sofas and reproductions of Elizabethan portraits in rather vulgar gilt frames. He had a mania for that period, you see, especially anything to do with Shakespeare. One of the parties we went to was a fancy-dress ball, and we all had to dress up as a character in a Shakespeare play. But it all turned sour because people drank too much, Victor Stratton worst of all. In the end he got into one of his moods and started screaming at some woman because she'd broken the rules and come as the Dark Lady of the Sonnets, who wasn't a character in one of the plays.'

'Did you think he was mentally unstable?'

139

'It was mostly the drink.' She looked at Celia sharply. 'Why are you asking me all this?'

'I've been manoeuvred into doing business with him,' said Celia, more or less truthfully, 'and I'm not sure I trust him.'

The guide gave her a warning look. 'I wouldn't trust him an inch beyond the end of my nose if I were you.'

She broke off to discourage a small child from scratching a mahogany chest of drawers with a toy aeroplane, then turned back to Celia. 'If you're doing business with him, he must be out of prison already.'

'Yes. He's been out for some time, living in Sussex.'

'Shocking, they should have kept him in for life. You know what happened?'

'Not really. Tell me.'

'It was awful, a tragedy. He'd been drinking more and more, till one morning he got paralytic and drove his car into a procession of children walking along the pavement outside the village school. The awful thing was, he didn't stop, he was too incapable. The car just ploughed its way through them till it hit a lamp post, and by then a whole year-group of Ashton Lacey children were dead or dying.'

Celia was horrified. She knew there had been a prison sentence for drunken driving. But this was monstrous beyond imagination.

'He never came back to the village,' the guide went on. 'If he had, one or other of the fathers would have killed him. His wife left here too, and various hangers-on; there was an uncle who lived with them and a man who looked after his finances, rather a feeble creature. After a bit the house was sold, for five or six million, according to rumour. But none of it went to the families in compensation; they just got what they could screw out of Stratton's insurance company.'

Five or six million, Celia thought. For Frank and Theo, the temptation to play the market must have been irresistible. All that loose cash was waiting to be invested: Victor, their bullying puppet-master, was in prison, it was their chance to break free. With the market going up and up in a seemingly endless boom, they could hardly lose.

But on the main point her curiosity was still unsatisfied. The only pictures on show at Ashton Lacey in Victor's time were the

Elizabethan reproductions in garish gilt frames that she had seen at Clintbury, and they did not belong to Theo. Any that did would have been handed to him by the executors of Victor's father's will. She needed to go back a generation.

'Did you know Donald Stratton?' she asked. 'Victor's father?'

'No, he was before my time. We moved into the village after my husband retired, and by then Victor and his wife were installed in the big house.'

Celia decided that the next person to try was the doctor who had received a legacy under Donald Stratton's will. The photocopy was in her handbag, but she managed to dredge the name up from her memory without consulting it. 'The family doctor was called Dixon. I wonder if he's still alive?'

'Oh yes, very much so.' The guide looked at her shrewdly. 'I'm sure he and Victor Stratton had dealings with each other.'

'Dealings?'

'Dixon was struck off, because of some illegal fiddle with drugs.' She leant forward confidentially. 'You're a plain-clothes detective, aren't you? Has Stratton been up to his old tricks?'

'Old tricks?' Celia echoed.

'Victor was an addict, you see. And Dixon was a pusher.'

'Oh. Where does he live?' she asked.

'That's easy. Turn left at the pub, and it's the third house on the left, with the scruffiest garden you've ever seen. But he's usually into his third bottle of whisky by tea time. You'd better go now if you want to get anything out of him.'

Following these directions, Celia drew up outside a tumbledown Elizabethan cottage with a gardenful of waist-high nettles and brambles and an air of malevolent neglect. Her normal panic at anything to do with drugs was heightened by this sinister setting, but she choked it back and battered on the door with a rusty wrought-iron knocker. It was opened by a very old man in a pullover with ragged holes in the elbows.

'Dr Dixon?' she asked.

He stared, breathing whisky at her. 'Go away, you silly interfering social worker.'

'I won't interfere and I'm not a social worker.'

He peered at her short-sightedly. 'You're sure?'

'No, really.'

141

'Then you're a busybody from the council, acting out some fantasy about the drains or putting me into a home.'

'No. I promise. I'm not an official of any kind.'

'You're not from Help the Aged? You don't want to counsel me about my grief because my smelly old dog got cancer and died, and about time too? No? What do you want, then?'

'I'd like to ask you a few things about Donald Stratton who lived at Ashton Lacey.'

He brightened into a twinkle of pleasure. 'Ah, that's a different kettle of fish. Come on in.'

He showed her into an untidy study which smelt strongly of cats. There were half-eaten platefuls of cat food on the floor, an evil-looking black tom on the window sill and a bottle of whisky on the desk with an empty glass beside it. He offered to fetch her a glass and fill it, but she refused.

Pouring a stiff tot for himself, he asked: 'Why d'you want to know about Don?'

'I'm doing some research for the county records,' she lied. 'They don't think they know enough about the history of the house after the Laceys left. How well did you know him?'

'Very well. I was his doctor, not that he needed one much. But we were buddies too: we cracked many a bottle together of an evening. He was my last real friend.' He sipped his whisky thoughtfully. 'Let's see now, when did he die? 1979, it must have been. The year after my poor old wife passed over and started twanging her harp. Damn boring occupation, I should think, but there's no accounting for tastes.'

He was not drunk, Celia decided. His speech was not slurred and he made perfect sense. He was merely maintaining himself in the state of alcoholism to which he was accustomed.

'Was he popular in the neighbourhood?' she asked.

'Popular?' He chuckled. 'Don was about as popular round here as an abortionist in a nunnery.' He picked up his glass, stared at it, and sipped. 'He was South African, that was the trouble. And even by South African standards he was what they call a rough diamond. Oh, yes. No airs and graces. Dirty fingernails. Funny accent. And why not? His father kept the store in an up-country township and walloped him for wild behaviour till he got big enough to wallop his dad and run away from home to make his fortune. He did too, though a lot of people's feet got trodden on and the partners in some of his businesses ended by wishing they'd never set eyes on him. After a time he decided to retire and enjoy his millions, and heaven knows why, he decided to do it here and not in South Africa. So he bought Ashton Lacey and settled down to get to know the neighbours and have a good time.

'It was the biggest mistake he could have made. The neighbours round here are a po-faced status-conscious lot. They're mostly not rich but they get very excited at the sight of money and they knew he had a lot. At first they were all over him like wasps at the jampot, and showered him with hospitality on account of the lavish parties they hoped to be invited to at Ashton Lacey and the massive contributions they hoped to collect for their pet charities. But they soon found out that his table manners were too disgusting, my dear, and he told blue jokes and drank too much and smoked big cigars in the wrong places at the wrong time. You see, the money hadn't changed Don. He didn't see why he should polish his image and clean his fingernails and pretend to be something he wasn't. Pretty soon they were telling each other he'd made his money out of brothels and fixing horse-races, and within three months they'd all cut him dead.'

With a sudden movement he emptied his glass and filled it again. 'Don was furious. Something similar had happened to him before; his damfool wife had told him he was too crude and vulgar for her, and run away with someone a step or two higher up the social ladder. Now he'd been snubbed again and the wild streak in him came out, he started behaving like a savage. When they asked for subscriptions to their charities he sent obscene messages back. To annoy the horsey brigade he gave a small fortune to some very violent animal-rights people who were sabotaging the local hunt. Then he cocked a snook at them all by giving huge parties with champagne and so on for the riff-raff, shopkeepers, people banned from decent society for being left wing, a family that everyone hated because they were running an unsightly dump for old cars at a local beauty spot.'

He was sipping steadily at his drink as he rambled on. At this rate of consumption, incoherence would soon set in. An opening would have to be found soon for putting the key question about the mystery of the pictures.

143

'The parties didn't last very long,' Dixon went on. 'Don soon found out that low life free-loaders could be just as unpleasant as the snooty sort. Then he hit on another wheeze for annoying the neighbours: he invited a whole tribe of gypsies to camp on his land. The neighbours hated that, because gypsies were supposed to be thieves and dirty and untidy and undesirable and a blot on the landscape. But I think Don liked having them there. They were social outcasts like him and he enjoyed their company.

'By then I'd arrived on the scene. One of my madder patients started telling a lot of lies about me, and some others joined in and there was a big scandal and suddenly I was an untouchable like Don, so we got to be buddies. He'd spend many an evening in that chair you're sitting in, or I'd go to his place and we'd crack a bottle there. Talking of which . . . ' he broke off, and held up the almost empty whisky bottle by its neck. 'I live on this stuff, but stock's getting a bit low.'

'Oh, is there anywhere in the village where I could get you some?'

'That's very kind of you, my dear, but there's no need. I've a few still in the cupboard, but if you'd care to give me the money . . . '

Celia handed over a ten-pound note and Dr Dixon pocketed it with dignity. 'Where was I, now?'

'You were telling me about your friendship with Mr Stratton.'

'Ah, so I was.' He thought for a moment, then shot a fierce glance at her. 'Don't get me wrong, we weren't just a couple of drivelling old soaks, we talked about politics, books, everything under the sun. Don was a bit rough on the outside, but he was a thinking man, well informed. Loved beautiful things, too.'

'Pictures?'

Suddenly he was on his guard, frowning. 'No,' he said. 'No pictures.'

But the frown faded gradually into a sly grin. What did it mean? That there were pictures, but they were obscene?

'You're sure?' she persisted. 'I thought he had quite a collection.'

'No, but he had some marvellous silver. Not just forks and spoons, but a lot of other stuff, even the plates for eating off

144

were silver, made by some quite famous Frenchman who lived in London. What was his name now?'

'Paul de Lamerie?' Celia suggested.

'That's it! He could afford beautiful things, but he didn't show them off. I was the only person who knew he had them, the everyday stuff was quite ordinary and tatty. But every so often we'd have what he called a blow-out, he'd buy some ready-made gourmet thing at a freezer shop and we'd eat it, just the two of us, off this marvellous silver. The rest of the time he kept it hidden away.'

'In one of the priests' holes?' Celia asked.

Dixon nodded. 'The one behind the dining-room fireplace. The others are all fakes, cooked up to amuse the customers by those bloody people who bought the place and turned it into a freak show. God knows what the world's coming to.' He lay back wearily in his chair and shut his eyes.

'There was a brother, wasn't there?' Celia asked. 'Called Theodore.'

'Oh Lord, yes, I'd forgotten him. Awful wet creature, couldn't make a go of it in South Africa and came here to sponge on Don.'

'Did he live in the house?'

'Heavens, no. Don couldn't stand him. Hc was a schoolmaster, but he couldn't keep order. Whenever he got sacked he came down on Don for money.'

And Don got his own back in the will, Celia decided. The legacy of 'my pictures' to Theo must be a malicious joke, like the arrangements for infuriating Victor and Nigel. But what was the joke, and where were the pictures?

'There were two children, weren't there?' she prompted.

'Children?' he echoed wearily. 'Oh dear me, yes. Boys. He had one by the snob of a wife who ran away. What was the awful little twerp's name now?'

'Victor, wasn't it?'

'That's right, my memory's getting awful. He was a silly prat with no brains and no guts. When Don lost his temper and shouted at him he used to pee his pants with fright. Don hated him. I bet he wondered who that god-awful bitch had cuckolded him with.'

145

'But he left Victor almost all his money,' she remarked.

'That's right, he reckoned that the sons of rich self-made men went to the bad when they got their hands on the money, and nothing could make Victor any worse, so he left him the lot to go to the bad with.'

'Were you Victor's doctor too?'

He looked at her with world-weary eyes. 'No.'

Because he had been struck off the register, she realised. For drug offences. He had had 'dealings' with Victor, but he had not been his doctor.

Dixon smiled uneasily and changed the subject. 'The other boy was called Amos. He was born much later. A lad after Don's heart, Amos was, wild as they come.'

'Who was his mother?'

'A gypsy. From one of the families that camped in the park. A lovely thing she was, hair and eyes as black as coal, marvellous body. Supposed to be some sort of gypsy princess, but it's all nonsense, they'll say anything when they're talking to a *gorgio*. The boy had inherited her wickedness, and her looks, naughty little devil.'

This, then, was the explanation of Nigel's dark beauty.

'It happened this way,' Dixon went on. 'Don was getting a bit sick of having the tribe making the hell of a mess in the park, and they were cheating him and doing a bit of thieving around the place on the side. They were afraid he'd turn them off his land, but there was a crisis because the woman who cooked and cleaned for him had left. So they got him to take on this raving beauty instead, and told her to get herself into his bed quick as she could, knowing that with a child on the way he wouldn't turn them out. Don was convinced it was his child, he may have been right. Later on he and the boy had frightful rows, and Amos in a temper looked and behaved exactly like Don in a temper: they both suddenly became savages.

'By then things were going from bad to worse, the house was in a mess and the gypsies went on cheating him. Then that lovely little slut got hold of the key to the priests' hole and he caught her helping herself to the silver. That was the last straw. He beat her black and blue and threw her out and told the lot of them to get off his land. There was a great row and in the end he had to fetch

146

the police. They went. But they put a Romany curse on him, and d'you know, tough old Don took it seriously; it worried him till the day he died.'

'They didn't take the boy with them, though?'

'No, that was one of the reasons for the curse. He was determined to hang on to Amos, thought the world of him and hid him at a flat he had in London till they'd gone. Even then he was nervous, sent the kid straight off to a posh boarding school and gave him a different name – what was it now? – so he couldn't be traced. What *was* Amos's other name?' He shook his head from side to side, as if to free it from the fumes of drink.

'I believe he's known now as Nigel Burke,' Celia suggested.

'That'sh right, Nigel!' he exclaimed as his speech suddenly became slurred. 'He was the one Don was fond of. And, d'you know, the worshe he behaved and the more rows they had, the fonder Don got. But then . . . ' he frowned and waved a stern finger at her, 'then Amos mishbehaved . . . onshe too often . . . there was a girl he'd got pregnant . . . crashed a car when he was shtinking drunk and she wash in it. Killed her, poor little thing.' Suddenly, he began to weep.

'So his father was furious and cut him out of his will?' she asked.

Dixon nodded tearfully. 'That was the shtupid businesh . . . Don . . . would have forgiven him after a bit, he alwaysh did . . . but he went and had a bloody heart attack too shoon, and that damn milkshop Victor shcooped the lot.'

'But you kept in touch with Victor after he inherited Ashton Lacey?'

He opened one eye warily. 'Don't . . . want to talk about him. He was a bore . . . oh dear me, such a bore . . . ' To end the interview, he settled down to sleep.

Celia gathered up her things to leave. But the performance was not quite over: Dixon was muttering to himself under his breath. She leant forward to listen, but only an occasional word or two was distinct enough for her to catch.

'Marvellous silver . . . candlesh . . . shnowing outshide . . . big log fire . . . how he could talk . . . ' He was reliving the great days of his friendship with Don Stratton. There were snatches of things they had said to each other about darling Amos and the scrapes he got into, about his lust-provoking but sluttish mother, followed by something about 'women like bloody shtatues with great big boobs'. Had they been to a brothel together? Presently it seemed to be summer, and they were going for a walk by a river. 'Sun shparkling on the damn water. Boatsh. Willow treesh on the bank. And Don shaid "that'sh how one ought to live".' A vision of a white tablecloth followed, with apples on it and bread and a bottle of wine: perhaps they had had a picnic, there were 'women in funny bonnets in a field'. Probably on another occasion, they had gone for a walk and got caught in a frightful storm. 'Long shtraight road,' he muttered, frowning. 'Treesh all waving about in a frightful wind, corn too, sky like ink, ooh, horrible . . . ' The frown vanished and a beatific smile replaced it. 'And then there were sunflowers.'

The effect on Celia was electric. 'In a vase?'

'A jug,' he corrected. 'With a handle.'

'And were there harlequins?'

He thought for a moment. 'Two. With their armsh round each other.'

'And they were all kept in the priests' hole, along with the Paul de Lamerie silver?'

Suddenly his bloodshot eyes looked horrified. 'No! I never shaid that, it'sh a shecret, Don shaid I mustn't tell.'

'But it's true, isn't it?'

'Go . . . away, damn you.' He shut his eyes firmly. 'Don't want to talk to you, I'm ashleep.'

In her excitement Celia was tempted to give him a sharp shaking, but decided against it. What he had said was quite enough. An enormous weight had been lifted from her.

She put another ten-pound note under the half-empty whisky bottle and let herself out of the house, feeling more cheerful than she had done for weeks. The riddle of Clintbury Park was all but solved, and it had nothing to do with drugs. She could think straight at last.

148

TEN

'There were six versions of the Van Gogh *Sunflowers*,' said the distinguished expert with the grey Vandyke beard. 'He painted them to decorate the house he'd rented in Arles. And you're quite right. After your phone call I rang the Rijksmuseum, they did the *Catalogue Raisonnée* of all Van Gogh's known works. According to them a picture in the *Sunflower* series was stolen from a private collection in Switzerland over twenty years ago, and has never been seen since.'

Richard Knowles was the sale-room correspondent of a reputable Sunday newspaper. Celia had approached him out of the blue on the understanding that he was to have the exclusive rights to the story when it broke, in exchange for providing her with his expertise. When she telephoned him and outlined her problem he invited her to come at once to his house in Chelsea, and let her pick his brains over a much-needed whisky.

'Why would anyone do it?' she asked. 'What's the point of having a secret collection of stolen masterpieces that you can't show to anybody?'

'You say "what's the point?",' he repeated. 'The answer is that nobody knows why people do it. Or rather did it, it couldn't happen now. Before the Getty Museum came into the market and drove prices sky-high, people didn't guard their pictures so carefully and it wasn't impossibly difficult to commission a professional thief to steal one or two for you. In those days stolen collections weren't all that uncommon: several have come to light since in the States, and at least one in Latin America.'

'What sort of people were the collectors?'

'The two or three I know of were very rich,' said Knowles. 'I suppose it was really a very grand form of shoplifting, the sporting sort when you get a kick out of stealing something you don't need and could afford to buy. And then there's the secret, almost sexual thrill of owning a masterpiece that nobody else will ever see, getting it out and gloating over it and hiding it away again.'

'A very kinky thrill, surely?'

He thought for a moment. 'We're talking about people whose personalities are in some way inadequate.'

'Such as latching on to pictures because they can't relate properly to people?'

'Possibly. Is that what's wrong with your chap?'

'He quarrelled with everyone, including his two sons, and left a very peculiar will.'

'He's dead then? Oh dear, this is the dangerous moment. The heirs are horrified when they discover papa's shameful secret. They would rather burn several Cézannes and a Monet or two than let the dear departed's memory be sullied by the publicity. Who has he left the pictures to?'

'His brother. All his legacies were devised to annoy and inconvenience the recipients, and this one was too. The brother is an eccentric bachelor in his late sixties, the sort you'd expect to be horribly embarrassed by this very hot testamentary potato.'

'Oh dear, we ought to get at him before he does anything drastic.'

'But the dangerous moment happened years ago: he inherited the pictures in 1979. I don't think he's destroyed them. He's more enterprising than one might expect. He seems to have been selling them lately.'

'In the open market, Mrs Grant? Surely not. If he tried to sell a version of the *Sunflowers* without a provenance, as if it had appeared out of the blue from nowhere, it would be dismissed as a fake at once. And he'd be clapped straight into prison if he gave the real provenance, namely "stolen from the home of Dr Julius Mendel, Villa Kantelberg, Lausanne in 1967".'

'Could he be negotiating with the original owners? If a picture that was worth thousands when it was stolen from them in the sixties is worth millions now, wouldn't they be happy to pay a few hundred thousand at least to get their property back?'

'In most cases it wouldn't belong to them any more. They

pocketed the insurance money at the time of the theft, and if the picture's recovered it belongs to the insurance company.'

'Wouldn't the insurance company pay up to get it back?'

'Oh no.' Knowles mimicked the shocked look on the faces of the insurance companies at this suggestion and mimicked their reaction: "It is against our policy to pay ransom for the return of stolen property". But of course they have ways of getting round that, especially when they settled a claim in thousands and are going to get a picture worth millions. They're perfectly happy to pay a reward for "information leading to the recovery of stolen goods".'

'Is that very different?' Celia asked.

'No. But they prefer it if the informant is a front man negotiating on behalf of the thieves, so that they can pretend not to know.'

'You mean, my enterprising old fuddy-duddy couldn't negotiate a ransom for the pictures himself?'

'Oh no, the insurance companies would insist on the decencies being observed. There has to be a front man.'

'Or woman?' she suggested as the obvious possibility struck her.

'Or woman,' Knowles echoed. 'How many pictures are we talking about?'

'I'm not sure. I've only had them described to me by an old rascal who was too drunk to know what he was saying, and when I tried to question him he realised that he'd let the cat out of the bag, and clammed up. Let me see now, there was one with a white tablecloth with apples on it and bread and a bottle of wine.'

'In other words, a still life by Cézanne.'

'I imagine so, yes. Another was a river scene with willow trees and boats and sun sparkling on the water.'

'Oh dear. That could be anybody. Monet? Pissaro? Sisley? It's anyone's guess. But we can check on the Cézanne, a man in New York called John Rewald is the world authority on him; he'll know if one of the still lifes has been stolen. What else did your drunk regurgitate?'

'A cornfield in a violent storm, with trees waving in the wind, and a road. If the trees were cypresses, it would have been another Van Gogh.'

151

'Yes, he did several of those. We must check with the Rijksmuseum whether one of them's been stolen. Go on, this is fascinating.'

'Two harlequins with their arms round each other.'

'Picasso. Harlequins turn up at various stages in his oeuvre, he even painted his little boy dressed up as one. Oh dear, this will be difficult.'

'Really. Why?'

'The authority in this case is the *Comité Picasso*, consisting of his widows, mistresses and various offspring. They quarrel a lot among themselves and getting sense out of them isn't always easy. However, we can try.'

'How about "women in funny bonnets in a field"? Who on earth would that be?'

'An early Gauguin, painted in Britanny before he went to Tahiti.'

A Gauguin, of course, Celia thought. Eavesdropping, Marcia had misheard the name as 'Gorgon'.

'The Fondation Wildenstein in Paris has done the *Catalogue Raisonnée* for Gauguin,' said Knowles, 'we'll have to ask them.'

'There's only one more that I remember: "Women like bloody statues with great big boobs".'

'Picasso again, I fear. There were several of those in a series called "The Dancers". Now, let's do some planning. I'll identify the stolen pictures for you, and find out who they were insured by.'

'Is that relevant?'

'Of course, don't you realise? You'll be in clover. Insurance companies usually pay ten per cent of the value for information leading to the recovery of stolen property. In your place I'd try to reach an understanding with them before you involve the police.'

'I can't. Someone's baby's been kidnapped. I've got to involve the police to get him back.'

'But unless you inform the insurance companies first, the thing will become an ordinary police operation and you won't collect the reward.'

'I can't help that, there's no time. Kidnappers sometimes kill babies if they don't get what they want quickly.'

'But how do the stolen pictures come into this?'

'The kidnappers are also blackmailers. They're demanding the

Sunflowers and the *Harlequins* by way of ransom for the baby.'

Knowles blinked. 'I'm sorry. Say that again more slowly.'

'The people who have been selling these pictures are being blackmailed. But they haven't any money with which to ransom the baby because the proceeds of the sale so far have been used to pay off a debt. The *Sunflowers* and the *Harlequins* seem to be the only two pictures that haven't been sold yet, and as far as I can make out, the blackmailers want them handed over in lieu of payment, so that they can collect from the insurance companies.'

'What an astonishing story. You seem to know everything. Do you know who these blackmailers are?'

'Yes, and I think I know how they fit in. Would any of the pictures have been stolen by what used to be called a cat burglar?'

'I've no idea, but I can find out. Why?'

'There's a cat burglar in the blackmailers' family. If he knew which pictures he'd stolen, he'd know they were being sold when they started reappearing on the market. And if he knew who he'd stolen them for, the family of the collector concerned would be a sitting duck for blackmail.'

Knowles frowned. 'You say the police know about this. Why aren't they dealing with it?'

Celia described Inspector Porter's fantasies about a drug war. 'I need chapter and verse about the stolen pictures if I'm to disabuse him. How soon can you start checking up?'

'I'll go down to the paper now and look at the press cuttings and ring a few contacts. Where can I contact you tomorrow morning?'

She gave him her home and office numbers. 'Be as quick as you can, won't you? I'm terrified for that baby. And not a syllable in your newspaper till it's been rescued.'

Back home at midnight she found that Bill had thrust a sheet of horrific trading figures through her letter-box. Accompanying it was a furious note, to the effect that her truancy had given Archerscroft the final push down the road to ruin. She spent a sleepless night worrying about Marcia's baby and the threat of bankruptcy.

It was mid-morning before Knowles telephoned. 'I've checked up as far as I can,' he reported. 'We still don't know about the river scene you mentioned or about the Picassos; the Picasso family committee says it can't answer until we put our query in writing. But the other five pictures were all stolen in the early sixties, in a series of thefts involving important works that happened round about that time. I'm at the paper, I have all the clippings from the morgue in front of me.'

'Oh, marvellous,' cried Celia.

'And I've even better news for you. Some months ago there was a lot of talk in the trade about pictures recorded as having been stolen coming back on the market for very discreet and low-key private sale. In all the cases the dealers were negotiating on behalf of insurance companies, which didn't want to auction them because the publicity would make people suspect that they'd paid what amounted to a ransom. I've checked, and according to my sources the works that there were rumours about included an early Gauguin and a Van Gogh, and a Seurat, which was probably the river scene we couldn't identify. Your fuddy-duddy bachelor seems to have been quite a clever operator after all.'

'I think he had help from a woman who works in the antique trade,' she said.

'This story gets more and more riveting every minute. Who?'

'She calls herself Alison Montgomery, but I don't think that's her real name.'

'Ah. There have been rumours about her.'

'Probably because she had a husband who was caught dealing in drugs, and killed himself in prison.'

'Maybe that was it. Anyway, I've been looking through old press cuttings. All the thefts were from private collections, and the method was rather interesting. A young woman claiming to be an art student, with a letter of introduction from the Courtauld Institute, would call on the owner asking to see the collection, and spend long enough studying it to become familiar with the house and decide on the best route for burgling it. Weeks later, the house would be broken into, often through an upstairs window, and one picture, never more, would be stolen. One assumes that a collector had commissioned the thieves to steal him one Gauguin, one Cézanne and so on. The picture they took was usually the best in the collection.'

An upstairs window, Celia thought. It fitted. 'But look here,' she objected. 'When the same young woman turned up at yet another victim's house and asked to study the masterpieces, surely the owner would ring the police at once?'

'That's what happened in the end, but she got away with it for quite a time. For one thing, the thefts were all from different parts of Europe and America, and liaison between police forces wasn't as close then as it is now. Also, there was always a time lapse of a month or two at least between the girl's visit and the break-in, and at first no one connected the two. She was caught in the end, spying out the land in a house in Hollywood with a Vuillard in it, and was arrested. But after sweating it out in various prisons while the American legal system pursued its usual meandering course, she got off on appeal.'

'Goodness me, on what grounds?'

'According to the press clippings, the evidence was circumstantial. All they had against her was that she'd visited houses from which pictures were stolen some time later. She was able to prove from her passport that she'd always moved on to some other country before the thefts occurred, so the stealing must have been done by a confederate. They tried very hard to make her identify the confederate, but she simply insisted that she was innocent. Unfortunately for the prosecution her letter of recommendation from the Courtauld Institute turned out to be genuine, and they knew all about the post-graduate thesis she claimed to be preparing. She'd always given her real name, which was Susanne Horton, when she called on a collector, and she insisted that she'd been the victim of an unfortunate series of coincidences.'

'When did all this happen, Mr Knowles?'

'In the sixties.'

'How old was she then?'

'Let's see. Oh, here we are. She was twenty-three.'

A woman who was twenty-three in the 1960s would be about fifty now. 'Is there a photo of her in any of the press reports?'

'Yes, the same one in several papers. Issued by the police, I imagine, so that she'd be recognised if she tried the same thing again.'

'There isn't a photo of Alison Montgomery in the files to compare it with?'

'Probably not, but I know her quite well by sight, let's look. Good Lord, yes, I think you could be right.'

Celia thought rapidly. If Alison Montgomery is Susanne Horton under an alias, it makes sense. Cat-burglar Krasinski sees the pictures he stole at her instigation coming back on to the market, and tells son Konrad to dun her for a big slice of the proceeds. But she's only getting a percentage, she's selling them as an agent for Theo and Co., it's their responsibility to choke Konrad off. In consultation with them, she lures him to a meeting-place, and helps carry out the murder plot that they've worked out together. But cat-burglar Krasinski knows that when the pictures were stolen all those years ago, Susanne Horton was only an intermediary between him and the collector: he or his heirs must now be selling them. When Theo turns up as an accomplice to the murder the Krasinskis decide, rightly, that the vendor of the stolen collection and the organiser of Konrad's murder is to be found at Clintbury. Their only mistake is to turn their vengeance on Victor as head of the family. The much more serious mistake made by Konrad's murderers is to assume that it will be the end of the matter if they kill one blackmailer.

After a longish silence on the line Knowles said: 'Hullo? Are you still there?'

'Yes, I'm sorry, I've been thinking. Can you meet me in Mayhurst at two, and help me destroy the illusions of a policeman with drugs on the brain?'

She arranged to meet his train at Mayhurst station, and was waiting there eagerly when it came in. 'The *Sunflowers* and the *Harlequins* were both insured at Lloyds,' he reported. 'I've had a word with both syndicates. They prefer to deal with the informant themselves, in fact they're not very happy about handing out a reward to someone who's already given the information to the police. But I've explained the circumstances and I hope you'll get your ten per cent.'

She was alarmed. 'Do the insurers realise what might happen if they don't keep their mouths shut?'

'My dear Mrs Grant, I made it quite clear to them that if they let the story get out they wouldn't get their pictures back.'

'You frightened them about the pictures, not about the baby?'

'Well, they haven't insured the baby.'

At the police station, the desk sergeant reported that Inspector Porter was not in his office. 'Why not?' she demanded. 'I left a message, saying I had to see him urgently. Does anyone know where he is?'

A constable pounding a typewriter in the background rose and murrnured something to the desk sergeant, who suggested that she 'might try the Red Lion down the street'. He sounded embarrassed and she wondered why.

Porter was sitting alone in a corner of the Red Lion's lounge bar, with an empty beer glass in front of him. His face was drawn and white and there were dark stains under his eyes. A look of hangdog panic crossed his face when he saw her. 'Something's gone very wrong,' she told Knowles. 'Wait here while I find out what it is.'

She left him and sat down opposite Porter.

'Hullo, Mrs Grant,' he muttered.

'Oh dear, what's happened, Inspector?' she asked.

'I'm done for, that's what's happened.'

'Oh, why?'

'They kept saying things I couldn't make sense of.'

'Who did?'

'The Clintbury lot. What they were saying on the phone and in the intercepts didn't make sense because I was still thinking about drugs, I must have been mad. I should have told the super days ago. He's furious. I've been wasting a huge drug-squad effort on a sordid wrangle between two picture dealers.'

'Not quite,' Celia began.

'Oh yes I have, just look at this.' He took a crumpled typewritten sheet from his pocket and pushed it across the table to her. It was a transcript of a taped conversation overheard at Clintbury on the microphone system she had helped to install, and an exchange halfway down the page was ringed:

' "C" is Frank Bradbury and "D" is Theodore Stratton,' he explained.

D. 'Well, here they are. Shall I unwrap them?'
C. 'Why? Nobody's going to see them, are they?'
                           (Both laugh)

D. 'Of course not, but they're very beautiful. I thought you'd like just a peep.'

C. 'No, we'd only have to parcel them up again. Which one is the *Harlequins*?'

D. 'The smaller one, I think. The vangoff (?) isn't much bigger, but it's in a very heavy frame.'

C. 'Better put them away before someone sees. Open up, will you?'

Porter almost snatched the paper back, and embarked on a fresh tirade of squirming self-reproach. Theo had been followed to London, he explained. He had gone to a bank with a safe deposit vault and emerged carrying two large flat parcels done up in brown paper and carefully sealed, with which he had returned to Clintbury. Porter, already puzzled by what he was hearing from Clintbury, had thought the parcels an odd shape for heroin and a bank vault an odd place to keep it. But the full truth had not dawned on him till he saw the transcript. 'I've made a complete patsy of myself,' he moaned. 'The whole force is laughing at me, I've wrecked my career.'

To hell with your squalid little career, Celia thought. But nothing could be achieved while his morale was in ruins, and she embarked on temporary repairs. 'What nonsense. Those pictures were stolen, and immensely valuable. This isn't quite what you expected, but you're still dealing with a major crime.'

He held grimly to his obsession. 'Nothing's major compared with drugs.'

'This is pretty major. There are lots more pictures involved besides the Van Gogh and the Picasso, and they've all got multi-million-pound price tags attached to them.' She beckoned to Knowles to come over. 'I've brought an expert with me who can fill in the details.'

Knowles joined them and gave Porter a thorough briefing on the state of the market in stolen Impressionist paintings. Porter listened glumly, and said nothing when it was over.

'Don't be so feeble, what are you waiting for?' Celia urged sharply. 'Get a warrant to search Clintbury for stolen goods. Get another to search the holiday camp for Marcia's baby and you're home and dry, with rounds of applause from your superiors and the insurers of the pictures. You'll be the darling of the media too. They dote on rescued babies.'

'No.'

'What do you mean, "no"?'

'You haven't heard the worst yet, Mrs Grant. The team watching the holiday camp were careless, the Krasinskis got frightened and made off. There was a high-speed chase and the police car crashed. The Krasinskis got away.'

'With the baby?' Celia asked, horrified.

'Yes, and we have no idea where they are.'

This was indeed disastrous. 'So what happens next?'

'God knows. There was another phone call last night in which Frank Bradbury agreed to hand over both pictures. He's going to get instructions tomorrow about where and when he's to exchange them for the child. Our only hope is to stake out the handover point.'

'But that sort of thing can easily go wrong,' cried Celia. 'They find out you're there and don't show up. Or they panic and kill the baby.'

'I know that!' cried Porter, almost in tears. 'But what else can I do?'

Celia had a nightmare vision of little Henry being killed during a midnight assignation with the kidnappers. She tried to dismiss it from her mind and think clearly. There was something that did not fit, something in Frank's remarks to Theo on the tape that had struck her as odd. What was it? She made Porter show her the transcript again, and as she re-read it an even more horrifying possibility than a bungled ambush struck chill into her. 'Look!' she cried, terrified. 'Look at this bit. Why does he say they needn't unwrap the pictures because nobody's going to see them, and why did that make them both laugh?'

Nobody answered.

'Surely the kidnappers would insist on seeing them? They wouldn't hand over Henry in exchange for two sealed brown-paper parcels that might contain oleographs of *The Stag at Bay* for all they know. This is an even worse stinker than I thought.'

A silence fell.

'Oh, my God! Oh no!' Porter moaned. 'I see what you mean. They don't intend to hand over the ransom!'

'Exactly. Put yourself in their place for a moment. They've cooked their goose with Victor. If he ever recovers from Helen's dope he'll have them off the payroll in a flash. Why should they hand over a Picasso and a Van Gogh in exchange for downtrodden Marcia's wretched little brat that they don't care a damn about? For that matter, why should they wait around for the Krasinskis to come back for more? Blackmailers always do. If they vanish abroad taking the pictures with them, they can get a ransom for them out of the insurance companies and live on it in modest comfort for life.'

'On ten per cent of the value of two pictures?' said Porter doubtfully.

'Everyone's saying the Impressionists are overpriced,' said Knowles. 'But we're still talking about two million at least.'

Porter was white to the lips. 'This is all very fine, but what the hell am I supposed to do?'

'Arrest the lot of them,' Celia suggested. 'Marcia can hand over the pictures and collect Henry.'

'No. If I do, the Krasinskis will soon find out. They're still manning their observation post on the church tower. When they see us arrive to make the arrests, they'll take alarm and kill the baby.'

'If you left it till after dark they wouldn't see you.'

'Who says they don't watch the gates from ground level after dark?' Porter paused. 'Anyway, what am I supposed to arrest them for?'

'Possession of stolen property, surely?'

'I've made a fool of myself once, I'm not doing it again,' Porter moaned. 'It's only your theory that there's stolen property at Clintbury. I've no evidence.'

'You will have, because I shall go there now and find it for you.'

Porter looked outraged. 'I can't allow that,' he snapped. 'Too dangerous.'

'You can't stop me, I'm not on your payroll any more.'

'I can refuse to give you police support.'

'If you do, I shall go over your head to Superintendent Marshall.'

'You can't,' Porter cried, triumphantly. 'He's at a conference in London.'

160

'Very well. If I'm on my own, I'm on my own.'

The police cellphone was still in her handbag. By way of an ultimatum she took it out and put it on the table in front of him. He ignored it, and stared at her hysterically. 'This is a police operation. Don't you dare interfere.'

'Interfere in what? There isn't a police operation. Go on, admit it, you haven't the faintest idea what to do next.'

He was furious. 'You want the reward, don't you?' he sneered. 'That's all you care about. You're going to barge in there and strike out on your own, and why? To get your hands on the reward. Two million from whoever insured those pictures would get that bankrupt nursery of yours nicely out of the red.'

For a moment she sat there, paralysed with anger. She had decided at once that Henry's life must not be put at risk, the pictures would have to be handed over to the Krasinskis in exchange for him, and to hell with the reward. But she knew only too well that she was too small and finicky-looking to lose her temper effectively. It made her look an utter fool, like the Queen of the Fairies in a tantrum, and she fought hard to control herself. She rose, hissed 'You filthy minded little wimp, how dare you!' in a tense undertone, and turned to go.

Knowles put a restraining hand on her arm. 'Steady on, both of you. Inspector, you owe Mrs Grant an apology, it's obvious that her main concern is to get Mrs Stratton's child back. If she was out for the reward, she'd have reached an understanding with the insurers before she brought her information to you. Please apologise.'

Porter said nothing. His eyes bulged with bad temper. Then suddenly he crumpled. 'I'm sorry,' he gasped, and passed the cellphone back to Celia. 'This has all been too much for me. I don't know what I'm saying.'

'That's better,' said Knowles. 'Now listen to me, you two. Forget how much you dislike each other and work together. If you don't you'll be responsible for a muddle and a disaster in which a baby is going to get killed, so for heaven's sake sit down calmly and think. I must get back to London now to write my column for the paper. I admit that I can't see an easy answer to your problem, but I hope you'll find one that I can tell my readers about when it's all over.'

He went, pursued by reminders that nothing must be published till Celia gave the word.

'He's right, you know,' she told the inspector. 'We must work together.'

Porter frowned. 'Do you dislike me very much?'

Wondering if he ever thought about anything but himself and people's opinions of him, she cast around for a tactful answer. 'I'm sorry for you, really. You're very young and unsure of yourself, and your promotion has come too soon for your own comfort. When you're trying to hide your worry about yourself you get arrogant, and that upsets people.'

Porter would happily have settled down to discuss his psyche with her, but she cut him short. 'Never mind about that. The problem is, how do we set about rescuing Henry?'

For almost an hour they discussed the narrow range of options. The variables were bewildering. For instance, how many Clintbury inmates besides Theo and Frank were in the plot to escape abroad?

'Helen Bradbury, for one,' said Celia. 'She more or less poisoned Victor Stratton when he found out too much about their goings-on. And what about Nigel Burke?'

'Would he want to leave his womanising and his vintage cars?'

Celia was convinced that Nigel had sneaked back from Hungary to break Konrad Krasinski's neck, and therefore had every reason to hide from Konrad's relatives' vengeance. But in the interests of peace she refrained from reopening this sorely controversial subject.

'I think he'll be off with the others,' she said. 'He's in it with them; he must have as much to hide as they do. When Marcia asked for his advice after the kidnapping, he was as anxious as Frank that the police shouldn't be told.'

'Don't let's forget Mrs Montgomery,' said Porter.

'Goodness no, she's got even more to fear from the Krasinskis. Konrad must have been keeping a date with her to discuss his blackmailing demand when he was killed. And another thing's just occurred to me: two million divided between five people isn't riches. Do you think Theo and Frank are planning to do the dirty on the others and leave them behind?'

These were not the only uncertainties. When would the kidnappers phone again with instructions for the handover of the ransom? Till they did, nothing must happen to alarm them, and a police search for the two stolen pictures was out of the question.

But receiving stolen property was the only ground Porter had for arresting Frank, so what if no stolen property could be found? And how did one arrest five people without the kidnappers finding out and taking fright?

After going round in circles in this quagmire of doubt, they hammered out an outline plan of action, or rather a set of possible plans of action to meet different sets of circumstances. Then they set to work. Celia rang Clintbury on Porter's office telephone.

It was answered by Briggs. 'I want to talk to Mrs Stratton,' she told him. 'And I don't want anyone else to know it's me.'

'Will do, madam,' said Briggs.

Presently Marcia came on the line. 'Oh, Mrs Grant, dear, where *are* you?' As always, her voice seemed to be ringing with insincerity, but the note of suppressed panic came through. 'You're my only hope, they've still got my precious Henry.'

'Yes, I've one or two things to tell you about that. You'll have to smuggle me in in the boot of your car, though.'

'Oh why? Never mind about Helen and her boiling oil, it's my house and I can invite who I like.'

'Yes, but I can be more use if the others don't know I'm there.'

'Oh, then I shall send Anderson with the Rolls. You can lie on the floor under a rug. Where shall he pick you up?'

'At Mayhurst station as soon as he can. There's one thing I need to know now. How's Victor?'

'Dreadful. Helen's still got him locked away in his suite. I think she's poisoning him slowly. Every so often he starts shouting and creating, like Malvolio in his prison.'

'Splendid, that makes everything a lot simpler.'

'Does it? How bewildering. Why?'

'I'll have to tell you later. 'Bye now.'

After a final review of tactics with Porter, she prepared to leave. As a last-minute afterthought he produced an impressive-looking gun from his desk drawer and handed it to her. 'In case you need to frighten anyone.'

'Horrors no, it frightens me,' she replied and tried to hand it back.

'Keep it, it's only a replica. A pathetic sixteen-year-old junkie tried to rob a bank with it.'

Stuffing this non-lethal armament into her handbag she hurried to the station, where Anderson was already waiting in the forecourt, a solid, reassuring figure beside the Rolls. He grinned broadly as he opened the rear door and stood by it with a carriage rug over his arm. 'Welcome, madam. Mrs Stratton will be pleased and so will all the household staff.'

'Thank you.'

'We're all on her side, madam. You can rely on us for any help you need.'

The butterflies in Celia's stomach rose in revolt. Marcia must have given her a build-up as a fairy godmother who would sort out the whole Clintbury carry-on with a wave of her wand.

Pompously installed in the back seat, she swept out of the station yard. 'If you don't mind, madam,' said Anderson over his shoulder, 'I suggest you get down on the floor now, under the rug. There's groceries to unload, so no one will think it odd if I drive right up to the back door for you to get out. Mrs Stratton's in the nursery. Briggs will take you up there.'

Plunging down on to the luxurious carpet, she lay cradled there till the car came to rest on the cobbles of the stable yard at Clintbury. Anderson murmured 'all clear now, madam,' and she dived into the dark doorway of the kitchen quarters, where the servants bustled about her like affectionate dogs. 'Ooh, we're all at sixes and sevens, madam,' said Lena. 'Thank goodness you're here.'

Wishing she was elsewhere and not hyped as a cure-all for Clintbury's criminalities, she let Briggs take her up the back stairs. In the nursery at the end of the passage, a woebegone Marcia sat on a dilapidated sofa clutching one of Henry's teddy bears with an impeccable sense of theatre. Briggs settled on the edge of a table and Anderson, who had followed them upstairs, leaned against the mantelpiece. Marcia's kitchen cabinet was in session.

Her welcome for Celia was warm, and she reported at once on the latest developments. 'The kidnappers phoned Theo again an hour ago. They've told him where to hand over the ransom. Ten tonight in Ashdown Forest. Frank's going into Mayhurst to collect it from the bank.'

'Is that what he told you?'

Marcia opened her eyes so wide that the whites showed all round. 'Why? Isn't it true?'

164

'No. For one thing the ransom isn't money; it's a pair of stolen pictures that Theo inherited from his brother.'

Marcia demanded details, with her eyes threatening to fall out of her head. Celia gave them, as briefly as she could. 'Just a minute, there's something I must check.' Celia produced the police cellphone and rang Porter. He answered at once. 'Yes, Mrs Grant?'

'Did the kidnappers call Clintbury this morning with details of where to hand over the ransom?'

'No. Why?'

'Theo has told Marcia they did.'

'Then we're right. He is cheating, he's getting out from under. What time did he say for the handover?'

'Ten tonight, in Ashdown Forest.'

'That's his alibi for a dash to one of the Channel Ports. We'll have to speed the whole operation up. But can I ring you back? Frank is having quite an interesting conversation with his wife and Theo downstairs somewhere, and I'm listening in.'

'What's going on?' wailed Marcia. 'Why is Frank telling frightful fibs? Who were you talking to?'

'The police.'

'But Frank said we must keep the police out of it, otherwise I'd never see Henry again.'

'He would say that. Frank isn't going to ransom Henry. He and the others are going to make a getaway abroad, taking the ransom with them.'

Marcia gave way to paroxysms of alarm. 'Oh Mrs Grant dear, what on earth are we to do?'

'Find the pictures and ransom Henry with them.'

'But Frank and the others will stop us.'

'Not if we all keep our heads,' said Celia with more confidence than she felt. 'But I'd better tell you the whole story from the beginning.'

In the ensuing catalogue of iniquity what registered most strongly with Marcia was not Konrad Krasinski's murder but Frank's double-dealing. He was a bastard, she cried, she would tear his eyes out, the blinding of Gloucester in *King Lear* would be nothing to it. And as she proclaimed that she would fry his

165

eyeballs and eat them, the door opened and Frank came into the room.

'What on earth's going on in here?' he asked.

Celia gasped with horror. The master-plan that she had worked out with Porter had gone drastically wrong.

ELEVEN

'What's happening?' Frank repeated. 'Is something wrong?'

'Oh no!' cried Marcia in an artificial drawing-room comedy hoot. 'Everything is in perfect order, except that you're proposing to rush off to France or somewhere with the ransom and let the kidnappers kill Henry.'

Frank's look of innocent shock was beautifully managed. 'Oh, my poor dear, what on earth can have put such a horrible suspicion into your head?'

'Your lies. The kidnappers didn't phone this morning. You're not going to take the ransom to them at ten tonight in Ashdown Forest. You made it all up.'

'Marcia dear, I know you've been under dreadful strain since Henry was kidnapped, and I'm prepared to make allowances. But you're doing me a horrible injustice. I drew the money this morning from Victor's bank.'

'Fine, except that the ransom isn't cash. It's a stolen Picasso and a Van Gogh, that Victor's father left to Theo.'

Frank's pained expression gave way to black fury. 'You bitch, I always knew you eavesdropped.'

For the first time he took his eyes off her and realised that there were two men twice his size in the room. Celia made urgent eye contact with Briggs and Anderson. They closed in on him and seized him by the arms. But unexpected hell broke loose. Surprisingly, Frank proved to be a pocket battleship of violent and skilful self-defence. Briggs ended up on the floor clinging to one of Frank's feet, a flying kick narrowly missed Anderson's groin, and in a moment the room became a whirlwind of flying male limbs and crashing furniture. When the confusion ceased to be total, Anderson was bent double clutching his stomach and Frank was kneeling on Briggs' chest, pummelling his face.

Celia decided that the moment had come to produce the toy gun. 'Stop that at once,' she ordered, levelling it at Frank, 'or I shall shoot you.'

He stopped pummelling Briggs and stared at her. 'Mrs Grant? What are you doing here?'

'Never you mind. Get off Briggs. No, don't stand up, Mr Bradbury. Lie down on the floor. No, on your stomach.'

Still covered by the gun, he obeyed.

'We need something to tie his hands and feet with, Marcia,' said Celia.

Marcia produced nylon tights from a drawer. Briggs and Anderson bound Frank hand and foot with them.

'Now, Mr Bradbury, where are the Van Gogh and the Picasso?' Celia asked.

'Aha. Wouldn't you like to know?'

'Bash his face against the floor, Briggs. Now. Where are they?'

He laughed harshly. 'Where you'll never find them, Mrs Grant.'

'We'll see about that,' Celia promised grimly.

Frank began to shout for help.

'Have to gag him too, won't we?' Briggs decided.

Marcia handed him yet another pair of tights. 'I wish it was a dirty nappy of Henry's, but I use disposable ones.'

Anderson and Briggs dragged Frank, securely trussed up, into Henry's walk-in toy cupboard and locked the door on him.

'Goodness me, Briggs, what a carry-on,' said Celia. 'Are you badly hurt?'

'Me manly beauty's suffered a bit, madam,' he replied, nursing what would soon be a colourful black eye.

'I'm sorry. He's such a dried-up little shrimp of a man, I didn't think he'd put up so much fight.'

'Oh, didn't you know, madam? He's into kung fu, martial arts and all that. That's what he gets up to in Mayhurst on Wednesdays.'

'But I thought his date on Wednesday afternoons was with a boyfriend?'

'Oh no, madam, his thing with Mr Simpson was over long ago, all passion spent, as you might say. The two of them run a martial-arts class for local homosexuals, so that they can defend themselves if they're attacked.'

She thought rapidly. 'Could he break a man's neck with his bare hands?'

'Easy, madam, he'd know how.'

So that bit of the puzzle was out of the way. She had been wrong in suspecting that Nigel Burke had sneaked back into the country to break Konrad Krasinski's neck. Frank, with his surprising martial-arts background, was competent to attend to that himself. But how, if at all, did Nigel fit into this conspiracy? And would he interfere effectively to support Frank?

She brought out the cellphone again to report progress. When told of Frank Bradbury's incarceration in the cupboard, Porter made peevish noises. 'I'd be up before a disciplinary board if I treated an arrested person like that.'

Celia giggled. 'Isn't it lucky that I'm not a member of the force?'

Porter was in anguish. All this was highly irregular. What would the super say when he got back and found out what had been going on? 'Have you found those pictures yet, Mrs Grant?' he snapped. 'We can't regularise the situation till you do.'

'I'm sorry, Bradbury refuses to tell me where they are, I think a little light torture may be necessary.'

Shocked, Porter made inarticulate choking noises.

'Oh, don't be such a fusspot,' Celia scolded. 'I'm sure worse things go on all the time in police stations. What's happening downstairs?'

'I've had an earful. Frank Bradbury was talking to his wife and Theo Stratton about the arrangements for tonight. They were all to cross the Channel by different routes in separate cars and meet up at a hotel in Abbeville, the Hotel de la Pay, it sounded like. But Mrs Bradbury said why not travel in one car? He said no, that wouldn't do because Marcia thought he was going to hand over the pictures to the blackmailers in Ashdown Forest. She'd want to see him off and she'd think it odd if there were three other people with him in the car. They argued about it for a while and he produced a lot more phoney reasons for doing it his way and travelling separately to Abbeville. Then he went off upstairs, saying he had to see Mrs Stratton—'

'To say he'd collected the ransom money from the bank?' she interrupted.

'Probably. When he'd gone Mrs Bradbury said her husband

169

was a perverted little toad who was going to give them the slip and keep the pictures and the money for himself, and Theo agreed. They're talking now about ways of outwitting him.'

Celia thought for a moment. 'Who are the other three that he doesn't want in his car?'

'Theo Stratton, Mrs Bradbury and Nigel Burke, I suppose.'

'Did anyone actually mention Nigel?'

'No.'

'Isn't that a bit odd, Inspector?'

'I suppose so, but – just a minute, something's happening. Oh yes, it's Mrs Bradbury, she's phoning someone. I'll call you back when I know what it's about.'

Celia turned to Anderson. 'Do you know if Mr Burke's on the premises?'

'He was in the coach house earlier, madam, tinkering with them old cars of his.'

'It'll be awkward if he interferes.'

'I don't think he will, madam,' Briggs interjected. 'He wouldn't be a party to any scheme of Mr Bradbury's; the pair of them don't get on.'

'But he must be in on it. Vintage cars are hellishly expensive. Where else could he have got the money?'

'I happen to know that Mrs Blow gave it to him, madam.'

'Mrs who?'

'I don't wonder you're confused, I can hardly keep up with it myself. Before she was Mrs Blow she was Mrs Small and before that there were one or two whose names I forget, and years back she was Mrs Doulton. The current stallion, name of Blow, is a weight-lifter and so full of steroids that he's no good to her, so she's divorcing him and marrying Mr Burke instead.'

'She isn't!' cried Celia in horror. 'Oh really, how disgusting.'

Muriel Doulton, alias Blow, was a disreputable soft-drinks heiress in her sixties, with a notorious appetite for virile young men.

'It would give me the creeps, madam,' Briggs agreed. 'But she's got her head screwed on all right. She gave Mr Burke just enough to buy the two cars, but not enough to finance the repairs. He's run out, and she won't give him any more unless he marries her.'

'Briggs, are you sure? How do you know all this?'

'My cousin's her butler, madam.'

Was Nigel, revolted by the prospect of marriage to a harridan, about to cut and run with the others? If not, who was the fourth member of the cross-channel party?

Beside her the cellphone burst into life. 'That phone call was to the Montgomery woman,' Porter reported. 'Mrs Bradbury told her to come to Clintbury instead of going straight to Abbeville, because Bradbury intended giving them the slip and they'd all have to keep an eye on him.'

Was Alison Montgomery the missing member of the party? Celia suggested it as a possibility, but Porter, tiresome as ever, clung to his idée fixe about Nigel.

'You've had your ear glued to his phone,' she protested sharply. 'Why the blazes didn't you tell me he was running after that filthy old mantrap and her millions?'

'He's been running after three or four women at once. I'd no idea any of them were important.'

Celia was tempted to remind him of what must surely have been lesson one on his training course: that in detection, everything is important till the contrary is proved. But she controlled herself. There was no point in quarrelling with her tiresome collaborator while enemies rampaged round them on every side.

'Have you found those pictures yet?' he demanded, sweating at the prospect of the super's withering disapproval.

'No, as I told you we have been otherwise engaged battening down Frank Bradbury under hatches.'

'Do hurry up and find them,' he said tetchily. 'Till you have, everything you're doing is against regulations.'

She managed not to say anything regrettable and cut him off. Where were the pictures, and how did one search for them in a house occupied by the enemy? 'Has anyone seen two largish brown-paper parcels in the shape of pictures?' she asked. 'Theo brought them down from London yesterday. They must be somewhere in the house.'

'I've seen two parcels like that,' said Anderson. 'Yesterday, it was. I was washing the car in the yard and Mr Theo drove in and got them out of his boot and took them indoors.'

'That's right, I've seen them too,' Briggs chimed in. 'Lena and

171

I was laying the tea in the drawing room and he came in and put them down on the table by the door.'

'What happened to them after that?' Marcia asked in a strained voice.

'I've no idea, madam. They'd gone when I went in to clear the tea.'

'Then they could be anywhere,' wailed Marcia. 'We'll have to search the whole house.'

'No,' said Celia suddenly. 'I've had an idea, let me think.' Her mind went back to the transcript Porter had shown her of a conversation between Theo and Frank. 'Better put them away before someone sees,' Frank had said. 'Open up, will you?'

Open up what? Some piece of furniture in the drawing room, or the business room, or the Great Hall? They were the only rooms she had managed to plant microphones in.

'It's funny you should say that,' Briggs remarked when she pointed this out. 'Things do tend to vanish from those rooms.'

'What sort of things?' Celia asked.

Briggs hesitated. 'Magazines with photographs in.' He went very red and added: 'Nudes.'

'Tit and bum magazines?' Marcia queried in a tragic wail.

'Oh no, madam. Real hard porn.'

'Where did you see them?' Celia asked.

'In the business room. Twice. They're Mr Stratton's. The first time, he was reading one when a visitor arrived unexpectedly, and he forgot and left it on the desk for almost an hour. On the other occasion it was with some post that he'd opened, and he was called away suddenly by Mrs Bradbury.'

'Whereupon you helped yourself to a horny eyeful,' said Marcia censoriously.

Briggs became very high-minded. 'I did glance at them out of curiosity, madam, but that sort of thing disgusts me rather, and I wouldn't have taken any more notice but for Lena. There were men with women in a lot of the pictures and I'm sorry to say that she went wild about them, wouldn't be satisfied till she'd found out where Mr Stratton kept the magazines, so she could have another look. She went on and on about it, making herself quite ill, so for the sake of peace and quiet I helped her search.'

This pretence of high-minded helpfulness was unbelievable,

but it hardly mattered. 'You didn't find them?' Celia asked.

'No, madam.'

'They aren't up in Mr Stratton's private suite?'

'No, madam. He wouldn't keep them there in case Mrs Bradbury saw them. And the second time it happened we were sure about that. When we went back to the business room later to look for them they'd gone, and he hadn't been upstairs.'

'So you're saying there must be some hiding place on the ground floor, probably in or near the business room?'

'Yes, but we looked in the bookshelves in there and the chest in the Great Hall where the croquet things are kept, and all sorts of other places, but we couldn't find them.'

'I wonder if anyone else in the household knows about this secret hoard,' Celia wondered. 'Theo, for example.'

If anyone had to be tortured to find the hiding place, Theo would be a less tough proposition than Frank.

'I think Mr Theo does know,' said Briggs. 'I've sometimes suspected him of teasing Mr Stratton about it.'

Celia stared at him wildly as an idea struck her like a thunderbolt. I have been blind, she told herself. Briggs is right, Theo did tease Victor about his secret hoard of filth; that was what the pelican joke had been about.

As a piece of Elizabethan iconography the pelican was a symbol of the Queen's position as head of the Anglican Church. What if the family that built Clintbury were Catholics, persecuted adherents of the old faith? In that case, it would be a gross historical error to introduce pelicans, a symbol of Protestant supremacy, into the garden at Clintbury. Why did Theo keep reminding Victor of this? Because in one of the downstairs rooms, probably the business room, there was a priests' hole, and like the ones at Ashton Lacey, it was part of the network of safe hiding places for itinerant Catholic clergy. Victor used it to house his secret pornographic hoard and Theo knew about it. Whenever he mentioned pelicans, Victor squirmed. It was a coded threat to make trouble if Victor tried to throw him out of the house.

And when Frank told Theo to 'open up' so that the pictures could be stowed away secretly, he was not referring to a piece of furniture.

Asked whether she knew if there was a priests' hole at Clintbury, Marcia shrugged her shoulders in astonished ignorance. 'Then Helen probably doesn't know either,' Celia concluded. 'So the person to put pressure on is Theo.'

She rang Porter. 'What's happening downstairs?' she asked.

'Nothing. Mrs Bradbury's gone up to mount guard over Victor Stratton.'

'And where's Theo?'

'Still down there, moaning to himself. What about the pictures?'

'Stand by for dramatic developments at any moment, Inspector.'

She had cast Marcia for the star part in the drama she intended to stage, and Marcia made hasty preparations for playing it, mussing her hair into wild disorder and undoing several buttons of her blouse. Then, attended by Celia, Briggs and Anderson in supporting rôles, she headed along the corridor with a mad glitter in her eyes, and strode down the great staircase with a grip on the fake gun as frenetic as Lady Macbeth's on the candle. She flung open the door of the business room, where Theo sat hunched gloomily in a chair behind the desk. She levelled the gun at him, and spoke like Lady Macbeth in her most bullying mood.

'You know where the Picasso and the Van Gogh are hidden. Get them out now and hand them over to me, or I shall shoot you.'

Theo surveyed her dolefully. 'Picasso? Van Gogh? I don't understand.'

'Oh, but you do, Theo, you do. If the ransom isn't paid and Henry gets killed I shall have nothing more to live for. Hand over the pictures or I shall shoot you like a dog, then shoot myself.'

Theo caught sight of Briggs and Anderson standing behind her in the doorway. 'The worry's unhinged her, poor thing. Could someone get the gun away from her?' When neither of them stirred, he said: 'Oh, I see. You think I should humour her. Yes. Exactly.' But he made no move.

'Better play ball, Mr Theo,' Briggs urged. 'Open up the porn cupboard like she says.'

To reinforce this demand Marcia broke into a stream of invective so vulgar that Anderson was appalled, and even Briggs looked surprised. Celia suspected that she was quoting lines from some

174

low-life part she had played in the experimental theatre.

'What on earth is going on in here?' demanded Helen Bradbury from the doorway.

Marcia spun round. 'Don't move, Helen,' she croaked, 'or I shall shoot you stone dead.'

Helen looked at her calmly. 'My dear Marcia, you should stick to light comedy. Melodrama isn't your line. Is that thing loaded?'

'Of course.'

'Briggs. Do something. Get it away from her,' Helen ordered.

'No, madam. If you speak out of turn and get shot, you'll deserve it.'

'I shall not overlook this, Briggs. Nor will Mr Stratton when I tell him. Marcia, pull yourself together. You're hysterical.'

'I don't think so,' Celia corrected. 'She's no angrier than one would expect in the circumstances.'

'I am not hysterical,' cried Marcia in her steely Lady Macbeth voice. 'I'm trying to save the life of my child. Unless the Picasso and the Van Gogh are handed over to me now, at once, this gun is going to do a great deal of damage.'

Helen attempted sweet reason. 'Marcia dear, you're having hallucinations. No one's going to kill Henry. The pictures are in a safe place, ready to ransom him. Do calm down and tell me what's bothering you.'

'What's bothering her, Mrs Bradbury,' Celia interrupted, 'is that several of you have a date to meet up as soon as possible at the Hôtel de la Paix in Abbeville with the pictures in your possession.'

As Helen struggled for speech, Anderson said: 'Come on, Mr Theo. Open up and give them to her.'

'Don't you dare, Theo,' shouted Helen.

'Going to make a nuisance of yourself, are you?' shouted Marcia. 'Briggs, take her away and lock her up somewhere.'

'You really are out of your mind, Marcia,' said Helen with dignity. 'Briggs will do no such thing.'

'Oh yes I will, madam,' said Briggs and seized her arm, twisting it behind her back.

Helen struggled, furious. 'Marcia, you pathetic little concubine, how dare you make this ridiculous fuss? Who cares a damn what happens to that mewling little creature that isn't Victor's anyway?'

'You might as well break her arm while you're about it,' Marcia suggested coldly.

Briggs gave Helen's arm a fiercer twist, making her wince. 'Now, dearie, you're going to come with me. Whether you do it now or after I've broken your arm is up to you.'

He led her away, screaming abuse, towards the kitchen quarters and locked her in the boot room, whereupon Lena shouted subversive remarks through the door, Jane asked in a frightened voice what was going on, and Adolphe wanted to know how many there would be for dinner.

'Only two that deserve any, the others can go without,' said Briggs.

In the business room Marcia rounded fiercely on Theo. 'If you don't take us to the secret hiding place now, you'll have to hop there on one foot, because I shall shoot you through the knee.'

'Why don't you do as she says?' Celia urged. 'You might as well because you're going to lose out anyway. If Bradbury doesn't give you the slip in Abbeville, he'll try something else.'

Faced with this uncomfortable truth, Theo nodded sadly. 'But how on earth did you— '

'Never mind about that, give us the pictures,' snapped Marcia.

Suddenly, to Celia's embarrassment, he began to weep noisily. Between sobs he gasped out excuses: he had been against the idea of speculating with the six million realised by the sale of Ashton Lacey, and horrified when they lost the lot. Selling the hoard of stolen pictures to replace the money had been Frank's idea, he had gone into it unwillingly, and now Frank was letting him down. Marcia waved the gun at him. 'Stop snivelling and get on with it.'

'Bring me that stool,' he quavered.

There were bookcases on either side of the fireplace. Placing the stool in front of the left-hand bookcase, Theo clambered on to it and twisted one of the lions' heads which projected from the frieze along the top. There was a click, and one side of the bookcase moved forward a few inches. Theo stepped down and pulled it open like a door, revealing the cavity behind.

It was small, even for a priests' hole, little more than a cupboard in which a man could stand, and it was stacked shoulder-high with copies of lurid-looking magazines. But Celia and Marcia had eyes only for the two flat brown-paper packages with sealing wax on all the knots, which lay on top of the pile. As Marcia lifted them down, magazines spilled out on to the floor. Anderson picked one up, looked disgustedly at the fornicating couple on the front cover, then began shovelling them all back into the cupboard.

Celia and Marcia cut string and tore at brown paper ruthlessly. Canvases worth several thousand pounds a square centimetre were revealed, but they were too busy checking that they had found what they were looking for to be overawed. While Marcia carried the pictures upstairs to lock them up in her desk, Celia called Porter. 'We've found them.'

'And about time too,' he grunted. 'We'll be with you in ten minutes.'

Frustratingly, the next step in the campaign was delayed because the door to Victor's suite was locked. Helen, incarcerated in the boot room downstairs, fought a tiresome rearguard action. Screaming defiance, she refused to say where the key was, even when Marcia threatened to let Lena strip her naked in search of it.

Theo, who had been following Celia around like a stray dog that thinks it has found a friend, plucked at her sleeve. 'She puts it on the ledge at the top of the door frame,' he volunteered with cringing helpfulness.

It was indeed on the ledge but above her reach. Theo got it down for her, then murmured something about needing a drink and wandered off to console himself with the sherry bottle hidden in his wardrobe.

Unlocking the door, Celia found herself in the library. Followed by Marcia, she hurried through it to the bedroom. Victor Stratton lay on the bed, apparently asleep. The sheets were filthy and he stank of urine.

Marcia bent over him. 'Oh my poor Victor.'

He opened his eyes in a fixed stare and made a small, frightened noise.

'Don't worry,' Marcia told him. 'No one's going to hurt you now.'

He seemed to be trying to say something but failed. Then he

177

struggled for a moment to get up from the bed, and sank back. 'Has she gone?' he croaked.

When Marcia told him that Helen was locked up in the boot room downstairs, he laughed weakly till tears came and he began to cry.

Leaving them together, Celia went downstairs to wait for Porter's arrival, but found Nigel Burke standing at the bottom of the stairs.

'You here, Mrs Grant? Where is everyone? I heard a lot of screaming and shouting. What's been going on?'

Celia tried not to panic. Would he turn ugly? She had no idea whether he was a prospective member of the Abbeville party or not. He might well have decided to cut and run rather than marry a vicious and unattractive woman over twice his age. And why, if he was innocent, had he been as keen as Frank to prevent Marcia from reporting Henry's kidnapping to the police?

She temporised. 'I'm not sure what's happening.'

'It was Marcia doing the shouting, wasn't it?'

'Yes. She . . . suspects that Frank intends to steal Henry's ransom and run away to France with it.'

Nigel frowned. 'I wouldn't put it past him. I've known for months that he was up to something crooked. The question was what? Can't he be stopped?'

'Would you like him to be?'

'Of course. I'm engaged to be married. A public scandal in the family is the last thing I want. If the ransom's paid and Marcia gets Henry back, the whole thing will be settled quietly. Let me talk to Frank. Where is he?'

'I think he's gone into Mayhurst,' she lied.

To her relief, Briggs appeared. 'An ambulance has arrived, madam, but there seem to be some policemen in it.'

'Quite right, there would be,' said Celia. 'I'm afraid you're out of luck, Mr Burke, there will be a public scandal. But Muriel Doulton isn't fussy about whom she marries. I'm sure you'll be able to talk her round.'

Two ambulance men entered, carrying a stretcher. As Briggs took them upstairs to collect Victor Stratton and take him to hospital, Porter strode into the Great Hall, followed by two uniformed constables. Seeing Nigel, he said, 'Ah, I want you. I'm going to take you to Mayhurst police station for questioning.'

Nigel looked bewildered. 'About what, for Pete's sake?'

'You'll find out when you get there,' said Porter severely.

Celia did not interfere. Porter would have to find out for himself, after much wasted breath, that Nigel was innocent except in matters of sex.

Along the corridor in the business room, the telephone was ringing. Briggs hurried downstairs to answer it. When he returned he reported: 'It's those people. They want to know what's going on and what the ambulance is for. I said Mr Stratton had been taken ill.'

Celia nodded. There was no point in telling the observers on the church tower that the ambulance had brought in policemen under their noses, and would also soon act as a disguised prison van.

'And they're asking to speak to Mr Bradbury,' Briggs added.

'Then fetch Mrs Stratton to take the call,' Celia ordered. 'And after that show the inspector where to find Theo and Mr Bradbury.'

They went. Nigel Burke asked Celia what he was to be questioned about.

'Stolen property, among other things. But don't worry, he's not very clever, you'll run rings round him.'

The two policemen enjoyed this slur on their superior, and sniggered. 'This way, please,' said one of them, and led Nigel away.

Marcia came hurtling downstairs and made for the telephone in the business room.

'You know what to say?' said Celia, following her.

Marcia nodded and picked up the phone. 'I'm sorry, Frank's not available. I'm Marcia Stratton, the baby's mother. Can I help? . . . I daresay, but the trouble is that Frank's a slippery customer. I don't trust him, so I've decided to take this operation in hand myself . . . Why not, damn it, it's my baby, and anyway it would be better if you told me the details, because I shall be coming to deliver the ransom myself . . . No, of course there won't be any tricks, I don't want you to kill him, do I? So tell me what I'm to do . . . Ten-fifteen tonight in the Market Square car park in Mayhurst, yes. But I don't drive, so I shall have a friend with

179

me, another woman. We'll be in her car . . . The registration number?'

Celia supplied the details, and she passed them on. 'I see, we're to leave the car unlocked with the pictures on the back seat, yes . . . Into the Queen's Head? No, damn you, where I come from unescorted women don't walk into a crowded pub fifteen minutes before closing time. We shall go into the County Hotel instead . . . I know you thought it would be Frank but it's me and a friend and you'll have to lump it. How long will it take you to collect the pictures from the car? . . . I see, so it'll be okay if we come out of the hotel again just after ten-thirty. And Henry will be in the car? . . . Why not? Of course the pictures will be the originals. I'd be mad to substitute copies, but I suppose we'll have to allow you to check before you hand him over . . . Trust you? Of course I don't, you must be crazy. But I know who you are, and I want Henry back within twelve hours. If you've killed him I shall put a contract out to have both of you and your mother shot through the stomach and left to die in agony. Is that clear?'

Celia was filled with admiration for Marcia's performance, which was delivered in a tough, clipped voice suggestive of an upper-class gangster's moll. But when it was over Marcia collapsed in panic-stricken tears. 'Oh Mrs Grant dear, they won't hand Henry over tonight, they want to check first that the pictures are genuine. Did I frighten them enough or will they kill him?'

'You sounded blood-curdling to me,' Celia assured her. 'But there's not much time to set things up before ten-fifteen. You'd better go and brief Inspector Porter about what you arranged with them.'

Marcia turned and ran, but collided in the doorway of the room with the thin, grim figure of Jeremy Elton. 'Marcia, what's happening?' he asked fiercely. 'The servants won't tell me. If it's about Henry you must let me help.'

'No! I've told you over and over again to clear out, you piffling little nuisance.' She tried to dodge past him, and failed. 'Get out of my way, I'm busy.'

'He's my son as well as yours. I've a right to know what is going on.'

'He's only your son because you were there, in the right

place at the right time. It could have been the milkman or a waiter I rather fancied at a restaurant in Mayhurst. Mrs Grant dear, do try to talk some sense into him and make him give up his nonsense.'

She dived under his outstretched arm and escaped into the corridor, leaving Celia to grapple with this unexpected addition to her case-load.

'She's quite a bit older than you, Jeremy,' she began, 'and married to a rich man. I should forget her if I were you.'

'How can I?'

'I'm afraid you'll have to. You're a nice boy and quite good looking. There will be lots of other girls.'

'I don't want lots of others, I want her,' he proclaimed. 'She ought to come away with me. She's not happily married, her husband's a brute. All the servants say so. He's no use to her in a crisis like this. I want to be with her and help her through it.'

'But the point is she doesn't want your help.'

'Henry's my son too!'

'She doesn't think that gives you any rights over him.'

'I don't agree.'

Deadlock seemed to have been reached. The only relevant thing that occurred to Celia was a quotation. 'Jeremy, listen to this:

"O what can ail thee, knight-at-arms,
Alone and palely loitering?
The sedge is withered from the lake
And no birds sing."

Keats. Do you know it?'

'No, I only like committed modern poetry.'

'I've always thought the knight-at-arms behaved rather stupidly. He met a beautiful fairy in a field, and after a lot of foreplay with garlands and wild honey etcetera she took him to her elfin grot and they made a night of it. In the end he fell asleep and dreamed that all her former lovers came and warned him:

" . . . death pale were they all;
Who cried – 'La Belle Dame sans Merci
Hath thee in thrall!' "

I've always wondered, Jeremy. Was La Belle Dame sans Merci really a fairy, or had the knight-at-arms made a mistake? He's had a night of love with a woman he's never seen before, and he knows nothing about her. For all he knows she could be a promiscuous little tease, or a sensible married lady who likes her fun but knows exactly which side her bread's buttered. But he makes up all sorts of fantasies about her and spends his time loitering by that dismal lake with no birds singing, instead of finding himself a nice bird he can get to know properly and have fun with day in day out.'

Jeremy treated her to a grim twinkle. 'This is a very sophisticated line of argument, but the parallel isn't exact. I may be loitering, but I'm not pale and *perestroika* has finally made knights-at-arms obsolete.'

'But the point is you don't know Marcia very well, and I'm sure you've made up fantasies about her.'

He shrugged, but did not deny it. 'There's Henry. What about him?'

'I respect your fatherly feelings, but can you see yourself changing his dirty nappies in some sordid bed-sitting room with a shared lavatory down the hallway, while Marcia goes out to work as a waitress?'

A silence fell.

Jeremy thought for a long time. 'I wonder if you're right about this,' he said, sounding surprised.

'Only you can decide. Why don't you go home and think about it?'

Another long silence. 'Thanks, Mrs Grant. I think I will.' He turned away dejectedly, looking very young and miserable.

When he had gone Celia went into the business room, where Marcia was locked in argument with Porter.

'I'm terrified, Inspector,' she cried with a sweeping Medea-like gesture. 'Must you set a trap? If anything went wrong they'd kill Henry. Why not let them have the pictures, I don't care.'

'That would be contrary to public policy, Mrs Stratton,' he replied pompously.

Moreover, Celia thought, it would not contribute to the glory of up-and-coming young Inspector Porter.

'I thought it was public policy to save life,' Marcia snapped.

'Without letting kidnappers get away with a ransom, Mrs Stratton. And now if you'll excuse me— '

The ambulance men were carrying Victor Stratton down the great staircase on a stretcher. He was strapped on it, and yelling in agonised panic. 'Had a time with him,' one of the ambulance men shouted. 'Terrified of us. Suicidal. Wanted to jump out of a window.'

Marcia went up to the stretcher. 'Don't worry, Victor. They're taking you to hospital. You'll be more comfortable there.'

'Don't let Helen near me.'

'No. She won't bother you any more.'

But Helen, Frank and Theo were already in the ambulance, supervised by the two police constables. At Marcia's suggestion, Porter was dissuaded from climbing in beside the driver, so that Helen could ride there out of Victor's sight. The ambulance drove away, and Celia and Marcia turned to go back into the house.

Briggs stood in the doorway, with two gin and tonics on a silver tray. 'From our private bottle in the kitchen. You deserve it, ladies. And Adolphe is doing a nice fillet steak each, with fruit salad to follow.' Marcia protested that she was not hungry, but he overrode her. 'You'll find you are when the time comes. You ladies need to keep your strength up.'

Waited on by Briggs and Lena, Celia enjoyed her steak and Marcia toyed with hers. As they embarked on the fruit salad, someone knocked loudly on the front door. Briggs answered it, and returned to report that a lady who refused to give her name was asking for Mr Bradbury. What should she be told?

Celia went, and found a smartly dressed, dark-haired woman pacing the Great Hall in an agitated state. After studying her for a moment she ventured a guess. 'Mrs Montgomery?'

'Yes. How did you know?'

This was a poser. 'Your photo was in the local paper after the inquest,' she managed.

'I need to see Mr Bradbury urgently,' said Alison Montgomery.

'I'm afraid Frank isn't here.'

'Then where the hell is he?'

Celia improvised a scenario hastily. 'He said something about a short continental holiday.'

'Oh my God, do you know where he's gone?'

'I'm sorry, no. But he was on the phone, booking his car on the Dover-Boulogne sailing at eleven tonight.'

Alison seemed to have trouble in framing her next question. 'Was . . . anyone with him when he left here?'

'No, but Theo Stratton and Mrs Bradbury left in a hurry shortly afterwards. They seemed rather cross.'

Muttering thanks, Alison rushed out of the house and drove away, crashing the gears in her haste. Having noted her registration number, Celia phoned Porter who received her report on the episode with another outburst of peevishness. 'You should have detained her. It would have saved me a lot of trouble.'

'Oh nonsense, when I shut people up in cupboards you make a long face and say it's irregular. Anyway, the harbour police at Dover can arrest her. What are they there for? Is everything ready for tonight in Mayhurst?'

'Of course.'

'Watch your step, won't you? If anything goes wrong, Marcia and I will chop you in tiny pieces and stuff you in the food processor.'

It was soon after ten when Porter rang Celia on the cellphone. 'All set?'

'We're just about to start.'

'The Krasinskis have just arrived. They're parked at the town-hall end of the square in front of the Queen's Head. When you get there, try to park as far away from them as possible, near the County Hotel.'

He was very excited. With any luck this would be his finest hour, a complex case brilliantly solved by the youngest inspector in the regional crime squad. But there were moments when visions of disaster broke through and his stomach turned over with fright.

Williams, Porter's driver, eased the car into a space ten yards from the Krasinskis'. Johnson, the electronics specialist, opened the door to get out. 'No, wait,' said Porter.

Mistake number one, Williams thought. Any criminal who saw three men sitting alertly in an unlit car would assume that they were policemen. Like the crews of all the cars on duty for this operation, he loathed jumped-up little Porter's guts. Porter had rubbed them all up the wrong way. But this time they would co-operate: there would be no fun and games at his expense. A kidnapped child put the whole force on its best behaviour.

The saloon bar of the Queen's Head was crowded, and on a hot June night customers had brought their beer out on to the pavement. The Krasinski brothers had locked their car and gone inside. 'Off you go, Johnson,' Porter ordered.

Johnson got out and strolled towards the Krasinskis' car. In his pocket was the small electronic device that he intended to fix to it inconspicuously. But the Krasinskis, carrying a pint tankard each, had just come out on to the pavement. Porter climbed out hastily and pulled Johnson back. 'Are you blind, didn't you see them?' he asked tetchily.

Johnson could hardly be blamed for failing to recognise two men whom he had seen for the first time a few minutes before, and then only under a street lamp. But he kept his resentment to himself and let Porter lead him back towards the car. Williams climbed out of the driving seat to meet them. 'What do we pretend to do now, Mr Porter?'

Porter considered. Three men standing about in the car park doing nothing would be very conspicuous, but no idea came to him.

Without saying anything, Williams opened up the bonnet of the car and made a show of fiddling with the engine while the other two looked on. Porter was in a frenzy of self-reproach for not having thought of this obvious ruse first.

Presently the Krasinskis looked at their watches, downed their beer and set off across the car park, presumably in search of Celia's Ford Sierra and its contents. 'Okay now, Johnson,' Porter muttered.

Sergeant Johnson strolled across to the Krasinskis' Vauxhall and took from his pocket a small radio beacon. Bending down, he clapped it under the Vauxhall's front bumper, where it attached itself magnetically. Until the battery ran out, it would send out a distinctive signal audible from several miles away. Five unmarked police cars had been detailed for this operation, all connected by radio telephone. If by some mischance they lost track of the Vauxhall, they would have little trouble in picking up its trail again.

After a few minutes the Krasinskis came back, each carrying

what was obviously a painting, loosely wrapped in brown paper. They put their burden in the boot of the Vauxhall and drove away. Porter was in no hurry to follow them. The squad cars were covering all the exits from the square. He would be told soon enough which way the quarry had gone.

He was in a mood of self-congratulation. Everything was going according to plan. Four people at Mayhurst police station awaiting questioning, the Montgomery woman was speeding into the welcoming arms of the harbour police at Dover, and the Krasinski brothers would soon be in the bag.

The trail led south out of the town, towards open country. Presently the leading squad car reported that the Vauxhall had pulled in to a filling station. Then came a correction. The filling station was attached to a small motel. The Vauxhall was parked by one of the rooms and the occupants had gone inside. Making Williams drive slowly past the spot, Porter surveyed the scene. There were lights at the filling station and the attendant was still on duty in his cabin. But the only light in the motel came from the curtained window with the Vauxhall parked outside it.

The squad cars were calling in, asking for instructions. He ordered two of them to station themselves half a mile away on either side of the motel, parked in lay-bys or on the verge. The others could wait in reserve further away, and he would set up his headquarters in one of the rooms of the motel, where he could also keep watch over the Krasinskis at close quarters.

Asked to provide a room for the night, the forecourt attendant unlocked a room with three beds in it, further along the row from the Krasinskis' but near enough for them to see the Vauxhall if it was moved. The place seemed to be fairly empty, and Porter remarked on this to the attendant. He agreed that they were the only customers, apart from 'two foreign gents' in number twenty who had been there almost a week, then left them to their own devices after demanding payment in advance.

Porter was appalled. If the 'two foreign gents' had had a baby with them, the attendant would surely have thought it worthy of mention. On any estimate of the probabilities, Mrs Krasinski and the child ought to be occupying an adjoining room. Why weren't they? He tried to persuade himself that success was still within his grasp; that the old lady was looking after Henry elsewhere, and would release him when her sons gave her the all-clear. But a vision of an infant's corpse lying in a ditch kept welling up at him from the bottom of a black hole of gloom.

Sick with tension, he took turns with Johnson and Williams to mount a watch at the window in case the Vauxhall was driven away. Meanwhile the Krasinski brothers, in their room a few doors away, were examining their haul. Unable to call in experts, they could not be sure that the pictures they had been given were the originals. But there were tiny cracks in the brushwork that looked old, and they reckoned that the Strattons were frightened enough not to try fobbing them off with worthless copies. So they made one quick phone call and settled down peacefully to sleep.

In a squad car parked on the verge half a mile from the motel Sergeant Nicholson and Constable Edwards were taking turns to catnap uncomfortably. At half past three in the morning Edwards, whose turn it was to be on watch, became anxious. An early summer dawn was breaking, and revealed what a moonless night had hidden. The motel and filling station stood alone, an isolated cluster of buildings dumped down incongruously amid the empty hedgeless fields of typical downland scenery. It struck him at once that by daylight the squad car would be the most conspicuous object in the view from the motel in such a deserted landscape, and he was worried enough to wake the sergeant and point this out to him.

Sergeant Nicholson was in two minds. It was unlikely that the suspects would be up admiring the view for some hours yet, and anyway an ordinary looking car parked by the roadside would not necessarily strike them as sinister. He would get a bollocking from Porter if he moved the car without permission, but he would also get a bollocking if Porter, woken from deep sleep by the phone, thought he was fussing unnecessarily. He decided to think about the problem before taking action.

All would have been well if Jan Krasinski had not found himself obliged to rise from his bed and dispose of the previous night's beer, and it was unfortunate that having done so he decided to part the bedroom curtains a little and examine the new day's weather. He saw the car parked by the roadside at once, and was curious enough to fetch the field glasses which had proved so useful on top of Clintbury church

187

tower. Moments later he was in a panic, shaking his brother's shoulder.

'Quick, Stash, there is trouble, come and see.'

Dragged over to the window, Stash was furious. 'A car? You wake me up to look at a car?'

Jan handed him the field glasses. 'Sitting in it are two men. We are betrayed.'

Stash argued with him in vain, pointing out that the Strattons would not dare to set a trap: they would be too afraid for the safety of the child. Jan was always taking alarm at imaginary dangers: he had made them move out of the seaside holiday camp because of one. But the trouble was that once Jan had got an idea into his head there was no holding him: his panic mounted till he was impossible to live with. In the end Stash had to give way. They packed, seized the pictures, and hurried out to the car.

By the time it had driven off, Porter had alerted the squad cars and they were moving into position to continue their shadowing operation. The two cars parked by the roadside on either side of the motel were to drive away unobtrusively to avoid causing alarm. Sergeant Nicholson started off accordingly, and was past the motel when the Vauxhall emerged from it and came up fast behind him. Jan, frantic to get past and away from what he saw as danger, overtook him on a blind bend and struck a glancing blow on the other squad car, which was making itself unobtrusively scarce by proceeding in the opposite direction. The Vauxhall ended up on its side in a ditch with its nearside wheels spinning.

The Krasinskis suffered cuts and bruises, but nothing more serious. Questioned by an embarrassed Porter, they denied indignantly that the pictures were stolen. But they also insisted that they knew nothing about any kidnapped child.

Porter was plunged even deeper into his black hole of despair. He continued to wallow in it till a phone message from Mayhurst police station informed him that a postman on his early rounds had found a pram outside the great gates of Clintbury Park containing a screaming baby.

TWELVE

The media gave wide coverage to the press conference at which Detective-Inspector Porter announced the arrest of six people, the recovery of two important pictures stolen over twenty years before, and the elaborate police operation in which the Strattons' baby had been rescued from kidnappers. It was the result, Porter explained, of months of patient undercover surveillance by a dedicated team of detectives, to whose work he paid fulsome tribute. His superiors in the regional crime squad were happy to bask in their share of the credit for a successful police operation, and saw no reason to mention that the dedicated team of detectives had wasted months investigating a mare's nest of suspected drug-dealing. As Porter omitted to tell them of Celia's part in putting him on the right lines, they showered him with public praise, and decided privately that he had been reasonably clever as well as lucky.

Bill Wilkins had maintained throughout that the prospect of a reward from the pictures' insurers was unreliable pie in a stormy sky. It was no surprise to him when they insisted that they owed Celia nothing because the donkey-work had been done by the police. 'I did warn you,' Knowles told her. 'You should have let me strike a deal with them at the beginning; they'll be much less forthcoming now that they've got their hands on the pictures. I'll see what I can get out of them for you, but I'm not hopeful.'

Gloom set in at Archerscroft Nurseries. Celia embarked on desperate financial shifts and appeals to the bank, amid Bill's bad-tempered sulks. At the end of the week Knowles phoned again. He had been putting pressure on the police by threatening to expose the lies Porter had told at his press conference, and publish the true story of the manic obsession with drugs from which Celia had rescued him. Rather than let all this appear embarrassingly in Knowles' Sunday column, the head of the regional crime squad had produced a letter addressed to the insurers, in which he admitted grudgingly that it was Celia who had discovered the existence of old Mr Stratton's hoard of stolen pictures and drawn it to Porter's attention.

'But I had to agree in return not to publish,' Knowles told her. 'So I'm afraid you won't get the credit you deserve.'

'I don't want that sort of credit, and I'm up to my neck in the other sort,' she replied. 'What I need is cash. How soon will the insurers come through if they're going to?'

He promised to put pressure on them, and after another agonising wait reported an offer of one hundred and fifty thousand for the *Sunflowers* and a hundred thousand for the *Harlequins*. 'It's not what you deserve,' he told her, 'but they won't budge. I've tried. They say Impressionists are overpriced and the market's collapsing. They're under no legal obligation, so I suggest that you accept.'

Celia agreed, but found that he expected a ten per cent commission on the deal. She beat him down to five per cent, paid off the bank loan and began thinking intensively about what to do with the balance.

Victor Stratton took several months to recover from deep depression. His convalescence was not helped by the alarming state of his financial affairs. Frank Bradbury had transferred several million pounds from Victor's bank into a Swiss numbered account in his own name. Victor's bankers, having made the transfer on the strength of Frank's forgery of Victor's signature, which was witnessed by Theo, were making frantic attempts to claw the money back from a bank in the Seychelles. To make matters worse, the money extorted from the insurers for the return of the other Impressionist pictures had been paid into Victor's bank account, to repay the money lost by Frank in the stock-market crash. Though most of it had vanished to the Seychelles, the insurers concerned were threatening to sue him for the return of the large sums they had paid out to people they now regarded as receivers of stolen property.

Marcia was sincerely sorry for Victor, and visited him daily in the nursing home. At her suggestion, Clintbury Park was put on the market, and Victor soon received an offer from an Australian property tycoon. She had decided to stand by Victor till he was through the worst of his troubles, possibly longer if he proved a wiser as well as sadder man. In the long term, she thought of trying for character parts on the stage, since she was old enough now to attempt them, and her mediocre looks would not hold her back.

By accusing Theo of having murdered Konrad Krasinski with his walking-stick, the police extracted from him an admission that Frank was the killer. Frank received a long prison sentence, Theo and Alison Montgomery slightly shorter ones as his accomplices. Sentences for all three for receiving stolen goods were to run concurrently. Helen Bradbury was released for lack of evidence. Before she could be rearrested and charged with the attempted murder of Victor with massive overdoses of Valium, she vanished to the Costa Brava, where she was later rumoured to be running a very shady bridge club.

Nigel was found to be innocent by a disgusted Porter, and he married Muriel Doulton. But he informed her on their honeymoon that out of respect for the wishes expressed in his father's will, and the resulting financial implications, he was obliged to live wherever his brother did for several more years.

In due course Celia was visited by the owner of the big garden centre on the main road which was the cause of her financial troubles. He wondered whether she had decided anything about his offer to rescue her from her sad predicament by buying her out. She replied cheerfully that she had just signed the contract to buy the derelict filling station next to his business premises, and was arranging to have it converted for her use. 'I've been wanting a main road selling point for some time,' she told him. 'And I don't think it matters our being side by side: antique shops rather like huddling together. If people want something more up-market they can always come next door to me.'